BLOOD TIED

JACOB Z. FLORES

Published by

DREAMSPINNER PRESS

5032 Capital Circle SW, Suite 2, PMB# 279, Tallahassee, FL 32305-7886 USA
www.dreamspinnerpress.com/

Blood Tied
© 2015 Jacob Z. Flores.

Cover Art
© 2015 by Paul Richmond .
http://www.paulrichmondstudio.com
Cover content is for illustrative purposes only and any person depicted on the cover is a model.

ISBN: 978-1-63476-520-6
Digital ISBN: 978-1-63476-521-3
Library of Congress Control Number: 2015945751
First Edition September 2015

Printed in the United States of America
∞
This paper meets the requirements of
ANSI/NISO Z39.48-1992 (Permanence of Paper).

Readers love *Please Remember Me*
by JACOB Z. FLORES

"With some very entertaining secondary characters, this story was a total hit for me.."

—The Novel Approach

"This was my first Flores novel, and to be honest, I was impressed. I loved the cover, the man helplessly watching the other walk into the distance. I loved the characters, the premise, and the stark realism of the world that I visited."

—Joyfully Jay

"... The power of true love is the sweetest balm, and I was left so full I thought I might burst."

—Boys in Our Books

"If you want a book that takes you on a roller coaster of emotions, this one is for you."

—Rainbow Gold Reviews

"Wow just simply wow. This story is what makes me love this genre; it's what makes reading the best feeling there is."

—Love Bytes

"Jacob Z. Flores gives readers a sexy story, with a little heartache, much compassion, and two love stories. I will definitely read another of his titles very soon."

—The Jeep Diva

"A well thought out love story with a great twist and one that's definitely put Mr Flores on my radar, so I'm off to check out more books of his."

—Sinfully Sexy Book Reviews

"Please Remember Me by Jacob Z Flores is a heartbreak and heartwarming look at love that is meant to be and could make any skeptic believe in true love."

—Prism Book Alliance

By Jacob Z. Flores

3
Being True
The Gifted One
Please Remember Me

Provincetown
When Love Takes Over
Chasing the Sun
When Love Gets Hairy
When Love Comes to Town

The Warlock Brothers of Havenbridge
Spell Bound
Blood Tied

Published by DREAMSPINNER PRESS
www.dreamspinnerpress.com

To Amy, Alma, and Dani: Your help has been invaluable. Thank you so much for being there when I needed you.

To Jacob's Junkies: Your encouragement and friendship makes me smile every day. I don't know where I would be without all of you.

To my family: Your support has made me the man I am today. I'm so happy to be blood tied to each and every one of you!

INTRODUCTION AND DRAMATIS PERSONAE

MAGIC HAS existed since the dawn of mankind. Its source is the Gate, a portal to the astral plane that powers the wonders of the world. From this gate, a new species—the *homo magus*—evolved from humans and divided into three different subspecies: *homo ater magus* or warlocks, *homo albus magus* or witches, and *homo neuter magus* or wizards.

From the first moment the humans witnessed the power of this new species, homo magus were hunted without mercy and brought to the brink of extinction.

But the homo magus survived by forming a secret society that lives amid humans.

The witch hunters still exist today, continuing their pursuit of eradicating magic. As long as they are hunted, warlocks, witches, and wizards will continue to live in secret, protecting themselves from extinction while saving humans from the new enemies and ancient threats they know nothing about.

The Blackmoors (Warlocks)

Pierce Blackmoor is the oldest of his siblings. Upon his father's death, he will assume the role of high priest of his coven. He commands lightning and often charges into battle without thinking, relying solely upon the powerful magic he wields to win the day.

Thad Blackmoor is the middle child. He is coolly logical and often aloof. He uses his ice abilities to strategic advantage. Knowledge is far more important to Thad than defeating his enemies.

Mason Blackmoor is the youngest of his siblings. Until recently he couldn't control his magic or access his active power. Mason has since learned he is a shadow weaver, which means he can bend the darkness to his will. This is a rare and powerful warlock ability that has led to the corruption of every warlock who has ever wielded it.

Drake Carpenter, a human and boyfriend of Mason, has recently been made an honorary member of the Blackmoor coven. His last surviving relative, Aunt Millie, was murdered by a vampyre. Drake is under the protection of the Blackmoors due to his part in the death of the vampyre that killed his aunt.

Oliver Blackmoor is the head of his family and the high priest of his coven. He is the most powerful warlock in the family, especially once he turns his entire body to stone. Though he is often distant and irritable, Oliver loves his sons and still grieves for his wife.

Priscilla Blackmoor was Oliver's wife and mother to Pierce, Thad, and Mason. She died from breast cancer nine months ago.

THE PROCTORS (Witches)

Charles and Camille Proctor are the high priests of their coven. Charles, who works for the Havenbridge Police Department as a detective, is capable of commanding fire, while Camille has dominion over plants. The Proctors pride themselves on the white magic they practice, which connects them to the spiritual forces of the universe.

Adam Proctor is the oldest of his siblings. His guiding element of magic is air, which allows him to use it as an offensive or defensive ability. Adam has a rocky past with former friend Pierce Blackmoor. He also nurses his wounds for the unrequited feelings he had for Mason Blackmoor.

Charlotte Proctor finds herself bookended by two strong-willed siblings. She is the peacemaker in the family, and this characteristic manifests itself in her powers. Charlotte taps into the element of water, which grants her astounding healing abilities.

Miranda Proctor fancies herself the rebel in her family. She is loud and opinionated, which often gets her in trouble and sets her at odds with her family. This likely explains why Miranda and Mason Blackmoor do not get along; they are two peas in a pod. Miranda's active ability derives from the spirit element, which grants her a unique ability to teleport objects and people at will.

THE STONEWALLS (Wizards)

Lawrence and Rachel Stonewall are the high priests of their coven. The gray magic of wizards gives them direct access to the spirit element, which allows them to tap into powerful abilities that are kept in check by their logical ways. Lawrence is able to control minds while Rachel can cast illusions.

Edith Stonewall is the eldest of her siblings. She can erect invisible force fields for protection. She is also the most like her parents. She rarely engages with others outside her coven and is closest with her twin brother, Elliot.

Elliot Stonewall is Edith's younger twin brother by three minutes. He is mute and cannot access his magic like others in the community. He does, however, have the ability to speak to others telepathically.

Kate and Keaton Stonewall are the youngest members of the family, and they are also twins. Neither of them has tapped into their active powers because they are still too young. Once they turn sixteen, they will learn what ability they will have at their disposal.

OTHER CHARACTERS and Entities

The Conclave is the governing body of the magical community. The three most powerful warlocks, witches, and wizards serve on the Conclave. They are charged with making and enforcing magical laws as well as ensuring the Gate is protected from all threats. The word of the Conclave is absolute, and their power is feared across the magical community.

Bartram and Ebenezer Kane lived during the Salem Witch Trials. Bartram was a powerful member of the Conclave of his time. He was also the last warlock to possess the abilities of a shadow weaver. When his son Ebenezer was burned at the stake, Bartram went mad. He spoke the forbidden *immortalitas* spell to resurrect his son, but turned him into a vampyre instead. As a vampyre, Ebenezer created other vampyren and almost destroyed the magical and human community. It took the combined might of the Conclave to end the threat of the Kane family.

CHAPTER 1

DARKNESS SURROUNDED me.

It engulfed everything, as if something had consumed all light in the universe, leaving behind only a black void as a landscape. I inched forward, my hands in front of me, searching for a wall, my dresser, anything that would tell me I was still in my dorm room at Southern Salem University.

I found only empty air, but still I shuffled forward. I had to find my way out of here and get home. My family needed me. I didn't know how I knew that, but I did. It resonated in my gut, my soul, my blood.

Something was coming. It was making its way toward us in silent bounds, and if we weren't ready, if we weren't together, we wouldn't survive.

Thump, tap, thump, tap.

I whirled to my left at the sound of footsteps. Someone was in here with me. "Who's there?"

Thump, tap, thump, tap.

I clenched my fists, and my hands tingled as frost coated my palms. I was ready to fight.

"Answer me or I'll turn you into an ice sculpture."

The slow, measured steps circled around me. I knew the drill. My enemy was sizing me up before devouring me whole. He'd quickly learn he was about to bite off more than he could chew.

I let loose my magic in the direction of the footsteps. Ice crackled from my fingertips, and I imagined the bastard would now be frozen solid. All it would take was a good kick and whoever he was would shatter into pieces.

Thump, tap, thump, tap.

It hadn't worked. How was that possible?

I uttered an immobilization spell, a sleeping spell, and even a warding spell, but nothing worked. It continued its leisurely stroll around me.

My magic was useless. Whoever or whatever was in here with me was either immune to my power or so beyond my abilities, I was little more than a mosquito buzzing around his head.

That was a terrifying prospect.

"What do you want?" I asked, embarrassed by the slight tremor in my voice.

"You will be mine." The four words echoed in the darkness, growing louder with each reverberation until they became a deafening wail.

I covered my ears, trying to block them out, but the words sliced through me like a razor. I fell to my knees, trembling as the words continued to explode around me and as the footsteps drew closer.

I opened my mouth to speak, to utter some spell that would save me, but the only sound to escape my constricted throat was a scream.

I sat up in bed, perspiration dripping down my back. The sheets were tangled around my clenched fists, and even though I was shivering, I wasn't cold.

Terror seized my heart in its iron grip and squeezed.

I took several deep breaths, trying to calm my jackhammering pulse. Once my heartbeat returned to normal, I could hopefully relax the muscles that refused to let loose of my bedding, which had suddenly become some lifeline that, once released, would send me tumbling into a pit of despair.

It was just that stupid dream again, so why did I want to throw the covers off my bed and turn on all the lights?

I wasn't some cowardly mouse, hiding away in the corners of life. I was Thad Blackmoor, a warlock, and my family was one of the covens elected to protect the Gate, the source of all magic, from harm.

We'd recently fought off a vampyre, one of the deadliest and most powerful magical creatures in existence, and won. I hadn't cowered when it attacked and almost killed me, so why couldn't I stop shaking?

It was the voice and what it said. Its words were spoken with such conviction, such absolute certainty, they'd chilled me to the bone.

"I will never be yours," I whispered to my empty room. "I belong to myself and no one else."

My response jumpstarted my confidence. I wasn't like my older brother Pierce or my father, both of whom relied on their powers or their muscles, and I sure as hell wasn't like my younger brother, Mason, who preferred to get by on a wing and a prayer.

Their dependence on external forces made them vulnerable.

That was not who I was. I relied on myself, on my intellect, to see me to success. That was what made me different from my family and every other warlock, and I wasn't about to let some silly recurring nightmare rob me of that.

I threw the covers off my naked body and stood up in an act of defiance against the dream I couldn't help but feel had seeped into the waking world.

Dark forces were gathering and unseen enemies waited. I already possessed knowledge of this, but there were too many unanswered questions.

I had to find the answers, but in order for me to do that, it was time for me to go home to Havenbridge.

A FEW hours later, I made my way from my dorm room to the Starbucks on the campus. I'd lived here for the past five years, working on my doctorate on witchcraft and historical occult practices. I'd narrowed my field of study to examining the historical conflict between mainstream religion and witchcraft.

It was important for me to understand our history, not just from a personal perspective, but also from an academic one. By studying our past through how humans viewed us, I hoped to gain knowledge on how to better deal with our hidden role in society and avoid the pitfalls when human and magical worlds collided.

This might be the only way to remain off the radar of the witch hunters who knew of our existence and sought to eradicate my species.

I still had two chapters left to complete on my dissertation, and with all the distractions in my life lately, namely that damned vampyre and the foe the Conclave, our governing body, had warned us about, I'd begun to doubt I'd finish them by the end of the semester.

But before I made progress on anything, I needed the magical elixir known as coffee.

It would clear away the lingering gloom that clung to me like spider webs and warm my body from the bone-chilling cold that had descended upon Massachusetts.

I threw open the door to the coffeehouse and entered the warm interior. The eye-opening aroma of coffee immediately filled my nasal passages. I already felt better by the time I placed my order and moved to the side, where the barista would hand me the one supernatural creation humans had managed to conjure.

"Long time, no see, handsome."

Hannah Bishop was standing behind me, and I internally cringed. Hannah and I had dated briefly last year, and though she was a beautiful woman, she wanted more than I was willing or able to give.

When I didn't immediately greet her in return, she regarded me with light green eyes—which I'd always been a sucker for on a woman or a man—and hands placed on her slender hips.

"Sorry," I managed in my usual flat tone. I wasn't one for expressing emotions. "Just surprised to see you. It's been a few months."

"Well, if you hung out in places other than the library or your dorm room, you might actually run into people." She held her chin high as she always did when she was angry, but when it trembled, I realized she was merely masking her hurt. Despite my best intentions, she'd fallen in love with me, and love was something I did not do.

Love, like most emotions, was a useless distraction. They kept us from our true goals and from being our true selves. How could we be who we really were if we constantly had to kowtow to someone else?

When I told Hannah I didn't return her feelings, she'd walked out of my dorm room. That had been the last time I'd seen her.

"Almost done with your dissertation?"

I nodded. "Just a couple more chapters."

"Good for you," she said with a forced smile. Hannah was also getting a doctorate, except her field was American literature. "I defend mine in a few weeks."

"That's wonderful," I said, offering her a smile I hoped came off as genuine.

I failed. She twisted her lips and sighed. "I guess these decorations upset you, huh?" she asked, glancing over my shoulder. She was clearly looking to explore all avenues of conversation.

"Decorations?" I asked, turning around, and that was when I noticed them. Halloween decorations were everywhere. Ghosts had been drawn on the chalkboard menu, and some narrow-minded employee had painted a witch on the glass wall to my right. She had green skin, a large hooked nose, and a huge hairy mole on her chin.

None of the witches I knew looked like that. No wonder their portrayal in modern popular culture always ticked them off, and it wasn't like warlocks were immune. Most everyone believed we were evil or demonic. While my species was definitely more selfish, we were most certainly *not* evil.

We were just a different race among my species. That was all.

"No need to answer," she said. "I can still read your expressions. Well, the few you have."

"You were always pretty good at that," I said.

"Considering the last time we talked about Halloween, you went into this long lecture on how the day wasn't about wearing a costume, getting drunk, or waking up next to some loser you didn't even know. It's one of your High Sabbats, right?"

"Good memory," I said. Although Hannah didn't know I was a warlock, she knew I was Wiccan. I didn't hide that from anyone. "Samhain to be exact." It was the end of our year, when the veil between the worlds thinned, and it was a time for honoring our dead. It was a sacred event, not this bastardized orgy of gluttony humans had turned it into.

"I guess I can't talk you into going to a Halloween party, then?"

"You would be correct," I replied. "I'm heading home."

"I'm sorry," she said. Sadness hooded her eyes. "I forgot about your mom. This is obviously going to be tough for you."

I swallowed hard. My mother was the one chink in my armor, and memories of her shattered the casual aloofness with which I greeted the world. The armor plating I kept over my heart slipped. I had to set it right before it fell off and left me completely vulnerable. "I don't wish to discuss that," I said with a break in my voice.

When Hannah heard the faintest sign of emotion, she pounced. She wrapped her arms around me and gave me a big hug. Although the gesture was sweet, I tensed. Expressing emotions around others made me uncomfortable. Being on the receiving end was even worse.

I patted her back. It was the universal sign that I would be fine, and she responded by letting me go. If I didn't change the course of this conversation, Hannah would find some way to steer us right back. "I take it you'll be attending this blasphemous Halloween party?"

"Sure am!" she said with far too much enthusiasm. She was clearly hoping I might take her up on her previous offer. "I'm going as a slutty vampire."

Why did humans insist on taking one of the most powerful creatures in existence and hyper-sexualizing it? Real vampyren weren't the hot-totrot, misunderstood anti-heroes portrayed in popular culture. They were vicious monsters with chalk-white skin, long talons, and rows of razor-sharp teeth. If one did happen to show up at the party, it would tear through them all before the DJ could play the next song.

"You know," said a man to our left. "Vampires aren't really how popular culture makes them out to be."

The intrusion surprised us.

When I turned to glare at the eavesdropper, the choice words I had prepared died in my throat. An attractive man sat on a stool, sipping from a cup of coffee. His jet-black hair was perfectly coiffed, and a crooked smile languished on his lips. He wore a purple button-down shirt underneath his black peacoat, and both had been tailored to perfection for his broad shoulders. He held a Starbucks cup in his hand and gazed at us with his piercing, chocolate-brown eyes. He wiggled his eyebrows at me before taking another drink.

His demeanor and appearance marked him as someone who clearly knew he was attractive. And while he might in fact be a hotter version of Zachary Quinto, neither his looks nor his attitude were what had given me pause.

This guy was a warlock too.

"AND HOW do you know so much about vampires?" Hannah asked. Whenever she felt challenged, she stood with both hands on her hips and cocked her head to one side.

"I read," he said with a gesture that meant the answer should be obvious.

She snuffed like a bull ready to charge. "And are you implying that I don't?"

"Not at all," he answered with a wave of a well-manicured hand. "I was merely answering your question." There was obvious condescension in his tone, and Hannah picked up on it right away. She pursed her lips.

As for the warlock, he sat there with an amused smile. He evidently enjoyed riling her up. That told me he had an aversion to humans, like many of our kind.

"I'm Ben," he said to me with an outstretched hand. His gaze traveled up and down my body enough times, he most likely had every inch of me already memorized.

What was he studying for, an oral exam?

"This is where you tell me your name, Red," he said after a few seconds of silence.

Why did people assume redheads enjoyed that little epithet?

"It's *not* Red, that's for sure," I replied, shaking his hand. For someone who'd been holding a cup of hot coffee, his skin was chilled. He must have just come in from outside. "I'm Thad, and this is Hannah." Just because I didn't express emotion didn't mean I allowed rudeness. He was deliberately ignoring Hannah, and that was uncalled for.

"Nice to meet you," he said to only me. I didn't often get angry, but Ben was pushing his luck. "Can I buy you a coffee?"

The barista called out my order. I took it from the shelf and presented it to him.

"Or reimburse you for that one." His crooked smile seemed permanently etched on his lips.

"Well, I'm out of here," Hannah said. She stepped between Ben and me. Her previously angry glare had softened. She evidently still hoped for a future for us. "I hope to see you around."

"That would be nice," I said, putting as much sentiment into the words as I could muster. I even gave her a hug.

"Call me," she said before tossing a sneer over her shoulder at Ben.

After I nodded, she walked away.

"Someone has a crush on you," Ben stated.

I stared after her and nodded. "We dated briefly." Now why did I just tell him that?

"What happened?" He leaned against the counter, grinning at me.

"Are you normally this rude?" I asked. "Strangers don't typically ask such personal questions."

"Not a stranger," he said with a shake of his head. "I'm Ben. We've been introduced." He scooted around in his chair to gently rub his knee against my thigh.

Ben was evidently looking to score. Too bad I wasn't going to take the field. "What do you think you're doing?"

"Hoping you'll invite me back to your place."

He had a big brass pair, I had to give him that. Not only was he blatantly coming on to me in public, he evidently had no reservation against casual sex with strangers. Unlike my older brother Pierce, I didn't jump into bed with someone I didn't know.

"Thanks, but I'm headed home for Samhain in a few hours."

He stood up and closed the distance between us. He was at least an inch taller than me, and I was just over six feet. For some reason though, that one inch difference in height seemed more like six.

"Aw, come on," he whispered. The scent of mint, aftershave, and something that reminded me of copper wafted in the air between us. My head spun as if I'd had one too many cocktails. "What better way to kick off the Sabbat?"

My thoughts suddenly filled with images of Ben naked in my bed. I shook them off, but my eyes developed a mind of their own. They scanned his broad shoulders and chest before settling on the bulge in his trousers. He brandished a pretty amazing staff.

How would it feel to have his cock press against me, to enter me while his lips and tongue drank in my flesh? What would it be like to abandon the control I normally sought and turn my body over to Ben to use as he saw fit? From the crooked smile and devilish glint in his eyes, he was evidently a warlock with some experience in the art of seduction.

He could no doubt make my toes curl in mind-blowing orgasm.

What? No. That wasn't going to happen.

I shook my head to clear the fog of lust that had briefly clouded my goal of getting back to Havenbridge. "I can't." My words came out low and throaty. Great. Now I was coming down with a cold. "I have to get home. I promised my father I'd be there in enough time to help him get everything ready." While that was true, it was a lie of omission. I was due back in Havenbridge tomorrow. It was my dream that made me want to arrive one day early.

"Samhain doesn't officially start till tomorrow," he said. "You'd have plenty of time."

I was beyond annoyed. Ben was obviously used to getting his way, just like my brothers. Pierce used his charm and looks to get people to do what he wanted while Mason relied on his youthful irresponsibility to get out of doing what had to be done.

"I said I can't." An irritated tone replaced my previous throatiness. Ben clearly clued in he was going nowhere fast. "I have things to accomplish."

He took a step back, but that wicked smile of his refused to be wiped away. "Are you always so responsible?"

As a matter of fact, I was. Someone in my family had to be. I grew up with a bunch of hotheads, who flew off the handle and rarely thought things through. It was usually up to me to either clean up the mess or be the voice of reason. Hell, if it weren't for me, we might not have survived the vampyre that almost killed us. "Yes, I am," I responded. I squared my shoulders and puffed out my chest.

"Come on," he prodded with a raffish glint in his eye. My stomach knotted under the full weight of his stare. He playfully flicked the tip of my nose with his index finger. "Live a little."

If I had found my voice, I'd have told him he didn't know me from Adam. That I resented his presumptuousness. Just because people like Ben and my entire family chose to live beyond the secure boundaries of logic and responsibility didn't make me some boring old nag.

I could let my hair down if I wanted to, but the simple truth was that I rarely wanted to.

Those were all the things I would have said had I been able to speak.

But Ben's piercing stare stripped me of speech. When he looked at me with those hard-candy chocolate eyes, he peeled back every single layer of my usual defenses. The aloof persona I'd cultivated for so many years had been chopped down with one cut of his gaze.

"I promise to show you a good time," he whispered in my ear. His warm breath swept across my neck, setting off a scorching fire that burned across my flesh and down into my groin. My cock hardened in tight black denim.

Ben glanced at the pronounced bulge in my jeans and grinned. He placed his hands on my waist and pulled me against his hardness.

Even though we were in the middle of Starbucks, he pounced on my lips. He groaned into the kiss and grabbed both sides of my head with his strong, smooth hands. As his fingers wound through my strawberry blond hair, his tongue came alive inside me. The bitterness of the coffee he'd consumed added a strange acidity to his taste.

I pulled out of Ben's embrace and kiss. "I said no," I repeated.

"Always the responsible one, huh?"

"Yes."

"Well, okay. I'll let you go home."

Nobody "lets" me do anything.

Before I could tell him that, he said, "But I'll definitely see you later."

I arched one eyebrow. If I saw him again, I wouldn't guarantee he'd remain breathing. "Will you now?"

He gave me a slow nod.

"There's a fine line between confidence and cockiness. I suggest you read up on that."

Ben leaned in close before muttering, "We're warlocks. We step over *every* line we come across."

The air between us sizzled, and I slowly backed away.

Being around Ben made me dizzy and lightheaded. I didn't enjoy that feeling at all, so why, then, did I suddenly want more?

TWENTY MINUTES after leaving Ben, I finally made it back to my dorm room. I tossed my keys into the bowl by the front door before adding my wallet and cell phone. I went to take off my scarf and realized it was no longer draped around my neck.

I searched the floor and opened the door again to check the hall. It wasn't there. I'd most likely dropped it at Starbucks when Hannah hugged me or when Ben practically ravaged me in the middle of the coffeehouse.

I'd been so flustered after that spectacle, I walked briskly home with my head down the entire way.

I blew out a lungful of air to center myself. I couldn't dwell on that now. It was over, and it was time for me to pack.

I took off my coat, grabbed my suitcase, and placed it on the small table to the right of my desk. As I carefully placed folded clothes into my luggage, I eyed my immaculately made bed. Images of Ben lying on top of it, naked, filled my mind, and I entertained what it would have been like to bring him back here.

We'd likely already be undressed and rolling around on my bed, him clutching my flesh and kissing my lips, which were still raw from his stubble.

My cock responded to the image. It lengthened and grew fat as it struggled for release from the constricting briefs and denim.

I managed to catch my reflection in the closet mirror. My chest heaved, and a noticeable flush reddened my usually creamy cheeks. I resembled Pierce right before he went out for a night on the prowl.

One moment I was me, but after meeting Ben, I'd become someone I didn't even recognize. It made me far too uncomfortable.

I shook my head and slapped my face hard, trying to get under control.

Managing my warlock instincts was a constant exercise for me—unlike the rest of my family, who gave in to the warlock tendencies that raged inside us. Just like the anger I constantly kept at bay, desire was another emotion that needed to remain in check.

Our history was littered with the corpses of dead warlocks who'd succumbed to their baser instincts and paid the ultimate price for their follies. I had no intention of being another statistic.

How else was I supposed to become more powerful than I already was? Where my father, Pierce, and now Mason had found their strength in their hammer strikes, mine would come from a source previously untapped by any warlock.

I'd grow from restraint and knowledge, not brutish power plays. That would ultimately make me the most powerful Blackmoor of them all.

Reminding myself of that helped return my previous calm. I completed my packing in just under an hour.

Someone knocked on the door. I didn't have time to listen to the lamentations of Stan, my neighbor down the hall. He'd been struggling with his dissertation and would most likely not be getting his doctorate. The first time he complained, I'd listened. I'd even offered advice.

After the fourth time of being trapped in the hall with him, I realized Stan was one of those people who preferred to whine about his problems rather than fix them.

I had no time for such nonsense.

"Little pig, little pig. Let me come in," the voice said from the other side. "I've got something for you."

I held my breath. Ben was here.

When he knocked again, my pulse quickened and my breathing turned ragged. Why the hell was I panting? I should be pissed off, not excited. I'd explicitly told him I didn't have time for company, and he'd shown up anyway?

"I know you're there, little pig."

Who was he calling a pig? I threw open the door to find Ben leaning against the doorframe. He arched his bushy eyebrows and grinned. "There's my little pig."

I crossed my arms. "Just so you know, I keep an extremely tidy room."

A grin hitched up the corners of his mouth. "Wrong type of pig."

"What do—" I asked before I realized he was referring to rutting around. "Oh." He chuckled at my obvious embarrassment.

"You're cute when you blush." He licked his pale lips as he once again looked me up and down. The foundation of my refortified self-control shuddered.

I gulped. "What are you doing here?"

He pulled his left hand from behind his back and held up my scarf. "You left this behind. I figured you might need it."

"Did I leave it or did you take it?"

He grinned. "I would never do such a thing."

And a vampyre never drinks blood. "How did you find me?"

He eyed me as if that was a ridiculous question. "Do you really need to ask?"

I shook my head. He'd obviously scried for my location. It was a basic spell most of our species mastered at quite a young age. In order to cast it, you needed a possession that belonged to the one you sought.

My scarf had led him right to me. I snatched it out of his hand. "I'm not a fan of being stalked."

His lips parted in a big grin. "Not stalking. I promise. Just trying to do a good deed." He glanced over my shoulder. "I see you're all packed, though."

I couldn't lie. I'd left the evidence in clear view of my open door.

"So, since I'm here…." He paused, letting his words and his waggling eyebrows deliver the final part of his message.

An immediate no sprang to my lips. He had to go. I had a long drive ahead of me, and I had to find the answers to the mysteries no one back home had taken the time to solve.

The logical part of my brain screamed at me to say the words and shut the door.

The problem was the blood to that part of my body had been diverted farther south.

I stepped back and motioned him inside.

Ben smiled and tilted his head to the side like an eagle who'd spotted his prey. "Really?" he asked. "Are you inviting me inside?"

"Would you prefer an engraved invitation?"

He chuckled and shook his head. "Just the words would suffice. I don't want there to be any misunderstanding."

I sighed, but mostly at myself. I couldn't believe I was doing this. "Please, Ben. Won't you come in?"

He strolled across the threshold with a huge grin stretched across his lips.

"What's with the Cheshire cat impersonation?" I asked as I closed the door.

He pushed me against the wall, sniffing my throat and groaning in pleasure. "Because that means I get to hold you in my arms again," he said. He licked and then nibbled at my neck. His swirling tongue caused me to moan. I'd never done that before. I clutched at his shoulders and ground my crotch against his. My hard-on slid against his erection, which throbbed in response to the contact.

"Ben, please." Why did I just say that? Ben didn't give me time to think. His hands found my ass and squeezed. The harness I'd managed to slide over my lustful yearnings unfastened and slipped.

"That's right. Beg. I like that," he said. His lips engulfed mine as he unfastened the buttons of my jeans and slowly led me over to my bed.

"Please," I repeated, clearly unable to stop saying that word. He shoved my pants and briefs down my hips, and my hard cock sprouted from its reddish nest. The big, angry head leaked a string of precum. Ben caught the silky thread and rubbed over the tip, coating the red crown and his finger before reaching around and using my own seminal fluid to lube my hole. I shuddered as he wormed his way inside.

"There you go," he said as he jammed the digit past the second knuckle. "I'm going to open you up good."

My head swam, and my knees threatened to buckle. I'd never relinquished this much control to another person before. Just as with everything else in my life, I sat in the driver's seat when it came to sex. Whoever I was with danced to the rhythm my fingers tapped out across their sweaty flesh. I didn't move to someone else's beat.

But here I was, pushing my ass back against Ben's hand and opening my mouth wider for his probing tongue.

"That feels so good," I muttered.

Ben broke the kiss and grinned before he once again nibbled a path to my neck. He bit and chewed until my flesh became so sensitive, it practically crawled beneath his urgings. "I could just eat you alive," he said before a sting of pain filled my world.

"What the fuck?" I pushed him away, and the lustful haze lifted.

"Holy shit, man," he said. "I'm sorry."

I put my hand to my neck and found a small spot of blood. The bastard had bitten me. What was he, a vampyre?

I tensed as I carefully studied Ben. He pulled a white handkerchief out of his pocket and handed it to me.

"I'm really sorry." Lust no longer blazed in his eyes. Some other emotion crouched in the shadows. "You just really got me going. I can't apologize enough."

As I wiped my neck, I shut down my human senses and opened up my magic. If Ben was a vampyre, I'd ferret it out, and if he was, I'd find a stake and rip his dead heart to shreds.

I poked and prodded around his aura. The black and silver bands that made up the magical energy of all warlocks swirled about him, but there was something else. I couldn't see it, but it reached out to me in invisible threads.

"Should I just go?" he asked. His words severed the invisible line that wrapped around me, and it retreated as if it had never existed.

And maybe it never had. But Ben did exist. He was here, his erection still straining against the fabric of his pants.

I tossed the handkerchief to the floor and kicked free of my clothes. Whatever control I'd relinquished earlier had reverted back to me. This I could handle.

"Take off your shirt," I commanded as I closed the gap between us.

"Really?"

I grabbed the back of his head and gripped his hair tight. "Do as I say. Now."

The confident take-charge stud morphed into a horse with a bit behind his teeth. He nodded eagerly and pulled his shirt off. Half-naked, he paused, his fingers at his zipper, awaiting the command that would set his boner free.

Before I could give the order, the golden chain that hung about his neck caught my attention. From it dangled an exquisite jade pendant. A lily with open petals had been carved across the face. It was beautiful, and for some reason, I didn't want any harm to come to it.

"I'd take that off if I were you," I said, nodding at the chain. "I'm going to get pretty rough, and it's liable to get broken."

Ben's eyes darted to the gem, which he lovingly caressed. "Don't worry about it," he said. "It's tougher than it looks."

"Suit yourself." I shoved him back onto my bed, stripped the jeans from his body, and fucked him good.

CHAPTER 2

THE SHRILL alarm of an impending nuclear meltdown yanked me out of my slumber. I tried to open my eyes, but they refused to obey. I couldn't even make my arms move. They were as stone-heavy as the rest of me. Had I been asleep or in a coma?

I finally managed to peel one eye open only to discover the world had suddenly turned fuzzy. Blurry objects populated my room, and no matter how hard I tried to focus, I couldn't clear my vision. I could finally move my arms, though. I rubbed my eyes vigorously as my cell phone continued to ring. It was Pierce's ringtone, the one he had chosen for himself. He claimed it was so I wouldn't miss any of his texts, but my brother chose it so I wouldn't ignore him when he did try to contact me.

Despite the infuriating racket of the phone, my one open eyelid drooped. I tried to block out the incessant wail by pulling the pillow over my head and burrowing deeper into the exhaustion that waited to claim me once again.

The phone switched over to voice mail, and I let out a relieved sigh when silence returned to my world. It was shattered two seconds later, when he called right back. The deafening buzz made my teeth ache.

I tossed the pillow across the room and sat up with my eyes still closed.

Pierce was evidently not going to be avoided. If I didn't answer, he was going to keep calling back until I did.

I felt around on the nightstand to my right and palmed my phone. "What do you want?" I asked curtly.

"Is that any way to greet your loving older brother?" he asked.

"When he calls, I'll be sure to be nicer to him," I teased. With everyone else, I remained steadfastly distant. My brothers were a different story. Playful hostility had been the hallmark of our relationship since we were kids.

Pierce snorted. "Fucker. So when are you getting your lazy ass home? Dad's been asking about you."

Did anyone listen to me? "I'm not supposed to be there until tomorrow, remember?"

"What?" he asked. "Since when?"

"Since always," I said as I attempted to shake the haze of sleep from my eyes. I'd never humped myself into complete unconsciousness before.

"What the fuck, Thad? Why in hell are you planning on missing Samhain?"

What was he talking about? "Excuse me?"

"No. Excuse you," he said. "You've got a duty to this coven to be here for our Sabbat. You know that."

Like I needed him to remind me. "I *do*," I replied. "In fact, I've forgotten more about Samhain than you've ever known."

"Then what's the deal?" he asked. "Why are you going to miss it?"

I was irritated. On the plus side, my aggravation slowly lifted the foggy veil from my vision. "How could I miss it when I'm getting there a whole day early?"

"Are you high or something?"

"I'm not going to even pretend to know what you're talking about," I said.

"Samhain is today."

I sighed. My brother's knowledge of our ways wasn't exactly perfect, but even he should have known the date of one of our highest holidays. "It's on the thirty-first, Pierce. Not the thirtieth."

"And just what do you think today is?" he asked.

I was beyond exasperated and had arrived at ticked off. My brothers typically affected me that way. "Buy a calendar and figure it out for yourself."

"I think you're the one who needs a calendar," he replied. "Go ahead. Look at your phone, and see for yourself."

I growled in frustration before I held the phone away from my ear. I pressed the home button, and all my icons appeared on the screen. When I clicked on the calendar, I gasped. It was the thirty-first. How the hell had that happened?

My gaze drifted over to the empty side of the bed where Ben had been a few hours ago. After our volcanic orgasms, he'd gotten up and dressed. He'd claimed he had out-of-town business to take care of and couldn't stay. Not that I would have asked him to anyway.

After I'd showed him out, a wave of fatigue had washed over me. I'd never felt so tired in my life. I'd intended to lie down and nap before hitting the road.

How the hell had I slept until the next day?

"Are you still there?"

I brought the phone back to my ear. "I'm here," I replied. Shock replaced my previous bluster.

"Believe me now?" he asked.

I nodded.

"I'll take your silence as a yes," he said. "What's going on, Thad?" His voice softened. He was no longer my bullheaded big brother, who plagued my existence. Genuine concern resonated in his tone.

"Nothing. I guess I just got too involved with my dissertation and lost track of time," I lied. I sure as hell wasn't going to tell him the truth. I'd never hear the end of it.

He snuffed. "You should spend more time with your nose in someone else's ass rather than shoving it in your books." And like that, Pierce-the-jackass returned.

"Do you have to be so crass all the time?"

He belched into the phone in response.

"Classy."

"I'm all about the class," he said. "Now get off the fucking phone and get over here. Dad's wound up about all the decorations, and he's planning on you to help."

"And what's wrong with you and Mason and Drake?" Although I knew Pierce and Mason were useless, Drake was not. Mason's boyfriend had been living with us since the vampyre killed his only living relative. That decision had brought about great controversy, especially when attempts to spell memories of our existence from his mind failed.

Drake's imperviousness to magic was yet another mystery that begged to be solved.

"I've got a business meeting," he said. Pierce worked as a vice president in the family business Dad was grooming him to take over. "And Mason and Drake are most likely playing hide the salami somewhere in the house."

I rolled my eyes. "I'll be there as soon as possible."

"Make it faster than that," he said before hanging up.

I tossed my phone on the bed and surveyed the room. Most people would likely descend into panic after learning they'd lost a good portion of a day, but I wasn't like most. As with anything else in life, clear thinking could produce the answers I sought.

Although it was bizarre and unusual for me to pass out like that, Ben and I had been going at it pretty hard for at least four hours. By the time we were spent, we'd dripped sweat and panted like bulldogs in the middle of a hot, humid day. I was exhausted after he left, and it had been somewhere around three in the afternoon if I remembered correctly.

While I'd planned on only taking a nap, the recent lack of sleep caused by my dreams, coupled with the intense sex, had more than likely caused my body to shut down. That had to be what happened.

Satisfied with my logic, I rose and entered the bathroom. I turned on the faucet, held my hands under the stream, and then splashed cold water onto my face.

As I toweled the drops of water from my pale cheeks, made slightly coarse from the reddish facial hair I'd yet to shave away, I noticed the small wound on my neck. I'd almost forgotten Ben had bitten me in the heat of the moment. The freak.

It wasn't infected or anything. In fact, it was little more than a scratch now. Still, I grabbed some Neosporin and rubbed it into the cut.

By tomorrow, all traces of it and Ben's short visit into my life would disappear forever.

AN HOUR later, I was on the road to Havenbridge in my black Mercedes Roadster. It was almost four o'clock, and home was still an hour away. Dad wasn't going to be pleased.

As we did every year, my family held the Samhain celebration at Blackmoor Manor. It was a lot of work that required a great deal of planning. The bonfire had to be set up in the backyard. Autumnal decorations had to be hung throughout the grounds and manor. Places needed to be cleared for the ancestor altars, and the table needed to be prepared for the Feast of the Dead.

Even though Dad hired a catering service to make the food and paid them extra to set up most of the decorations, he'd been relying on my help with the final touches.

As if on cue, my father's ringtone, "Magic Carpet Ride" by Steppenwolf, started playing. I took a deep breath before answering. "I'm on my way."

"You were supposed to be here hours ago," my father said. His tone was low, almost a whisper. Oliver Blackmoor didn't yell when he was furious. He became deadly calm.

"I got held up. You know I'm working on my dissertation, and I just lost track of time." I couldn't very well tell my father the truth. Being late due to important schoolwork was one thing. Telling him it was because I'd fucked my brains out and then passed out would likely result in a mushroom cloud where my house used to be.

He exhaled before replying. "I know you've been busy trying to finish up your dissertation, son." His tone had returned to his usual baritone. "I shouldn't have gotten upset."

Why couldn't he be his typical self and fly off the handle? I knew how to handle him when he was belligerent. He was evidently taking my advice and trying to control his warlock temper. It was something I'd asked my family to work on the last time I was home. Getting riled up had almost cost my father and Pierce their lives in our battle with the vampyre. "I'll get there as soon as I can."

"Well, don't speed," he said. "I want you home safely."

I stared into the phone. Who was this man? "Have Pierce and Mason been helping?"

He grunted into the phone. "Pierce scheduled a business meeting and has been out the last few hours. As for Mason, well, he and Drake hung up some of the fall wreaths, but then they started making out. I don't know where they are now."

Leave it to my brothers to shirk responsibility as often as possible. Didn't they realize this Samhain would be a tough one for Dad? It was the first one without Mom. But instead of thinking about anyone else, my brothers thought only of themselves. Typical warlocks. "I'll finish up once I get there."

"Don't worry about it. I think I can get it done." He didn't sound convincing. "I just can't find where your mother stored the candles for the altar."

"Check the attic." Even though she'd lost her battle with cancer in March, it seemed like it happened yesterday. "I think they're in the black chest next to where she stored our baby clothes."

"Right," he replied. His voice broke, and a heavy weight landed on my chest. Although my father and I hadn't had the relationship he and Pierce enjoyed, I felt for him. She had been my best friend, the one person I was closest to in our entire family. But she had been his wife, the woman he'd been spell bound to the moment he saw her.

I couldn't begin to imagine the emptiness that threatened to swallow him up from inside.

"What time are the Stonewalls and the Proctors arriving?" I asked. Changing the subject would distract us both from the swell of emotions that threatened to drown us, especially since my father didn't care for the heads of the other protector covens. It was part of our culture for warlocks, wizards, and witches to not get along. Our different types of magic necessitated such staunch divisions.

At least that was what I'd always been led to believe. After everything we'd gone through recently, I had my doubts.

"Eight o'clock," he answered through gritted teeth.

And they'd all be on time too.

"Well, we've got plenty of time to get things ready," I finally replied. "I'll be there no later than six, and, I'll take over and make my brothers toe the line."

He snorted. "Good luck with that."

They'd listen all right. Or they'd be walking around with freeze-dried nuts for the rest of their lives. "Don't worry, Dad. I've got it covered."

"Thanks, Thad. I appreciate it." The tension in his voice had disappeared, and I was relieved. "I'll see you at six."

"See you then," I said before I ended the call.

A road sign up ahead revealed Havenbridge was fifty miles away. In just under an hour, I'd be home with a family that was often more frustrating than getting a cat to obey. Still, it would be nice to be home again. So why did the weight that sat upon my chest only grow heavier?

WHEN I crossed the Havenbridge town line, I was about five minutes from home, and the woods that made up the rear of our estate stretched to my right. I pushed down on the accelerator, causing the scenery to flash by in a blur of orange and brown.

I foolishly hoped that if I drove faster, I could outrace the strange sensation that had overcome me a few miles back. It wasn't working. The bizarre feeling persisted and had only gotten worse. Unease had settled across my skin like frostbite.

I shook uncontrollably, as if my body couldn't get warm enough, and it felt as if some unseen entity was stabbing me with dozens of sharp needles.

The last couple of times this happened had been when we got news of my mother's prognosis and right before the vampyre attacked us at our house.

Something bad was coming. Its presence drifted outside the cone of light my headlights cast onto the darkening road, and no matter how wide I opened my magical senses, I couldn't detect what lay in wait out there.

It couldn't be the vampyre. Drake had run a stake through its heart. No, that vile creature was most definitely dead. Was it some new threat? Perhaps it was the shadow weaver that had almost killed Mason and Drake or even the mysterious enemy that worried the Conclave.

A fireball suddenly flew out of the woods and bounced off the hood of my car. The impact caused me to swerve. I slammed on my brakes and the rear end fishtailed before skidding to a stop on the shoulder. I was about two feet away from rolling over into the ditch.

A second fireball exited the woods and slammed into the speed limit sign on the other side of the road.

I scrambled out of my car.

A cry of pain shattered the eerie darkness that had suddenly enveloped the woods. I rushed toward the sound on instinct. The only sound I could hear was my pounding heart.

I sprinted through the woods, leaping over fallen logs and praying my trench coat didn't trip me up and cause me to stumble. I ducked past the withered limbs of saplings that had succumbed to the advancing cold, my breath pluming in front of me. I was winded, but why couldn't I hear myself panting anymore as I ran?

I trampled over dead leaves, but they didn't crunch. I stopped and snatched a thin branch off one of the younger trees and bent it in two. No snap.

Slowly, the noise of the woods came back as if some deity had his hand on the volume button of the world and gradually turned the knob back up to normal. But he didn't stop there. He moved the dial from a normal five all the way up to ten.

My panting echoed around me as if I were screaming. The crunching of leaves beneath my feet became explosions. I placed my hands over my ears, hoping to drown out the deafening cacophony, but it didn't work.

The world continued to grow louder and louder until it became white noise, which vibrated my bones.

I sank to the ground, the cold, damp mud seeping into my jeans. I swept my gaze left and right, trying to discern what the hell was happening to me, but all I saw was the darkened woods.

But something was doing this. I was being attacked, and if I didn't stop the awful screeching, my head might explode. When my mouth filled with the taste of copper and blood flowed from my nose, I realized I didn't have much time before whatever was attacking me killed me. I had to act.

Whatever was responsible had to be close by, but I didn't know the exact location so a straightforward counterattack was impossible. But I wasn't helpless. I'd been playing with the limits of my powers lately, trying to use them in ways beyond a frontal assault that encased my enemies in ice.

If this worked, I might just have a shot.

Instead of focusing my ability through my hands as I usually did, I imagined it radiating out of me in rippling waves of chill. Whatever it touched, it would freeze.

It froze the ground and trees within a three-foot diameter of me, but that wasn't enough. The screaming persisted, and blood poured out of my nose. I forced my power out even farther. Six feet. Still nothing but an ever-growing ice patch around me.

At nine feet, my vision blurred. In a few moments, this would all be over. I had the reserves for one last push, and if it didn't work, I hoped when my family found my corpse, I would be more than just liquefied ooze.

I dug my fingers into the frozen ground and let out a silent scream as I radiated my power as far as I could.

The wailing stopped, and the world returned to normal.

My breath wheezed from my lungs in a normal decibel, and when I scratched the ice, it cracked.

I tore my gaze from the ground to the woods. Approximately fifteen feet away stood a figure encased in ice. It was a woman with long white hair that hung past her waist. Her flesh reminded me of ash, and her eyes glowed an eerie yellow. Her mouth hung open an inhuman ten inches in a wide silent scream.

I'd seen this creature before. Not in real life, but in my family's Grimoire. It was a banshee. Its presence meant death was near.

I slowly rose to my feet and drew closer. "What are you doing here?" I asked.

Since she was frozen, she obviously couldn't reply, but her yellow eyes tracked my movement. She was pissed. Banshees, like most of the fae, didn't take kindly to being caught. Fairies didn't live in our world, but they had important functions to perform in order to make ours run smoothly.

Had she stumbled from her realm into ours by accident? It wasn't uncommon for a random fairy to cross over on Samhain, when the veil between our worlds grew thin.

If she'd been an elf or a brownie, I'd just ask her. The light fae were mischievous, but they were usually gentle and kind-hearted. A banshee, however, was a dark fae. Their ways were often sinister and wicked. She couldn't be trusted not to attack me again.

A low hum filled my ears. I placed my hand on the ice surrounding her, and it vibrated. She was trying to get free.

"Don't do it," I told her.

Her yellow eyes turned to slits. If she could have screamed, she'd most likely shatter my bones.

The humming grew louder, and the ice surrounding her started to crack.

"Stop it," I warned.

She didn't listen. The sound increased in decibel until tiny fissures worked their way through the ice.

"Damn it." I hated cursing. To me, it was a sign of limited intelligence, but right now, it was the only way I could think to get her attention. "If you don't fucking stop, I'll have to kill you."

The hum turned into a steady drone. Ice chipped and fell off her prison. She was less than a minute from freeing herself. I had no choice.

With a gesture of my hand, the ice prison collapsed in on itself, crushing the banshee within.

Chunks of ice fell away from her broken body, and as I stared down at her corpse, a dense fog sprang up around her. When it dissipated, she was gone.

Great. Now I'd never find out what she'd been doing here.

A low moan behind me drew my attention. I spun around, bracing for another attack. How stupid could I be? I'd forgotten all about the fireball that had struck my car. Banshees couldn't project fire. Something else had been with her.

I scanned the area, sweeping past the ice patch I'd created, the silent trees that stood like gnarled soldiers all around me, and the carpet of dead leaves that crunched beneath my feet.

A groan came from a tangle of bushes about twenty feet away on my left. I clenched my hands into fists, and a spell was ready on my lips for whatever might leap out at me. No attack came, only another mumble of pain.

Maybe whoever was in there had been battling the banshee and had no wish to fight me. Still, I had to be prepared. I headed toward the sound, ready to defend myself.

I stepped through the bramble. Stretched out on the ground before me was the unconscious, naked body of a man.

I KNEW I should check to see if he was okay, but I could only stand there, transfixed by the man's stunning beauty. He looked to be in his midtwenties. Claw marks scratched crimson tracks across his pale, bare flesh, but it didn't detract from the innate attraction that shot through me like a rocket.

He had obviously been fighting the banshee and hadn't been winning. Why did I suddenly want to find a spell that would bring that wicked fae back from the dead so I could kill her again?

I rubbed my temples. Where was all this outpouring of emotion coming from?

I took several deep breaths to clear my mind before kneeling next to him. His pulse was normal, and besides the cuts, he didn't look to have any serious injuries.

That was good. I ran my hands along his broad shoulders, over the Celtic tattoos that encircled his strong biceps, and down his flat, chiseled stomach. A few inches from his cock, I stopped and withdrew. He was hurt and needed medical help, not for me to help myself.

I shook my head, forcing the inappropriate thoughts and lustful urgings from my mind. I had to maintain control.

"Tell me your name, warlock."

I started. I'd been so busy ogling his naked body and his perfectly sized prick that I hadn't even realized he'd awoken. I prepared to answer, but then I gazed into his eyes. They were a deep, vivid green that reminded me of the sea glass that washed up on the coast. "M-My name's, uh," I stammered. Since when couldn't I remember my own name?

An impish smile danced upon his pale pink lips. It held all the confidence of Ben's smile without the cockiness. It made me unbearably thirsty. "Take your time." He placed his hand on my thigh. If I'd been butter, I would have melted.

"I'm Thaddeus," I answered, suddenly remembering. "Thad."

He sat up and cupped my cheek in his palm. "Thank you for your help, Thaddeus."

"Any time," I said with a smile. To my surprise, I meant it. Both the words and the smile, and I didn't even have to fake either of them.

"Just breathe," he said as he stood. I still knelt before him, my gaze wandering from his entrancing eyes to his cock. It was a good seven inches and sprouted from a small thatch of black hair. Since his dick dangled only a few inches from my face, all I would have had to do was move forward slightly to take the entire length of his shaft down my throat.

He towered over me, a sparkle glinting off his bottle-green eyes. "Here," he said, offering me his hand. "Let me help you up."

When his hand closed over mine, I couldn't stand. My legs had turned to noodles. "I can't," I replied. "I don't know what's happening to me."

His grip grew tighter, and he pulled me to my feet. I lost my balance and fell into him. He wrapped his hands around my waist and pulled me against him. A low moan escaped my throat. I should be naked right now too.

"You must focus," he said. No anger flashed in his eyes, only concern and a hint of amusement. He'd no doubt had this effect on others. "Remember why you are here."

"I was attacked," I said. My voice sounded far away, as if I was listening to myself from the opposite end of a tunnel.

He nodded. A dark strand of his raven black hair fell onto his forehead, where it contrasted sharply with the paleness of his extremely fair skin. "And do you know what it was?"

I stood taller, no longer leaning my entire weight against him, but he was still at least three inches taller than me. "A banshee." For some reason, recalling the previous events acted as an anchor that kept me from sinking further into the ocean this man had created.

"There you go," he said with a slight nod. "You're coming out of it."

I was. The dreamlike quality that had suddenly become my world started to fade. The reality beyond this man came back into focus, and my logical side, which had been straining in vain against the riptide of attraction, started to make some progress in keeping me grounded.

"What are you?" I asked.

He grinned before stepping back and letting me stand on my own. "Do you even need to ask?"

I opened my magical senses. A golden aura surrounded him, and a dozen tiny, sun-shaped particles orbited around him. "You're a light fae."

"A fire fairy, to be exact."

And he was definitely not what most humans pictured a fairy to be. He was at least six foot three, not six inches high. He wasn't thin or effeminate. Strong, masculine lines shaped his face, and lean muscles defined his frame. The combination made him appear more of a rogue than a sprite.

Being a fire fairy did explain the fireballs and my almost instant attraction, though. Not only were his kind charged with keeping the home hearths burning, but they sparked the fires of creativity and passion.

That must be why I'd suddenly turned into a horny teenager and was sporting more wood than the forest. The knowledge relieved me. Now if only I could relieve myself of the persistent erection that bent at an uncomfortable angle. It was getting painful.

He grinned down at my bulging denim. "Impressive," he said with a nod at my groin. "But we can deal with that some other time."

With my boner? That sure as hell didn't alleviate my raging erection. It only made it worse. I was slightly worried my cock might burst out of my pants like a jack-in-the-box.

"Did you dispatch the banshee?" he asked in a tone far more regal than you'd expect from someone standing naked in the woods. He exuded confidence that had clearly come from a lifetime of freedom and privilege.

I nodded, unable to speak. His poise captivated me because his bearing was unlike mine. He was warm and comfortable in his own skin, and it most likely drew others to him like a moth to a flame.

I was the complete opposite. I stood aloof and was often cool and distant, a by-product of my constant war against the brutish nature that swirled within.

Being at ease with my nature wasn't in the cards for me. The true me was far too dangerous and unpredictable. I'd only let him out once, and I'd regretted it ever since.

"You must be very powerful," he said, looking quite impressed with me. "Banshees are not easy to defeat. I have firsthand experience with that."

"I belong to one of the three protector covens," I said with a smug jut of my chin. I might as well have been a peacock fanning my tail feathers.

His eyes widened. The protector covens were legendary in the magical community. Without the Gate, warlocks, witches, wizards, and even fairies would cease to exist. "Then I consider myself most lucky to have stumbled upon a warlock such as you." The formality in his speech intrigued me. It was like he was a naked ambassador sent here by his people.

"And why are you here?" I asked.

He surveyed his surroundings, and an emerald fire danced in his eyes. "I'm not certain how I got here, and I find that infuriating." His right hand burst into flame before he quickly snuffed it out.

Like most of his kind, he was a hothead. "I don't understand."

He chuckled, but it communicated frustration instead of amusement. His broad, muscular chest heaved, and his respiration increased. He was getting more worked up by the minute. "Yes, well, neither do I," he admitted with a grimace. "All I remember is falling asleep in my chambers at the Hearth, and when I awoke, there was only darkness." He shivered, and I suddenly remembered it was in the midthirties and he was naked. I took off my fur-lined trench coat and offered it to him, but he waved it away. "I'm a fire fairy. I don't get cold."

I eyed his trembling body. "But you're shivering."

He waved away my concern. "In anger. Nothing more."

"Tell me about the darkness," I asked, putting my coat back on. I didn't have the luxury of not getting cold.

He gritted his teeth before replying. "It was everywhere, like some damned plague I couldn't escape. I couldn't breathe, and there was this voice, speaking to me in a strange language." His anger continued to grow in his retelling. He clenched his hands as if he were ready to strike out and punch a tree. "Its hands were all over me, and then pain I'd never felt before shot through me. Afterward, I woke up here with that bitch of a banshee standing guard. I was too weak at the time to fight her, and I don't *do* weak." He locked onto my eyes, and I nodded. He apparently wanted me to know he was capable of defending himself.

But as quickly as his rage ignited, it blew out. Tranquility returned to his gaze. His mood swings made me dizzy. "If you hadn't come along, she would have killed me." He held my cheeks in both hands. The warmth of his touch spread across my body. "Thank you," he said.

He bridged the small gap between us. His breath, which reminded me of cedar and honeysuckle, plumed across my face, and then his mouth brushed tenderly against mine.

His velvety lips and the sweetness of his kisses filled me with joy and need. It was a stark contrast to what I'd experienced with Ben.

When he pulled out of the kiss, I tried to bring his lips back to mine. Instead of succumbing to me as I had to him, he placed his hand on my chest and gently pushed. "I am forever in your debt, and while I would enjoy making love, I'm afraid I don't have the time. I must return at once to Otherworld."

What? No. How could I let him return to the land of the fairies? "Please, don't."

"I must," he said. He removed my hands from his smooth waist, but even though his almost regal tone had returned, there was a moment of hesitation, as if he seriously considered my request. When his dilated pupils returned to normal, he shook his head. "Trouble is obviously brewing back home. I must return."

I understood the pull of duty. That was why I'd come home, and I couldn't stand in his way any more than I could let him stand in mine.

He waved his hand. In response a fiery pinwheel floated in the air. It rotated clockwise, and as it did, it grew larger until it was at least seven feet high. "Good-bye, Thaddeus. I hope our paths will cross again."

"I don't even know your name," I said.

"I'm Aiden," he said and stepped through the flaming portal. Once he entered, the flaming blades spun counterclockwise, shrinking with each turn until it disappeared in a puff of smoke.

CHAPTER 3

I DROVE the rest of the way home with a clarity I hadn't had in a while. Since my nightmares began, I'd been walking around as if the world were muted. It had gotten worse when I ran into Ben. My muffled world had been thrown askew, and I'd reacted to him in a way that was definitely *not* me.

But in the few moments I'd spent with Aiden, that changed. It was like sipping a tonic that flushed the poison I'd inadvertently drunk from my body. The heaviness that had settled upon my chest, and the unease I had been carrying around, vanished.

The comfortable control I'd cultivated all these years had returned, and Aiden had had something to do with that. It wasn't just his kiss, which had been pretty damn amazing. It was like a refreshing spring breeze had cleared all the cobwebs in my soul.

Aiden's presence and self-confidence weren't like the smug warlock self-assurance I found so aggravating, which probably explained why my brother Pierce and Ben rubbed me the wrong way.

Aiden's assurance was pure, almost untainted. It reminded me of my mother. Though she'd had more power in her pinkie than most had in their entire bodies, she'd never let it distort the image she presented to the world.

Perhaps one day I'd learn how to find the balance that would set me free.

But now that I once again found my center, I could focus on what needed to be done—solving the burning questions my family needed answered.

I turned onto the cobblestone driveway that led to my house. The three-story colonial estate and the spectacular grounds opened up before me. The gray-shingled roof with the white wooden trim welcomed me back in the role I always assumed—the responsible one.

I had a lot of work to accomplish while I was here, and that was where my mind needed to stay. The task ahead of me wasn't going to be easy, but I would find the answers. Of that I had no doubt.

I pulled into the four-car garage, and the door to the house immediately opened. Mason and Pierce stood on the porch. They were both almost the spitting image of our father. They had inherited his dark locks and blue eyes while I had my mother to thank for my strawberry blond hair and hazel eyes. I looked and acted so differently from them, it was sometimes difficult to believe we were brothers, especially when they were glaring at me with their arms crossed. Ah, home.

They were both dressed for the Samhain celebration. Pierce wore a form-fitting, blue plaid button-down with the sleeves rolled up and tight khaki denim. He naturally chose clothing that displayed the muscular body he worked so hard on. Surprisingly, Mason hadn't donned his favorite pair of jeans and a T-shirt. That had to be Drake's doing. A black collared shirt showed underneath his gray cashmere sweater, and he was actually wearing black slacks.

Would miracles never cease?

"What cheery tidings do you bring me?" I asked as I exited my vehicle.

"Took you long enough, Brainiac," Pierce quipped. A playful scowl wrinkled his upper lip. I hated that nickname, and he knew it. But this was what we did. The Blackmoor brothers didn't greet each other with hugs or pats on the back. Teasing and hostility were how we embraced.

"I talked to Dad on the way here," I replied, choosing to not take the bait Pierce dangled in front of me. "So simmer down."

"Simmer down?" Mason asked. Of my two brothers, he and I were the most distant. It was probably because he lived life with his thumb up his ass. How he tapped into the power of darkness was beyond me. I shivered at the thought of the immense power he possessed. "Because of you, we've been busting our asses."

I couldn't feel any less sorry for him if I tried. "What? You two actually had to get off your butts and do some work?" I shot them both a blank stare. "My trip here wasn't exactly a piece of cake. I ran into some trouble on the road."

That got their attention. Their pretend pissiness vanished. After our most recent problems, we'd all been waiting for impending doom to come crashing down around us.

"What happened?" Pierce asked. As usual, my older brother thought with his fists. His hands clenched, and the hum of his electrical powers buzzed.

"Was it the shadow weaver?" A dark aura surrounded Mason. While he had yet to truly explore his shadow weaver abilities, I was pleased to see he no longer had trouble summoning his active power.

"No. A banshee."

Pierce and Mason locked eyes with each other before gaping at me. "A fairy?" They asked almost in unison. The incredulity in their question couldn't have been more apparent.

"Considering how little you two study our Grimoire, I'm surprised you even knew that."

Mason's bushy eyebrows slanted, but before he could respond to my dig, Pierce, clueless as ever, spoke first. "What trouble can a fucking fairy cause?" he asked.

His question proved how little my brothers read our magical texts. They believed fairies to be androgynous sprites with high-pitched voices, flitting about on paper-thin wings. That was definitely not the banshee and most certainly *not* Aiden. "You'd be surprised," I answered as I shouldered past them after ascending the porch steps.

When I entered the house, I inhaled deeply. I hoped to find traces of my mother's perfume still lingering on the air, but the comforting scent of orange blossoms and sweet spices had vanished long ago. Still, I couldn't help but sniff like a bloodhound every time I came home.

The door slammed shut, and Mason circled to stand in front of me. "Should we be worried?"

The concern in his tone was evident. He and Drake had been through a lot with the vampyre and the shadow weaver. They'd both almost been killed. Hell, we were all almost sliced to pieces, but Mason had seen exactly what a vampyre could do. Not only had he battled it multiple times, but it had killed Drake's Aunt Millie.

I wasn't entirely convinced my encounter with the banshee was something we shouldn't be worried about, but I had to assuage his concern. "It was just a fairy," I said with a nod. "I took care of it."

"Why do I get the feeling there's more to this story than you're telling us?" Pierce asked.

He stood beside me, leaning his bulky frame against the wall. For someone who was usually oblivious, he was pretty on the money right now. "We can talk about it later," I said. "We need to get ready before the Stonewalls and the Proctors get here."

Mason moaned. Out of all of us, he hated these rituals the most because whenever we got together with the witches and the wizards that made up the other two protector covens, he was forced to deal with Miranda Proctor, the witch who burrowed under his skin like a bot fly.

"Don't worry," Pierce said with a pat to Mason's back. "You've got Drake to help keep you occupied."

"Speaking of your boyfriend," I said. "Where is he?"

"In the living room with Dad," Mason said with a nod down the hall. "They're entertaining Pierce's business associate."

"Why did you bring a coworker home?" I asked. "Samhain is a private holiday for us."

"Really?" he asked. He stuck a finger up his nose and crossed his eyes, pretending he was the idiot I'd basically just called him.

"Relax," Mason said. "He's a solitary warlock with no coven to celebrate with."

I nodded. Solitary warlocks weren't rare, but they were uncommon. They often glommed on to other covens during high Sabbats to partake in the celebration. While it was annoying, we were honor-bound to make him feel welcome.

"Thad, is that you?" My father's gravelly voice drifted down the hall from the living room.

"Yes," I called back.

"It's about time. Now get in here and meet our guest."

I abhorred newcomers, and my brothers knew that.

"He's a nice guy," Pierce said as he shoved me forward with a playful smile.

"And he's hot," Mason added.

"I'm going to tell Drake you said that."

Mason wasn't pleased with my comment. "Do that, and I'll hit you with a shadow blast."

I chuffed at the threat. Mason couldn't hit the bottom of the pool if he jumped in. I was about to tell him that, but as I entered the living room, I went mute.

"Red!" said the man sitting next to my father. His chocolate-brown eyes widened, and a wicked smile tugged across his lips. "Long time no see."

"YOU TWO know each other?" My father asked. His steel blue gaze shifted between Ben, who had a pleased smirk on his face, and me. My face flushed hot, but I did my best to maintain my composure. Just seeing Ben rattled the foundation of my newly built self-control.

"We sure do," Ben answered. He rose from where he sat across from my father and strode over to me. He pulled me into a hug, and I went rigid. Ben either didn't care or didn't notice. Instead of releasing me, he lingered.

I looked around the room. I made a concerted effort not to put my private life on display. What I did behind closed doors was no one's business but mine, but here I was with Ben pressing his body against mine. To make matters worse, his cock slowly hardened against my thigh.

This was not going to go well.

My father glued his wide eyes to the floor and scratched his fingers through his thick facial hair. My brothers, like the jerks they were, snickered behind me.

"No need to tell us how," Pierce commented.

Ben chuckled before finally releasing me. "Why does your mind always go straight to the gutter?" he asked.

"Because that's where my brother lives," I replied. I shot him an even stare that told him to drop it or else.

Pierce answered my threat with a big, goofy grin. He was clearly not done being an ass.

Mason patted my shoulder before squeezing by Ben and me to get to Drake. "I'm just glad you're getting some," he said. "Since I've never seen you with anyone but us, I was beginning to think you were either a hermit or a serial masturbator."

"Mason!" Our father reprimanded from where he sat. He ran his big hand through his short-cropped dark hair before straightening the creases in the black pants he wore for the Sabbat.

"Will all y'all stop teasin' him?" Drake asked in his Texas twang. Dressed in a long-sleeved shirt and sweater vest, he rose from the couch and gave me a big hug. "It's good to see you again. It's been too long."

"Thank you, Drake," I replied. Even though Mason was a pain, I liked Drake. Despite the hurt he had suffered, he had a ready smile on his lips, and true kindness reflected in his cornflower blue eyes. I turned from his warmth and leered at Pierce and Mason, who giggled like schoolkids. "I would say it's good to be home, but since my brothers are here, I'd be lying."

"Can we get back to the business at hand?" Pierce asked.

My father nodded. "Yes, let's."

"So how *did* you two meet?" Pierce asked.

"Pierce!" In about half a second, Dad was going to send my older brother flying through the window into the backyard.

"What?" he asked, a look of pretend innocence widening his expression. "You can't tell me you're not wondering the same thing."

"It's none of our business," my father answered. "And frankly, I don't need the details."

Before I could agree with him, Ben opened his big mouth. "It's not a secret. We met at Starbucks yesterday," he said as he returned to his seat.

"A coffeehouse?" Pierce asked. "I didn't know you trolled Starbucks for tail. I'm gonna have to give that a try."

Everyone laughed except my father. His bearded face twisted in revulsion. "That's enough," he said. He eyed Pierce, silently telling him if he continued, there would be hell to pay. I half hoped Pierce would. Nothing would make me happier right now than to see my older brother brought down a couple of pegs.

Pierce evidently got the hint. He shoved his hands in the pockets of his slacks like a little kid. "All right. No need to get violent."

I exhaled in relief. The teasing had finally ceased, so I plopped down in the wingback chair across from the couch where Mason, Drake, and Ben sat.

"I still can't believe you're Pierce's brother," Ben said. He locked his gaze on mine and unconsciously licked his lips. The seductive gesture triggered a flush that spread across my body. It wasn't embarrassment but an overwhelming desire to jump his bones.

I shook it off and nodded. "Neither can I."

"How could you not?" Pierce asked. He took the empty spot on the loveseat next to Dad. "Blackmoor isn't that common a last name."

"True. But it's not like we exchanged last names or anything." He locked eyes with me. "And mine's Crane, by the way."

Was he trying to piss me off? If so, he was doing a damn good job of it. I arched my eyebrow at him before glancing at my father.

"My apologies, Oliver. I didn't mean to offend." My father refused to meet Ben's gaze. "I'm evidently rattled and not thinking clearly."

"I guess we all know why you were *really* late today, don't we?" Pierce asked.

I glared at Pierce for that comment before looking at my father. He'd obviously not put two and two together, but thanks to my oaf of a big brother, he did. His even stare told me we'd be talking about this later. "Either we change the subject, or every single one of you will be spitting out rock."

That shut us all up. Oliver Blackmoor was the most powerful warlock in this room.

"What's your active power?" Ben asked. He leaned forward, clearly willing to change the subject. "Since warlock abilities come from an amalgamation of two different elements, I've always been fascinated with how that manifests in others."

"Stone," my father answered.

"So you draw your abilities from fire and earth," Ben said. "Mine is earth-based too. Sand."

"Manipulation or dermal?" I asked. My father didn't manipulate stone; he actually turned into rock.

"Manipulation and projection," Ben said with a grin. "I tap into earth and air."

I was impressed. That meant Ben could not only bend sand to his will, but he could create powerful sandstorms. That could definitely come in handy if we needed it.

"What about you, Thad?"

"Ice," I replied.

Ben turned to Pierce, whose fist crackled with blue electricity. "Got it," he said. "You're a living lightning rod." When he turned to Mason, the hairs on the back of my arm stood at attention.

"Mason hasn't discovered his active ability yet," I said before Ben could ask.

"Really?" Ben asked. He didn't sound convinced. "It's unusual but not uncommon for someone your age not to have found his active power yet. Don't worry. It'll come," he said with a smile.

No one responded to Ben's comment. They were too busy being shocked that I'd just lied, and they weren't hiding it very well, either. They stared at me with mouths agape. Only Drake managed to school his face, even though his tilted head and pursed lips gave him away.

The stigma of potential corruption might come with Mason's rare shadow-weaving abilities, but that wasn't the reason I'd lied.

Although I couldn't understand it, I didn't want Ben to know.

I DIDN'T have time to figure out why I suddenly distrusted Ben. Shortly after I'd stunned everyone into silence, my father announced we needed to finish setting up for the Samhain celebration.

I set everyone to task. I charged my brothers with assembling our family's altar in the library and Drake with hanging the remaining decorations still in boxes. Mason wanted to work with Drake, but there was no way I was letting that happen. Left to their own devices, they'd be sucking face and then running off to one of the many bedrooms.

While I supervised the setup of the bonfire in the backyard, I asked Ben to help organize the offering table for the feast. He'd clearly wanted to work with me out back, but I needed space from him. His sudden appearance in my home still had me rattled.

My dad wanted to help, but I made him go upstairs and take a nap. He needed his rest before leading us through the ritual.

By the time the front doorbell rang, everything was ready. My father descended the staircase, offered me a smile, and then proceeded to open the door to let the Proctors and the Stonewalls inside.

As usual, my father greeted the heads of the two families with cool cordiality before welcoming them into our home. He didn't like them, and they didn't like him. Still, we were the protector covens, and together we guarded the Gate and celebrated the Sabbats like one big, extended, dysfunctional family.

But unlike our parents, the children they had produced didn't follow the established tradition of intolerance among the different types of magic. Though we tried to keep it from our parents, we liked each other well enough. Well, except for Mason and Miranda Proctor. The same went for Pierce and Miranda's brother, Adam. When we were younger, they used to be close. Now, they could barely stand to be in the same room with each other. Once, I asked Pierce what had happened, but he'd told me to "mind my own fucking business." I never brought it up again.

"Should I set this up at the usual spot?" Adam Proctor asked, holding up a triangular table that would serve as the altar for their dead. He was the oldest of his witchy siblings, with eyes so light blue they were almost gray. He wore black pants and a white button-down that made him look like a waiter.

"Yeah, same place as last year," I answered with a nod down the hall to the library.

Edith and Elliot Stonewall, one of the sets of twin wizards, followed Adam, carrying their altar between them. They were in Mason's class at high school. Elliot, who was mute, smiled at me as he passed in his gray corduroy pants and beige shirt. Even though he couldn't speak, he used his telepathy to hold a conversation. The problem was it usually resulted in a migraine for whomever he chatted with. He was a sweet guy, and we used to study together at the library. His sister took a little getting used to. She had on a long skirt and frilly blouse in the exact same color scheme as her brother's, but she didn't bother to acknowledge me. She was a typical gray-magic wizard, aloof and coldly logical. She and I had at least that much in common.

"You seem distracted."

I turned to find Charlotte Proctor standing behind me. The glint in her brown eyes matched the friendly smile on her lips. As always, she wore modest clothing—white blouse and a long yellow skirt—unlike her younger sister, Miranda, who preferred a more seductive appearance. Charlotte was the friendliest of the Proctor coven and one of the nicest people I knew. She was also a middle child like I was, so the two of us had often commiserated about the inherent joys of being bookended by siblings who irritated us.

"I am," I reluctantly admitted.

"What have your brothers done now?" she asked, brushing a stray bang out of her eyes.

"Just their usual teasing," I said. My gaze drifted from Charlotte to Ben, who was in the middle of introducing himself to Charlotte's parents in the living room. "But it's not them. It's him," I said gesturing toward Ben.

She casually stole a glance behind her. "He's cute. No wonder you're distracted." Besides sharing our sibling woes, Charlotte was the only person in Havenbridge with any knowledge about my personal life. She knew I dated both men and women, and she had never let on to anyone that she knew more than she did.

I always appreciated her discretion. "It's not that."

She crossed her arms and glared up at me.

"Okay, it's not *just* that."

"Then what?"

I told her the story of how Ben and I had met and how he'd come to Havenbridge.

"I'll admit it's a big coincidence, but what about it has you so irritated?"

"It doesn't feel right." That didn't quite express what I was feeling. It felt all kinds of wrong.

Charlotte placed her hand on my forearm and patted me, trying to give me the comfort I needed. She had always been a mother hen. "I think you might be reading too much into this," she said. "After everything we've been through since Mabon, it's no wonder. Vampyre attacks and a mysterious shadow weaver."

"Not to mention the Conclave's complete incompetence dealing with those situations," I added.

She inhaled sharply. Like a good little soldier, Charlotte followed whatever our superiors said. If they told us not to worry, she didn't. If they told us to jump off a bridge, she'd leap over the railing. The wizards were the same way. For being so logical, they were far too trusting of the Conclave's motives.

Warlocks didn't blindly follow anyone. Not anymore. Not since Bartram Kane.

"Anyway," she said, completely sidestepping my insult of her precious Conclave, "you and your family have been through a lot. You almost died. It makes sense you'd be constantly looking over your shoulder."

Was that what I was being? Overly cautious? I hadn't acted that way with Aiden in the woods. Maybe Charlotte was right.

"So what you're saying is I need to take a chill pill?"

"That would be a start," she said with a grin. "You've always been too serious for your own good. Let your hair down every now and then."

I glared at her. "Why do people keep telling me that?"

"Maybe it's because we can all see you're wound tighter than a jittery Chihuahua."

I frowned at the analogy. I considered myself more of a German shepherd, cautious and alert. I was *not* a temperamental yelper!

She gently shoved me in Ben's direction. "Go talk to him," she said. He'd just finished being introduced to Kate and Keaton, the younger Stonewall twins. Their big white smiles beamed against the ebony skin they'd inherited from their father. "Get to know him with clothes on. That might make you feel better."

I did need to get to know him better but not how Charlotte thought I should. Ben presented yet another mystery I needed to solve.

I made my way over to where Ben chatted with Mrs. Stonewall, and his dark eyes drifted over to me. A huge smile hitched up his lips. My heart fluttered and familiar warmth spread in my groin.

"I WAS beginning to think you were ignoring me," Ben said after I'd interrupted his conversation with Mrs. Stonewall and escorted him into the kitchen. It had taken me a few moments and half a dozen deep breaths to get my hormones under control. I stood with the granite counter between us, because that was the only way I wasn't going to grab him and bend him over.

Undeterred, Ben rounded the island until only a few inches separated us.

The overwhelming scent of copper slammed into me as he leaned closer, a naughty smile dangling from his perfectly symmetrical lips. He was clearly angling for another round of sweaty fun, and as the overpowering metallic aroma that hung about him filled my lungs, the more I craved his flesh on mine, my tongue on his neck, and my dick in his ass.

I had to bite the inside of my cheek to regain focus.

"What are you doing here?" I asked. My tone was more biting than I intended, but at least I was no longer remembering the warm tightness of Ben's hole.

Ben stepped back, a strange look on his face, as if my sudden restraint was unexpected. Not that it surprised me that much. Ben struck me as a warlock who was used to getting his way. Still, he put a respectful distance between us and leaned against the island. He pulled the chain with the green pendant out of his shirt and fidgeted with the stone. "I'm here on business with your brother, but you already knew that." He paused, studying me. "What's going on?"

"How long have you been working with Pierce?"

He strummed his fingers across the counter in thought. "A few weeks. I recently acquired a software company in California, and your brother approached me about buying me out. It seems that Blackmoor Enterprises is interested in snatching up what I have to offer." He wiggled his eyebrows. "Kinda like you yesterday." He paused, studying me with a knowing half grin as he fingered the emerald encased in gold. "And if I'm right, you're ready for a bit more too."

I forced the sensual curve of his lips from my mind and focused on his words. I'd heard Pierce and Dad talking about an electronics company in Silicon Valley a few weeks ago. They had a computer chip that was supposed to revolutionize the industry. "And you didn't know who I was when we met yesterday?"

"No, I didn't." He stared at me as if I'd just thrown a bucket of water on him. The cocksure demeanor vanished as if it had never been there. "Just what are you accusing me of?"

That was a good question. Why was I acting like a conspiracy theorist? "I guess I find your sudden presence here too coincidental for my liking."

Ben's lips parted in the smile that he'd first flashed at me over his coffee. It made my head spin. "That's right," he said, once again drawing closer to me. "You're tightly wound. Like a Chihuahua."

I crossed my arms. If one more person compared me to that rat breed of a dog, they'd find themselves turned into a permanent ice sculpture. "You don't know me well enough to make such an unflattering observation."

"Maybe not," he answered. He leaned against the island and ran his index finger along my forearm. I held my breath as his touch sent chills down my spine. "But I remember how you responded to my suggestion of going back to your place. Way too serious and responsible to cut loose and have fun."

"Then why did I fuck you stupid after you showed up at my place?" I asked with one raised eyebrow. "That doesn't sound like someone who can't cut loose."

"That was lust," he said. "Pure and simple. That's not really cutting loose. Most guys are occasionally led around by their boners. Otherwise we wouldn't be men, or warlocks, would we? Those types of casual encounters are easy for someone like you."

Ben's comment halted the seductive burn his finger had ignited across my flesh. "What the hell does that mean?"

He held up his hands to indicate he meant no offense when it had been nothing but offensive. "I'm not judging. I've known lots of men who prefer the old come and go. They get their rocks off and then have no desire to see you again. It's hard for guys like that to deal with anything other than superficial, anonymous encounters because they can be forgotten as soon as it's over. But seeing me here upsets that for you."

Ben couldn't be more wrong if he tried. My sex life could never be described as a series of random one-night stands. Especially since I didn't really have a sex life.

"You're really starting to piss me off." I pulled my arm from his wandering finger and took a step back, the reins once again safely in my hands. "You don't know a damn thing about me."

Despite my strident tone, his smile never faltered. Was he enjoying this? "Maybe not, but I'd like to," he said, kissing the back of the pendant before tucking it beneath his shirt.

I eyed him suspiciously. "You'd like to what?"

"Get to know you better," he said, his voice barely above a whisper. He slid into the space I'd created between us, and the scent of copper grew even stronger. What kind of cologne was he wearing? "I'd like to get past the protective iceberg you've built around yourself. The one you use to keep others, including your family, at a safe distance. I want to get to know the real Thad Blackmoor, the one no one else gets to see."

How did he know these things about me? Was I that much of an open book? "This doesn't make any sense," I finally replied.

"What? That I want to get to know you?"

I shook my head. "That you would want this from someone you don't even know."

He grinned at me as if I'd just said the cutest thing in the world. "That's what getting to know someone is all about, right? I know real emotion is scary for someone as protective of himself as you are, but why not give it a shot and get to know me?"

"Because this is weird and unsettling," I replied. "You shouldn't be here."

"Are we back to that?" he asked. His tone lacked irritation. He seemed to find this humorous, as if no matter what obstacle I placed in his path, he'd simply bound over it in pursuit of me. "Is it coincidental that I've been working with your brother and I'm here the night after we hooked up? There's no doubt about it. But where you see ulterior motives and conspiracy, I see opportunity. In case you've forgotten, we live in a magical world. Couldn't this be the Gate's way of telling us we might have more in common than just the hots for each other?"

I snuffed. "I don't have 'the hots' for you."

Ben grabbed my groin and tugged on the erection I hadn't even realized I'd been sporting. "Are you sure about that?" he asked with a wicked leer.

As my dick throbbed in his grasp, I had to admit I wasn't too sure about anything.

MY FATHER'S voice rescued me from my uncomfortable encounter with Ben in the kitchen. It was time for us to honor our ancestors.

My brothers elbowed each other and grinned like idiots when Ben and I entered the library where everyone else waited on us. They evidently believed we'd been going at it. Would they ever outgrow their adolescent tendencies?

I ignored their childishness and swept my gaze around the room that had been set up for the ritual.

The leather couches and red wingback chair had been moved to the perimeter of the room. To the right of the couches, a small feast had been prepared. Dark bread, apples, fall vegetables, cheeses, nuts, cider, and red wine were offered in tribute to our departed loved ones. In the center of the room were four altars with unlit candles. Each family had set up their altar with photos of their deceased relatives and heirlooms passed down through the generations.

The Proctors had prominently placed the harmonica that William, Charlotte's grandfather and former High Priest of the coven, used to play. The instrument was lovingly set between a photo of William and his wife, Elizabeth, who'd both passed to the spirit world when I was in third grade. Charlotte had cried her way through most of the school year. She had been incredibly close to her grandparents.

A tabletop grandfather clock belonging to Lawrence Stonewall's great-great-great-grandmother, Perrine, adorned the center of their family's tribute. She had been one of the most powerful wizards of all time. In fact, she had been one of the only members of the Conclave who survived the battle with Bartram Kane, the warlock shadow weaver responsible for unleashing the vampyren during the Salem witch trials. Other photos decorated the Stonewall family altar, but their stern visages faded away when my gaze drew too close to my family's altar.

In the middle of the many loved ones we'd lost over the years, I saw only one photo, the one belonging to Priscilla Blackmoor, my mother. Her luminous red hair cascaded over her creamy shoulders. As a child, whenever I snuggled into the crook of her neck, the bouquet of rose petals and cinnamon had always brought me great comfort. When she'd smiled, mischievousness glinted in her hazel eyes. No one ever knew if they were going to be on the receiving end of a giant momma bear hug or a practical joke. She'd loved a good prank almost as much as she loved us.

But now that she had been reduced to photos and memories, I couldn't swallow the bowling ball-sized lump lodged in my throat.

To the best of my ability, I choked back the tears that threatened to make me a blubbering mess and focused on the fourth altar. It had been set up to honor our predecessors, the past protector covens. It was the longest altar of the four, since it contained photos and mementos that dated back to the birth of our species. It represented a symbolic assemblage of the most powerful warlocks, witches, and wizards who had ever existed.

The four altars signified everything we were as individual covens and the legacy of the station we had been elevated to in our community.

My father, dressed in a black button-down and tan pants, stepped forward. He regarded each of us with his steel blue gaze before focusing his attention on the altars before him. Since Samhain was a Sabbat dominated by black magic, it was up to him as the High Priest of our coven to initiate the ritual. "Let us begin," he said.

He proceeded toward the altars, where Charles Proctor and Lawrence Stonewall, the high priests of their respective covens, joined him. The three men held hands, and all the candles across the four altars lit at once.

All of us then joined hands in one big circle around them.

"On this night, the gateway between our world and the spirit world grows thin," my father began. "Tonight is the night to call out to those who came before us, and tonight we honor those ancestors."

For a moment, silence engulfed the room as we each called to mind the memories of our loved ones.

"Spirits of our ancestors, we call to you. We welcome you. Join us this night. You watch over us and protect us and guide us, and we thank you by offering to share in our meal."

With magical synchronicity, we all turned to gaze upon the table, each of us offering a silent invitation to our lost loved ones before returning our gaze to the High Priests.

"This is the cup of remembrance," my father said before picking up the chalice on our family's altar. He raised it high for all to see. "We remember you. You are dead but never forgotten," he said with a slight crack in his voice. I shot my gaze to my brothers, who stared back at me. Though we all wanted to go to him and soothe the pain of missing our mother, we could not. We had to be strong. He had to be strong. At least until the ritual was over. "And you live on within us."

He then brought the chalice to his bearded lips and drank.

With the ceremony concluded, we released hands and broke the circle. Everyone proceeded to their family's altar to pay their respects. My brothers were at Dad's side before I could even move. Mason patted his back while Pierce squeezed his shoulder.

I should have been there too, offering my father the comfort he required, but I couldn't move.

A fiery pinprick had formed a few feet above the altar. Everyone was too focused on their conversations to notice. It grew bigger and brighter with each turn of the pinwheel's fiery blades.

It had to be Aiden, but why was he coming back to our world again? I held my breath, my attention fixed upon the growing light. I shivered with excitement at the possibility that he had returned to see me.

IT DIDN'T take long for the flaming pinwheel to attract attention. It grew in size quickly, radiating enough heat and light to rival a small sun. Tendrils of flame snaked outward from the spinning blades, and with each revolution, a loud *whoosh* echoed off the cherry wood walls of the library.

For a room full of magical beings, I found their silent captivation both humorous and bothersome. Although I knew its appearance signified no threat, they did not. Someone should be sounding the alarm.

"Get behind me!" my father commanded. His body immediately turned to stone as he thudded closer to the spinning flame. It did my warlock pride good to see someone from my family spring into action. Since warlocks were typically the first to jump into a fight, I wasn't all that surprised.

"I think this is more up my alley," Charles Proctor said as he rushed to my father's side. His active power was fire, and it made him a rather formidable witch. His disdain for my father was well documented, and he enjoyed attempting to one-up him whenever the occasion merited it.

Lawrence Stonewall snuffed at them both. A sneer curled up the right corner of his dark lips. As was commonplace with wizards and their gray magic, he believed he was the only one capable of handling any threat that presented itself, and with his ability to control the minds of his enemies, he most likely could.

Right now, though, none of them were needed.

"Stand down," I said with far more severity in my voice than I had intended. All eyes quickly turned to me. My father's rocky lips widened in surprise, and Mr. Proctor gazed at me in disbelief. As High Priests, neither of them was accustomed to taking orders. Mr. Stonewall appeared to be only irritated by what he no doubt considered my petulance. "It isn't a threat. I promise."

"How could you possibly know this?" Lawrence Stonewall asked in his typical condescending tone.

"Because I met the being responsible for this portal on my way here."

"You what?" my father asked. "And when were you planning on telling me?"

Only renouncing my magic could make him any more disappointed in me right now. Perhaps I should have revealed what happened, but seeing Ben in my home had blindsided me so hard, it distracted me from the wailing banshee and the sexy fire fairy I'd encountered in the woods.

"You told us you fought a banshee," Pierce said. He suddenly stood at my side, his eyebrows stitched in confusion.

"A banshee?" Mr. Proctor asked. He and the rest of his coven darted their eyes around the room. White magic celebrated the connective spiritual aspects of life. Since banshees heralded death and the end of such connections, they were a species the witches didn't enjoy being around.

"We could play twenty questions, or we can prepare to meet our guest," I said.

As if on cue, a tiny fireball appeared in the middle of the flaming pinwheel. It shot out from the center and hovered above us, flitting like a hummingbird from one part of the room to the other. The ball of flame morphed into a small man with wings trailing fire behind him.

Even though he was no taller than three inches, I could definitely tell it was Aiden. His wide green eyes searched the crowd below, and when he settled his gaze on me, he darted toward me while increasing in size. By the time he flew in front of me, he had adjusted his size to the same tall, muscular man I'd found lying naked in the woods.

To my surprise, not only was he still unclothed, but he looked to be in even worse shape since the last time I'd seen him. A purplish bruise marred his snow-white right cheek, his pink lips were cracked and bloodied, and claw marks cut a nasty trail across his smooth chest and legs.

"Thaddeus," he panted as his fiery wings suddenly disappeared. He landed roughly on his feet, clearly unable to stand on his own. I wrapped my arms around his larger frame, and he leaned against me for support. It surprised me how comforting and comfortable his body felt against mine.

"Aiden, what happened to you?"

Tears welled in his wide green eyes before spilling down his pallid flesh, but they weren't tears of sadness or fear. His eyes burned with rage. "Otherworld is under attack."

"By whom?"

"We don't have time," he said, a scowl forming on his lips. "They're coming."

I snapped my gaze to my father and brothers. They immediately surveyed the room, preparing for an attack. My father, still in his stone form, waited to take on anyone who might come flying out of the spinning pinwheel, which was slowly closing. While Mason placed himself in front of Drake to protect him, arcs of blue lightning snaked out of Pierce's clenched fists.

The other covens did the same, switching on their active powers and preparing to meet the threat. Even though we didn't get along very well, they quickly formed a defensive circle around us.

Only Ben stood on the periphery, wearing a rather odd expression. He arched one eyebrow at seeing Aiden in my arms, and his lips twisted as if he was in deep thought. Was he jealous?

I shook my head and turned my attention to Aiden. "Who's coming?"

Though Aiden's lips moved in response to my question, no sound issued forth. That was all the answer I needed. The banshees were here.

A FEW seconds later, silent chaos erupted all around us. Six banshees with white, waist-length hair blinked into existence inside the library. Before anyone could act, they let loose an ear-piercing scream that put most of the room out of commission.

Those closest to the banshees when they appeared were hit the hardest. The sheer force of the sonic scream sent them tumbling across the room, where they fell. Among the unconscious heap were Mr. Proctor and his daughters, Charlotte and Miranda, as well as Mr. and Mrs. Stonewall. And Ben.

In just one move, the banshees had managed to take out two of the High Priests. Individually they could steamroll over most. When they worked together, they became a tank.

Edith Stonewall found that out the hard way. She had erected a force field around herself and her two younger siblings, but she had been unable to maintain the barrier under the concentrated scream. She and the young Kate and Keaton fell to their knees before passing out.

The banshees closed their mouths to gather their breath and surveyed those they still needed to put down.

Thad, get out of here! a voice wailed inside my head. It was even louder than the banshees' screams, and it made my teeth hurt. It was Elliot, using his telepathy. *They've come here for Aiden, and they intend to kill him.*

My gaze met Elliot's, who kneeled next to his fallen family. His eyes were saucer wide in terror. Whatever he saw in the dark fae's minds was evidently not good.

I wrapped my arm around Aiden's naked waist and pulled him close.

"What are you doing?" he asked. Fiery tendrils snaked off his fists. He was clearly ready to fight, not retreat.

"We need to get out of here. They want to kill you."

"Let them try," he said. His temper raged as hot as the fire burning from his palms.

"I have to keep you safe."

He shrugged out of my embrace. "I don't need anyone to keep me safe."

Was he kidding? Now wasn't exactly the best time to be arguing or be offended that I'd inadvertently challenged his manhood, or fairyhood, or whatever he called it.

Thad! Elliot yelled inside my head again. *Move it!*

One glance over my shoulder revealed the cause of Elliot's unease. The banshees had set their gazes upon Aiden and me, and their yellow eyes burned in hatred. They flew toward us, their gray, tattered dresses fluttering about them as they joyously prepared to bring death.

I shielded Aiden with my body and erected a wall of ice. The banshees tore through the barrier with their silent screams, and the force of the explosion sent Aiden and me careening away from the exit.

As I struggled to get to my feet, one of the screaming dark fairies spasmed in pain. Pierce, who still appeared wobbly from the initial onslaught, unleashed a thousand volts of electricity that instantly fried her. She disappeared in a puff of fog.

The remaining banshees howled in silent grief. Two of them converged on my older brother, clawing at his skin. As Pierce fought them off with my father's assistance, the three remaining dark fae advanced toward where I crouched over Aiden.

Before I could summon my powers again, a sudden rush of wind slammed into the banshees. They crashed into the table that had been set for our feast. Adam Proctor stood to my left, his hands outstretched. He'd tapped into his air abilities to keep them pinned against the wall.

Roots exploded through the wood flooring. They wrapped around the trapped banshees' necks and snaked across their open mouths, gagging them and rendering them unable to access their power. Adam's mother, Camille, who had the ability to manipulate plants, had evidently made use of the trees that grew around Blackmoor Manor to silence them.

I focused my attention on where Pierce and my father battled the remaining two banshees. In his stone form, my father yanked them off Pierce and hurled them across the room. The shadows along the wall formed into a giant black spike that skewered them both. Black blood gurgled out of their mouths as they writhed in their death throes.

Mason stood off to the side, a wicked grin on his face. His shadow weaving talents had evidently grown since the last time I'd been home. Although his projections quickly reverted to their harmless form, he'd managed to manipulate the shadows long enough to do what needed to be done.

"Holy shit!" Pierce said, as the banshees' corpses turned to mist. His voice sounded tinny, and there was a constant ringing in my ears, a side effect of a banshee attack. "That was fucking awesome."

I glared at my brother, as did most everyone else in the room.

"Are you serious, Pierce?" Drake asked. Whenever he was rattled, his Texas twang often made it difficult to understand him. "We were just attacked by a whole mess o' pissed off ghouls. I wouldn't exactly be callin' that awesome."

"Banshees," Mrs. Proctor corrected.

"Whatever," Drake said, dismissing her with a wave of his hand. His obvious dislike for Camille Proctor couldn't be more evident. After all, she had been the one who'd attempted to wipe his memories a few weeks ago. "My point is this is about as far from awesome as anythin' can get in my book. First a vampyre and now a gaggle o' banshees. What's next?"

"What's next indeed?" Camille asked. She tore her gaze from Aiden and glared at me. While Mrs. Proctor's brown eyes usually reflected the maternal kindness she was famous for, when she was a pissed off witch who'd seen her family assaulted, she evidently turned ice cold. "What new hell have the Blackmoors brought to our lives?"

"That's enough, Camille," my father said. He'd reverted to his normal form and crossed to stand by my side. "This isn't Thad's fault."

"I beg to differ," a pained voice said from across the room. It was Mr. Stonewall. He and the others were waking up and untangling themselves from the heap they'd been turned into.

"As do I," Mrs. Stonewall agreed. Her husband helped her stand up. "If Thad had shared his previous misadventure with us, we would have been prepared for what just happened, and my children would not have been harmed." She lifted the young Keaton in her arms. He had begun to stir. She stroked his head while Mr. Stonewall kneeled beside Edith, who held her sobbing sister, Kate, in her arms.

While the youngest Stonewalls would grow up to be powerful wizards, Keaton and Kate had yet to come into their powers. Right now they were vulnerable, and I had unknowingly brought them into harm's way.

Perhaps I should do something I rarely ever did: apologize.

"Your children belong to the family chosen by the Order of the Gray to be its protector coven," Ben told the Stonewalls. "Being born to the two of you is what put them in harm's way. Don't try and pass that off onto anyone else."

All eyes turned to Ben as he wove his way to me. The closer he got, the more I wanted to be by his side.

"What your families do is dangerous, and it's a duty you accepted. Or have you forgotten that?" Ben asked.

"You're a solitary warlock," Mr. Stonewall said. Even though he seethed, his voice never rose or strained. He spoke in cold, measured tones. "You have no voice here."

Mr. and Mrs. Proctor nodded in agreement before turning their gazes to my father. "I think it's time for your guest to depart," Mr. Proctor said.

My father's eyes turned to slits. The control he'd been struggling to maintain on his emotions slipped free. "You will not come into my house, into *my* coven, and tell me what to do. I run this family, *not* you."

Mrs. Stonewall snorted in reply.

"What the hell is wrong with you?" Aiden asked. He strolled into the fray with a regal jut to his chin and met everyone's gaze. "Is this how the much-vaunted protector covens act? Like goblins arguing over a stack of gold?" He turned up his nose. "It's pathetic."

No one spoke. They were just as stunned as I was. We weren't used to being reprimanded by other magical beings. As members of the protector covens, we held a status that most respected and even feared. Well, everyone except Aiden.

"Just who do you think you are, little fae?" Mrs. Stonewall asked.

He puffed out his chest and stretched to his full height of six-foot three. He was clearly making a point. "I'm Prince Aiden Teine, son of Oberon, king of the Salamander Tribe." He looked down his nose at her. "You may call me Your Highness."

Mrs. Stonewall quickly shut her mouth. As a member of the Royal Fae Court, Aiden had direct access to the Conclave if he so desired, and the Conclave insisted on peace between our two species. A war with the fairies was definitely something we didn't need right now.

"We could argue about this all evening," I said. "But I think we have more important matters to attend to." I nodded toward the three banshees still held by the roots Camille Proctor had summoned. They gagged the dark fae into silence, but that didn't stop them from struggling against the steely grip of their wooden restraints.

"It's time for us to get some answers," I said.

CHAPTER 4

WHILE OUR parents and Aiden discussed how best to proceed, I stood off to the side, still in shock. Aiden was a fae prince? Why hadn't he told me that when we first met?

Well, we hadn't had a lot of time for formalities, that was for sure. He was eager to return home and deal with the banshee attack. I understood why now even more than before. He had to return to his people, to be the prince they needed to fight alongside them in whatever battle waged in Otherworld.

I wasn't completely surprised, though. Now that I thought back on our initial encounter, it explained a lot about Aiden and my reaction to him. The way he carried himself had a noble bearing, as if he were accustomed to speaking his mind and having his wishes transformed into action. That was likely at the heart of his confident nature. He would one day be king of his people. He had no choice but to adopt an attitude that would not only draw others to him but also make them want to do his bidding.

He was accustomed to commanding respect, as Mrs. Stonewall had learned. The memory of him bringing her down a couple of pegs made me smile.

From across the room, I studied Aiden as he spoke to the High Priests. He wore a pair of old sweatpants I'd had Mason retrieve from my room. How did he manage to make the cheap cotton look majestic, as if it was a princely robe made from the most expensive silk? I also had presented him with a sweatshirt, but he'd drawn the line. "I'm not ashamed of my body," he told me.

Neither was I. I sure didn't mind looking at it, but we weren't exactly alone in the woods anymore.

Unlike Pierce, who pushed the limits of his workout to achieve muscle mass, Aiden's body was strong yet lean. Well-defined shoulders extended into bulging biceps that were surrounded by Celtic tattoos. If I could, I'd lick a trail around the ink, across his smooth, defined chest, and down the ridges of his abdominal muscles. From there, I'd follow the light dusting of dark hair that cut a tantalizing path beneath the waistband of the sweats that hid his seven-inch cock and tight, plump ass.

His jet-black hair lay in a tangled mess, and with every gesticulation, wispy strands fell in front of his eyes before he brushed them away.

How would it feel to surf my fingertips down his thin nose and along the rough cut of his jaw? How would he respond if I pushed my finger into the button on his chin before trailing a path to his mouth? Would he allow me to follow the soft line of his pale pink lips before kissing them once again?

My blood turned into a lava stream that charted a speedy course to my swollen cock. If I didn't regain some semblance of control, I was going to hyperventilate.

"He's very handsome."

I jumped at the sound of Ben's voice behind me.

"Sorry," he said. "I didn't mean to startle you."

"You didn't," I lied. Was that disappointment I saw in his eyes?

Whatever the emotion was, he blinked it away. "I can see why you're so taken with him."

"I'm not. I'm just...." I didn't know how to finish that statement.

He nudged into my shoulder, leaning against me. "For a warlock, you're not a very good liar."

The weight and warmth of Ben's body set my already churning passions on a tilt-a-whirl. Images of Ben naked underneath me replaced my fantasies of Aiden. It was Ben's body I touched. His coppery kisses I tasted. His ass wrapped around my cock. My sudden desire for him returned like a tsunami threatening to drown me in one massive wave if I didn't get out of its way. "Well, he is a fire fairy," I finally managed. "I'm sure you feel the same thing."

"I don't," Ben replied with a firm shake of his head. "I mean, is he hot? Yeah. If he asked me to fuck him, I would. Other than that?" He shrugged before locking his gaze on mine. "Why?"

"You don't feel drawn to him?" I asked, glancing at Aiden. Like a beacon in the middle of treacherous, rock-laden waters, he called to me. His presence cut through the musky fog of desire Ben's touch and proximity had briefly created.

"No," he replied. The tautness of his reply caught my attention. He studied Aiden intently, as if searching for a solution to some complicated situation. A scowl slowly crept across his lips, and his eyes drew into slits.

Was this the jealousy I had sensed earlier? Ben had made it clear in the kitchen he wanted to pursue something with me, but ever since Aiden's arrival, a scowl had taken permanent residence on his face.

"I think we need to talk," I said.

"Later," Ben said. "I think the others are ready to get started." He walked away without another word.

I followed him to the other side of the library, where Mr. Stonewall cast one final judgmental glance my way before clearing his voice. "Are we ready to begin?"

"What's the plan?" I asked.

Mrs. Stonewall shook her head slowly at me. "If you weren't so distracted by your suitors, you wouldn't need to ask such questions."

I visibly bristled, and my face grew hot. Who the hell did she think she was? I was a fucking warlock, and no damn wizard was going to get away with talking to me that way. I was just about to launch a return salvo when a hand rested on my shoulder.

It was Charlotte. She'd realized I was about to lose control. Her comforting gesture turned a hose on my hot temper. She was right. Now was not the time, so I clung tightly to the reins I used to keep me in check. When was this emotional roller coaster I'd boarded ever going to stop?

"I still think this will be faster if you just let me electrocute them," Pierce said with a smirk.

"I would agree," Aiden said. He stood at the front with my brother. He clearly preferred Pierce's method of interrogation.

"We have already discussed this," Mr. Stonewall said. Whenever he spoke this seriously, the light in his blue eyes faded until they were almost as dark as his skin. "You're powerful, but you lack the finesse that is needed here, and it is finesse that I can provide."

Their exchange told me all I needed to know. Lawrence Stonewall planned on using his mind control abilities. It was a rare yet powerful wizard trait. Unlike most warlocks and witches, who received their gifts from the four elements, wizards tapped into the fifth and more ethereal element—spirit.

It was considered the most powerful of the five, which was why gray magic could harness it. Since wizards took a more logical and neutral perspective on life, the gift would most likely not be corrupted because it couldn't be swayed by the pull of white or black magic.

Mr. Stonewall nodded to his coven, and they fell in behind him like soldiers. Edith held her arms wide and erected a shield around all of us. That was a cautionary measure in case the banshees broke free and resumed their attack. While Edith's barrier might not hold for long, it would give the rest of us the few seconds we needed to mount a counterattack.

Mrs. Stonewall rested the tips of her fingers on her fair temples. It was how she focused her illusion-based abilities. She was preparing to launch the banshees into some unseen world if her husband was unsuccessful.

It was Elliot, however, who stood by his father's side. He had an integral part. He bit his bottom lip and glanced nervously around the room. Whatever he planned to do was clearly new to him. After a quick exhalation, he squared his shoulders and closed his eyes.

Can everyone hear me? he asked inside my head.

Everyone except the Stonewalls jumped as Elliot spoke in our minds.

Sorry about that, he said sheepishly.

My head throbbed in pain, which was the usual response to Elliot's ability. Others around me winced as well.

When my dad gives the word, he said, *I'll do my best to link a banshee's mind with ours. I've never cast such a wide telepathic link before, so I'm uncertain what will happen or how this will work. Things may get... unpleasant.*

That wasn't the vote of confidence I'd been hoping to hear, but that was Elliot. His handicap severely affected his self-assurance. When we used to study together, he told me he felt like a lame wizard because he couldn't use spoken words to cast spells like the rest of us.

I had no doubt his power would evolve like our parents, who didn't need to speak in Latin to access their magic. Unless it was an extremely difficult spell, hand gestures did the trick.

I will begin. This time it was Lawrence Stonewall's cold voice speaking to us using his son's abilities.

He approached one of the banshees. She writhed against her restraints, eager to gain her freedom and tear him to shreds. Her sisters convulsed at her side. Their eyes had turned into yellow flames of pure hate.

The dark fae weren't the friendliest creatures, yet they acted as if we were sworn enemies.

Mr. Stonewall held his palm a few inches from the face of the banshee in the middle. *Aperi mentem ad me*, he said, commanding in Latin for her to open her mind to him. The banshee grunted in pain. She struggled against the roots that held her fast. She clawed against the wood so violently, she left trails of blood across its surface.

Go away! she suddenly wailed. Her thoughts were as ragged and sharp as her scream. Her hammering voice in my head was worse than unpleasant. It caused my brain to throb as if it might explode. *Get out of my head.*

I will not, Mr. Stonewall responded. *You will do my bidding and answer my questions.*

I'd rather kill you instead!

He placed his hand against her forehead and thought, *The only thing you will do is obey.*

The banshee ceased struggling. She stared at Mr. Stonewall as if she could see through him. He had finally managed to get her under his control.

The two dark fae on either side of their now calm sister grew even more hysterical. They wriggled and squirmed, hoping to find some weakness in the roots. Mrs. Proctor narrowed her eyes, and with a gesture, the roots constricted even more tightly around her captives.

Why did you attack us? Mr. Stonewall asked.

Because you must die. You must all die.

That revelation set off a low murmur through all of us. Mrs. Stonewall shushed the room into silence.

Why? he asked.

So the dark fae can take what is rightfully ours. Our world and yours.

This time a low roar traveled through the room that not even Mrs. Stonewall's constant shushing could stop. The whole reason behind the banshee attack was to increase their territory? That didn't ring true to me. It wasn't the way of the fae, light or dark.

Something else was going on here. Aiden clearly agreed. His gaze met mine, and he shook his head.

Why are you lying? I asked through the link.

Mr. Stonewall glanced over his shoulder at me, perspiration dripped from his forehead and his eyes narrowed in displeasure. His wife stepped forward and turned me to face her.

She grabbed my forearm and yanked me toward her. "What do you think you're doing?"

"Getting to the truth," I replied, tearing free of her grip.

Aiden appeared by my side. If he'd been any angrier, Mrs. Stonewall would be a pillar of flame. "She's lying, you idiot." He spoke to her as if she were one of his subjects, which wasn't making things easier. He clearly had to learn to control his temper. "The fae don't concern themselves with territorial wars. If you knew anything about my kind, you would realize that. We have always lived in harmony."

She arched one eyebrow at Aiden. "Perhaps *you* don't know the dark fae as well as you think you do," she replied. "My husband's power prevents her from lying."

"Enough!" Mr. Stonewall shouted from where he struggled to hold sway over the banshee. "You're breaking my concentration."

I paid no attention to the warning. We had to get answers, and if the banshee couldn't lie, I had to make use of the opportunity. *Answer me*, I commanded. *Why are you lying?*

The banshee's gaze shifted from Mr. Stonewall to me. The dead, faraway glare changed, and the glimmer of hate resparked. *Because that is the answer I'm supposed to give.*

Who told you to say that? Aiden asked. He stood next to me, and I drew strength from his presence.

She shut her eyes and let loose a muffled scream of protest. *I cannot say!*

Tell us, Mr. Stonewall commanded. He squinted, and his entire body shook as he forced his magic into her in order to get the answers we needed.

No, she pleaded. *Don't make me.*

Answer! Aiden said. He spoke with stately finality. *I am a prince, and all fae fall under my sway.*

The banshee glanced at her sisters, who shook their heads in response. The aggravation at being held captive and the anger in their yellow eyes had been replaced by terror.

This was the information we needed, what would likely lead us to the answers about the vampyre and the shadow weaver that had attacked us during Mabon.

Tell us! Aiden commanded.

It was E—, she began, and then her eyes darted around the room as if she sensed a familiar presence. Her sisters followed her gaze, and a few seconds later their golden eyes grew wide in fright.

Instead of fighting against the roots that held them, they gripped tightly to them as if they'd become a lifeline.

I'm sorry, she pleaded. *It's not our fault.*

In reply, the shadows around us coalesced until a huge head the size of an overgrown pumpkin emerged upside down from the ceiling. "*Siopāte,*" it said in a language foreign to my ears.

The shadows around the gaping mouth turned into ragged rows of sharp teeth before the figure lurched forward and descended upon the banshees. I leaped toward Mr. Stonewall, shoving him out of the way as the jaws snapped shut around the banshees, cutting them in half.

The pumpkin head turned to regard each of us before its gaze settled upon me. "*Ései emós,*" it said before it merged back with the shadows upon the wall.

FOR A few moments, no one spoke. The surprise and violence of the attack had caught everyone off guard. The banshees' corpses turned into puffs of fog and vanished.

Pierce was the first to speak. "What the hell was that?"

"It was the shadow weaver," Mason answered. He darted his eyes around the room, uncertain if the threat still remained. "That's what it looked like when it attacked Elliot and me at school, and then again here in the library before Drake killed the vampyre."

All eyes suddenly turned to Elliot and Drake for confirmation. When they nodded, everyone spoke at once.

"What does it want?"

"We need to contact the Conclave."

"Um, guys. I have somethin' to say."

"Will the Conclave even have answers? They haven't had any so far."

"Why did it kill them?"

"Are any of y'all even listenin' to me?"

"How come no one sensed its presence? How powerful is this shadow weaver?"

"What hold does it have over the banshees?"

I couldn't keep track of who said what. Their voices became white noise as a tidal wave of confusion washed over me. I'd been hoping to finally have answers, but like everyone else, all I had were more questions, the most important being: what had it said to me?

"Are you okay?"

Aiden gripped my shoulder as he kneeled beside me. His touch was strong yet gentle, and when I gazed up into the green pasture of his eyes, I couldn't help but feel safe and secure. "I'm uncertain," I replied.

He nodded. He could undoubtedly relate. "A shadow weaver?" he asked. His eyes widened in concern. Knowledge of these rare warlocks had evidently traveled as far as Otherworld. "The situation is more grave than I expected."

"Tell me about it," I said, taking his hand and being helped up. Once I was on my feet, I couldn't bring myself to remove my hand from his, so I left it where it was, waiting for Aiden to release me. When he didn't, I smiled. "Are you okay?"

"Surprisingly so," he muttered, as if he was shocked by his answer. He glanced at our joined hands and beamed. "There must be magic in your touch."

A childlike smile spread wide across my lips. "I was thinking the same thing about you."

He squeezed my hand tighter. "Then we'd best not let go."

"Will all y'all shut your traps and listen for a minute?" Drake stood on the leather couch, cupping his hands around his mouth in a makeshift megaphone.

That got everyone's attention, especially Mason's. His wide eyes told us all how surprised he was by his boyfriend's words.

"I've got somethin' to say."

"What could you possibly have to say about any of this?" Mrs. Stonewall asked. "You are not one of us."

Mason bristled. "Yes, he is. My father made him a member of our coven, remember?"

Silence was her only reply.

"Oh my God," Drake complained. "Can all y'all stop bickerin' for just one second so I can say my piece?"

"What is it, Drake?" my father asked.

"I know we don't have a ton of answers right now, but that thing just spoke to us, right?" He paused, clearly waiting for someone to agree with him. When only Mason nodded, he continued, "Well, I don't know what it said to Thad any more than the rest of you, but I do know one thing. It spoke Greek."

While the Stonewalls proceeded to question Drake, I stopped listening. I'd forgotten that Drake had an inherent gift for language. It came as easy to him as free running. When Mason had first told me about Drake's affinity for dialect, I'd put Drake to the test. I presented him with a book written in Latin, and he'd translated the words quite easily. He'd done the same with texts in Spanish, French, and German.

It wasn't a bona fide answer, but it certainly pointed us in the right direction.

"Can you remember what it said?" I asked, interrupting the wizardly interrogation.

Drake thought for a moment before answering. "I believe it said, 'Aníkete se ména.'"

That sounded about right. I rushed over to one of the shelves, found a Greek dictionary, and placed it in his hands. "Think you can tell us what it means?"

He grinned at me as if that were a silly question and then opened the book.

"CAN YOU do it?" I asked Charlotte with a nod toward where Aiden reclined on the couch. "Can you heal him?" Aiden still had some nasty wounds from his previous run in with the banshees, and he needed to be in top form for whatever might come next.

She arched her left eyebrow. "Are you serious?"

I was being silly. Of course, she could. Her water powers allowed her to heal most injuries, as long as they weren't fatal. "Right. Dumb question."

She nodded. "They don't come much dumber than that one."

But instead of going over to where Aiden waited for us, she continued to stare at me until both eyebrows had arched. "What?"

"I'm just trying to figure out what's going on."

"You and me both," I said.

She shook her head. "Not with that," she said with a gesture to where Drake worked on translating the shadow weaver's words. "With you."

"What are you talking about?"

She glanced over to Ben, who stood talking to Pierce and then turned her attention to Aiden. "Well, you've got Ben, who's obviously got a thing for you, and then this hunky fire fairy shows up. The moment he flew into our world, your eyes lit up and you wrapped your arms around him as if he were the most important person in the world."

Had everyone seen that? No wonder Ben was jealous. "I think you're overexaggerating."

"And I think you're in denial," she replied.

I shot her my disapproving stare.

"Not judging," she said, waving her hands as if they were white flags. "I get it. Aiden's hot. There's innocence under the muscle and bravado. It's a pretty intoxicating combination. And Ben? Well, he's a warlock, so he's much darker. More mysterious but just as yummy. Like that piece of chocolate cake that will destroy your diet, but you want to eat it anyway." Her long, drawn-out sigh communicated her envy. "If only I had your problems."

"Will you just heal him already?"

"I will." She hooked my chin in her fingers and forced my gaze to hers. "But if you're not interested in Ben, you should tell him. No one likes being strung along."

I wasn't stringing anyone along. Ben and I had hooked up. It wasn't like I'd asked him to spend the Sabbat with me and then ignored him once Aiden came along. As far as I was concerned, Ben and I had been a one-time thing.

So then why did getting close to Ben make me want to strip naked and fuck?

I glanced over my shoulder and found Ben studying me intently. He obviously wasn't paying attention to anything Pierce was saying. When he noticed me staring at him, he gave me a nod and a big smile.

At exactly what moment had this bizarre love triangle formed?

Wait. No. Love triangle was *not* the right word. I didn't do love. This was attraction, pure and simple. I was insanely, *uncontrollably* attracted to Ben. And Aiden? Well, his appeal went beyond the physical. What that meant, I had absolutely no clue.

An aquamarine glow filled the library as Charlotte kneeled over Aiden. "*Sana*," she muttered, and at the uttering of the Latin word for heal, a small pool of water appeared. It floated above him, skimming over his body as if it were alive instead of a manifestation of Charlotte's abilities.

It hovered over him, searching for the areas that begged to be refreshed. On those spots, a bead of water dropped from the floating pool and landed in a sparkle of blue. Drop after drop fell, onto his bruised lips, swollen eye, and along his cut flesh until the spell dissipated and the pool disappeared.

Aiden's healed lips parted in a smile. "Thank you, Charlotte." When he gazed up at me, the light of his smile dazzled in his eyes. "Thaddeus, you seem different."

I glanced down at my clothes. They were a bit wrinkled from the banshee attack, but my appearance was otherwise unchanged. "What do you mean?"

"There's a lightness about you I haven't seen before now."

I glanced from him to Charlotte in confusion. "Does he have a concussion?"

She giggled and shook her head. "He sees what everyone else can see," she said, standing. "You, Mr. I-Don't-Do-Relationships, like the half-naked fairy."

My cheeks grew unbearably hot. Why did she have to say that? I darted my eyes from Charlotte to Aiden, mortified he might get up and walk away.

A big grin broke across his expression, but he didn't speak. It only added to the awkwardness.

"Well, alrighty then," Charlotte said. "I think I'll give the two of you some privacy.

When she walked away, I had no clue what to say or do. Did I tell him Charlotte had too many bats in her belfry, or did I just play it off with a chuckle? Instead of playing it cool and doing either of those things, I got up and left the room.

I DIDN'T storm out the front door like I planned. I plopped down in the antique Queen Anne chair in the hallway. I couldn't leave, no matter how embarrassed I was. I had to stay and see what Drake might uncover.

I buried my face in my hands and groaned. How could Charlotte have done that to me? She knew how guarded I was with my feelings. Hell, she was the only person until a few hours ago who'd had any knowledge I even dated.

I kept my private life and my feelings to myself. They belonged to me. They were mine to deal with and work through. As long as I understood what I felt and processed it, I could keep myself under check.

It kept those I loved safe.

What Charlotte had done undermined all the precautions I'd taken. Plus, it was pretty bitchy. I'd expect that from Miranda but not from someone I considered a friend.

"I don't think she meant any harm."

Aiden stood over me. His earlier smile had been replaced with a thin grin that clearly communicated his discomfort with the situation.

"I know," I said with a sigh. There wasn't a malicious bone in Charlotte's body. She most likely believed she was helping me, pushing me beyond my comfort zone. But that wasn't her place. "I don't have many friends, so I won't hold it against her for too long."

"Why is that?" he asked. He sat down on the blue carpet that lined the middle of the hallway.

"Because despite the fact she sometimes speaks before thinking, she's a good person."

"I have no doubt," he replied. "But that wasn't what I was asking. Why don't you have many friends?"

I shrugged. "Not really a people person. Too busy. More of a lone wolf. Take your pick."

He scrunched up his lips. "I choose none of the above."

Interesting answer.

Aiden scanned me, practically piercing through the barriers I had erected. He was worming his way into territory no one but my mother had ever entered.

"What are you doing?" I asked.

"Seeing you," he replied as if it were no big deal. "The real you."

"What you see is what you get." I stood up. This conversation was making me uneasy, even more than Charlotte's grand reveal. I had to get back to the library, where topics like shadow weavers and banshees were being discussed. Those made more sense to me.

Aiden wrapped his fingers around mine as I tried to pass. He didn't clutch them as if he was preventing me from leaving. If I wanted to leave, he wouldn't stop me, but his soft lingering touch was asking me to stay. How could I say no to that?

"Do you have something on your mind?" I asked, not withdrawing my hand from his. His warmth was too comforting.

"There's more to you than what can be seen," he said. His big smile returned, and it lit up his green eyes like the sun. "I can sense it. It's hidden behind so many barriers, though, it makes you a tough read, but it's there like a seed waiting for the rain to set it loose."

Of course. Fire fairies dealt with emotions. They were not only good at kindling them but also sensing them in others.

"I like to be mysterious," I said with a wink. Perhaps a playful approach might put an end to this conversation.

"It's not mystery I sense, Thaddeus. It's sadness." His eyes welled, and a stray tear slipped down the angular lines of his face. While the fire fae weren't empathic, they were sometimes affected by what those around them felt. "It's overwhelming, and it's what keeps you separate from everyone else. It's what makes you feel so alone."

I opened my mouth to deny it, to tell him his fairy senses were on the fritz, but I couldn't speak.

I could only stand there and watch as Aiden shed tears for the pain that twisted my soul. It was odd to have such a big man so freely express emotions, especially since I did everything in my power to avoid just that.

He rose from the floor. He placed his massive hands on my shoulders and rubbed them. "Don't live in the pain of loss. Your mother wouldn't have wanted that."

I recoiled from him, and my response startled him. "Stop right there," I said through gritted teeth. "My mother is off-limits."

"Your mother should never be off-limits," he replied. "You should talk about her with everybody. Every day if you have to. You should visit her grave, sit on the grass next to her and carry on conversations. Tell her what you're feeling or what happened during your day. She's not with you physically, but she hasn't completely vanished." He closed the distance I'd created between us and placed his hand on my chest. "She lives inside you, and she always will."

"Stop it."

"Why?" he asked.

"Because I don't talk about my mother." I brushed his hand away, and he made no move to put it back.

"Why does talking about her scare you?"

I clenched my jaw until it popped. My anger threatened to boil over and spill out. "I'm not afraid of a damn thing." My voice was low but stern. He was pushing the wrong buttons. "And you're a fae, not a psychologist, so back off."

"I will respect your wishes," he said with a sigh. "But I have one more thing to say."

I eyed him with one cocked eyebrow. "And what is that?"

"This half-naked fairy likes you too."

I FOLLOWED Aiden back to the library. I couldn't just let him drop that bombshell and walk away. After the way I'd treated him, how could he possibly like me?

I didn't like me right now.

Drake ran in with the book in his hand. "I've figured it out." A triumphant grin snaked across his face as he sneered at Mrs. Proctor and Mrs. Stonewall, who were obviously not members of the Drake Carpenter Fan Club.

My conversation with Aiden was going to have to wait.

"What did the shadow weaver's words mean?" Mason asked.

Drake turned to the pages of the dictionary he bookmarked with his fingers. "It took me a while to figure out. I had to familiarize myself with the Greek alphabet and then try to match up their symbols to what the words sounded like to us. It wasn't easy."

"And?" Mr. Stonewall asked, tapping his foot.

"Well, if I'm right, what it said was somethin' like 'you belong to me.'"

That sounded vaguely familiar but also not quite right.

"But after checkin' online," he continued, "I realized that was a literal translation. I think what it was trying to say was—"

"You will be mine?" I asked.

Drake's stitched eyebrows told me I was right. "How'd you know?"

"Because I've heard that before."

Everyone's eyes were suddenly glued to me. Ben and Aiden stepped forward but when each witnessed the other make the same move, they stopped.

"When?" Mason asked. "Because I've heard those words too. In my dreams a few days after Mabon."

After I told everyone about the nightmares I'd been having, the room grew deadly quiet. The Proctors and the Stonewalls exchanged glances with each other that accused me of once again withholding information. My brothers glanced at each other before gazing into the storm that silently raged in my father's blue eyes.

"And you didn't think to tell us this before?" he asked.

"It was a dream," I answered with a shrug. "How often do you share your dreams with me? Or anyone?"

"Considering all we've gone through, and the fact that Mason had a similar dream over a month ago, I would think you'd recognize a warning that obvious." Although he didn't say the words outright, his tone condemned me for my stupidity. My father, who'd been reining in his emotions the past few weeks, stepped back, and Oliver Blackmoor, the impatient, hotheaded warlock took his place.

Maybe it was foolish of me for not considering the nightmares a bad omen, but bad dreams had become a regular occurrence since Mom died. In them, my loved ones were always in danger, hunted by creatures I could hear but not see. How was I to know *this* dream was any different?

"You're not being fair," Aiden said. He stood by me and crossed his arms. It was a posture I'd seen Mason take many times over the past few weeks. He was trying to protect me, but why? I had basically bitten off his head a few moments ago. Plus I didn't need anyone to come to my rescue. So why did tiny fluttering wings suddenly tickle my stomach?

"Fair?" Mrs. Proctor asked. "This isn't about being fair. This is about withholding vital information."

"Camille is right," Mr. Stonewall said. "Had we known about this, we might have been prepared for what happened here tonight."

"You think too much of yourself. As is typical of your species." Aiden met Mr. Stonewall's cool indifference with an emerald fire in his eyes. Only dismounting a white steed and drawing his sword would make his intentions any clearer. He was ready to defend me with words or weapons.

"Where was your preparedness when the shadow weaver attacked?" Aiden asked. "You knew of its existence, yet each and every one of you stood there like dim-witted trolls. Foreknowledge clearly doesn't provide you with what you think it does. It seems to me you're using Thad as your convenient scapegoat."

I couldn't have said it better myself, and for once, I didn't have to. Aiden evidently had my back. The only other person who had ever defended me so fiercely was my mother.

"He's right," Pierce said. He trotted over to stand next to Aiden and me. My brother's sudden show of support surprised me. He rarely openly defied the High Priests. He saved his massive size and big mouth for our enemies or for tormenting Mason and me. "We're all to blame for this. We've known for weeks that some unseen enemy is out there, and we've done nothing about it. And why?"

"Because the Conclave told us not to," Mason answered before joining Pierce at my side. Both brothers supported me. Maybe Aiden had been right earlier. Perhaps I wasn't as alone as I'd believed I was.

"Are you questioning the motives of the most powerful of us all?" Mr. Proctor asked.

We were, and my family had been for some time now. Admitting that, though, was not an easy thing to do. The Conclave included warlocks, witches, and wizards capable of turning every one of us inside out with but a stray thought, and they didn't take kindly to being second-guessed.

Their word was law. No middle ground existed.

Aiden was right about one thing. I hid my emotions and perhaps that was wrong. Denying what I felt didn't solve anything. Only admitting what rang true could fix what was inherently wrong. "Yes," I finally answered. "We are."

"And that is why we are here now."

Nine hooded and robed figures, three in black, three in white, and three in gray suddenly shimmered into existence before us.

The Conclave had arrived.

CHAPTER 5

FOR SEVERAL minutes, we all stood in silence. No one knew what to say or do.

Even though they were our governing body, personal audiences with the Conclave were uncommon. They only appeared when a threat needing our attention turned up, and then they usually only spoke to our parents. They rarely, if ever, addressed us.

I'd never understood why. We were members of the protector covens too, but whenever I asked my father that question, the answer I had always received was, "That is the way of the Conclave."

And it was those mysterious ways that had inevitably led to my distrust of them and their actions. How were we to blindly follow people who didn't address us or even let us see their faces?

Since the days after the mad warlock, Bartram Kane, they preferred to govern in secret and from afar, and while that may have worked as the magical community rebuilt its decimated ranks, it no longer worked for me. Or my brothers.

"Your thoughts betray you, Thaddeus," one of the Conclave spoke. His gray robes marked him a wizard, and he stood dead center in the foreboding line of power that was assembled before us.

But it wasn't the words he spoke that caused me to step away from my brothers, who stood as bookends of protection on either side of me. I recognized the voice.

"Who are you?" I asked, inching closer. "You sound familiar."

"I will not stand for this insolence any longer," Mr. Stonewall said. His typical indifference melted into a blaze of anger. He pointed his hand at me, and a sudden force of unseen energy compelled me to my knees.

My head exploded in pain. He was using his active power on me, forcing me into submission.

"Oh, fuck no!" Pierce said. Sparks of energy snaked from his fists. "This shit is on!" He let loose an explosion of electricity that slammed into an invisible barrier around Lawrence Stonewall.

Edith had projected her force field around her father.

To make matters worse, a dozen vampyren suddenly surrounded my brother. They hissed and pounced on him. My father and Mason immediately responded, but their powers passed through them without causing any damage.

I settled my gaze on Mrs. Stonewall, who held her fingers to her temples. The vampyren weren't real. They were illusions she had created.

"Stop attacking my son!" my father yelled. With a wave of his hand, Rachel Stonewall flew backward and slammed into one of the bookcases. Her projections immediately disappeared.

After that, chaos erupted. For the first time in centuries, warlock fought wizard and witch.

"Your entire species is unstable," Mr. Proctor said after hurling a fireball at my father. He managed to switch to his stone form just in time. The attack bounced harmlessly off his earthen armor.

"Us?" Mason asked. He crafted inky tentacles from the shadows that wrapped around Mr. Proctor. "We were attacked first."

Adam Proctor, who'd once had a thing for him, slammed Mason with a gale-force wind that sent him rolling across the library.

"Now this is what I'm talking about!" Ben shouted before joining the brawl. A satisfied smirk tugged his lips when he created a small sandstorm and sent it barreling toward Adam. It swept him away and up to the second floor of the library, where he landed with a crash.

The roots that had once secured the banshees shot toward Ben as Camille got her revenge for the attack against her son. They wrapped around his arms and legs until he couldn't move.

A dome of fire suddenly surrounded me where I still knelt on the floor. "I'll keep you safe," Aiden said. He stood over me and studied the maelstrom for any sign the tide of battle was coming our way.

I smiled in thanks, because I didn't know what else to do. I was used to standing on my own and taking care of myself. It was a learned behavior fashioned after years of feeling as if I was the odd person out within my own family.

It had only gotten worse after my mother died. But not only had my family sprung to my aid, but Aiden put himself between me and the battle that raged around us.

Even though I couldn't speak or move—Mr. Stonewall's power kept me glued to where I knelt—confidence I'd only pretended to have before filled my soul.

"That is enough," the familiar voice in the gray robes announced. He and the others didn't move. They remained in the same pose they had arrived in, but their thoughts reached out around them. In an instant, every person in the room, with the exception of Aiden and me, was lifted off the ground and dangled like naughty kittens before the Conclave.

Their hidden eyes studied us intently before they turned to each other and nodded. They lowered everyone to the wooden floor of the library, and the power that had previously kept me on my knees faded.

Aiden helped me to my feet and then stood by my side as the gazes of the Conclave settled upon me.

"This is what you have wrought," said the white-robed figure on the far right. "Dissension among those elected to safeguard magic."

"It wasn't my intention," I said. Although I still distrusted them, I would be a fool not to fear their collective might. "I merely seek answers. That's all."

"No, you do not." This time it was one of the warlocks in the Conclave who spoke. Her voice was stern and cold. "You question us and see us as the enemy. Do not enrage us further by lying."

"I don't see you as the enemy," I replied. I scanned the shadows that hid their faces, hoping for some sign that one of them believed me. "But I do see you as an obstacle."

"Why?" asked the voice I still couldn't place. The sleeves of his gray robe moved as he dropped his hands from the folds and let them lie at his sides. It was the first glimpse any of us had ever had of the individuals beneath the robes.

"Well, for one, you hide your identities from us. Why?" I asked.

"To protect us," he answered, looking down the line of warlocks to his left. "And you."

"That doesn't make any sense." This time it was my father's turn to speak. "What do we need to be protected from? And what could you, the most powerful of us all, be frightened of?"

"That is an answer for another day," he said. "But what I do now, I do for the sake of us all."

The heads of every single member of the Conclave turned to stare at the wizard who'd stepped out of the line. He pulled back the hood to reveal himself, and a collective gasp filled the room.

Not only was his voice familiar, but so were his gray eyes, white hair, and wizened face. He had come to Havenbridge as a solitary wizard when I was a teenager, and I'd spent many summer evenings at his small cottage discussing magic and the differences between our species. He had been a confidant and trusted advisor to a young warlock trying to find his place in the world.

"Gerald Wa?" Mrs. Stonewall asked. "How can it be? You died."

"A necessary deception," he said. "To hide my ascension to the Conclave."

"Wait a fuckin' minute," Drake grumbled. He stormed right up to Gerald despite the protests of everyone and the rigid bodies of the rest of the Conclave. The old wizard held up his hand to silence everyone.

He'd most likely already guessed the cause of Drake's anger. "You're the one my aunt Millie fell in love with?"

He nodded. "Millicent was a wonderful woman. Far too good for someone like me." His gray eyes drooped in sadness. "I was sorry to hear of her passing."

"Passin'?" Drake asked. Venom dripped from his question. "She was killed. Her throat slashed open because of the vampyre you did nothin' to stop."

"Drake," Mason said. He sprinted to his boyfriend's side and wrapped his arms around him. "Stop. It's not his fault."

"Yes it is!" he railed. He shrugged out of Mason's embrace and wrapped his fists in Gerald's robe. The remaining members of the Conclave quickly circled them, but Drake paid them no attention. His anger and grief had evidently swept aside any fear he might have about their powers. "If he's this all-powerful wizard, he could have done somethin' to save her. If he hadn't faked his death, he would have been there. That damned vampyre wouldn't have gotten close to her." His voice cracked.

"You're right," he said. He wrapped his arms around Drake and allowed him to sob into his chest. "For that I am truly sorry."

The members of the Conclave, sensing no threat, backed off.

As we stood there watching Drake release his pent-up grief, I wiped tears that suddenly fell from my eyes. I understood his pain. His misery called to the gut-wrenching torment losing my mother had created, and I had yet to fully release. It was like a bottomless pit nothing in the world could ever hope to fill.

Aiden grabbed my hand and offered me a small smile. He most likely saw the newly formed chinks in my emotional armor. I wiped the tears away, hating how vulnerable they made me, but at the same time, spilling them made the hole inside me not as deep as it had been before.

I inhaled the rest of the emotions that threatened to spill out. I wasn't ready to let go of my restraint. Perhaps I never would, but I took some comfort in the release, and in the strength and reassurance Aiden offered.

SHORTLY AFTER Drake's breakdown, the Conclave pulled Gerald aside, and they quietly conversed in the corner. They were no doubt expressing their displeasure that he had revealed himself to the rest of us.

I, for one, was glad he had. Now that the Conclave had a face, it made them less ominous and more like us. It was a bold, logical, and much-needed move.

We still didn't have the answers we needed from them, but before we could get those, other fences needed mending.

"Are we good?" my father asked the Stonewalls and the Proctors. Since warlocks didn't apologize, that was as much an act of contrition they were going to get.

The reluctant smile that slid across Mr. Proctor's face communicated his understanding of that. "Yes," he said. He shook my father's hand. "Emotions ran a bit high for all of us."

"Speak for yourself," Mr. Stonewall replied. "But apology accepted. We can't afford to be at each other's throats. Not when we have mutual enemies."

"I agree," my father said. He patted Lawrence Stonewall on his back, which elicited a slight scowl. Most wizards found physical contact with others not of their coven uncomfortable.

"Are we good too?" Mason asked Adam, Charlotte, and Miranda.

Adam, who'd developed feelings for Mason during Mabon, smiled at him and nodded. Although Adam clearly had yet to move past those emotions, he respected my brother enough to be happy for him and Drake.

Charlotte replied by giving us all a hug and a kiss.

Miranda snuffed in reply. "You and I are never good." She crossed her arms and glared at Mason.

He nodded. "Then things are back to normal." He wrapped an arm around her shoulders and kissed her cheek.

"Gross!" she said as she shoved him away. "I don't need your cooties."

"I love his cooties," Drake replied. Even though his tears had dried, he still hadn't fully recovered.

"You doing okay?" my father asked. He clearly cared for Drake as if he was one of his own, and I admired him for that. He might be cranky and hot-tempered, but he was a dad first and a warlock second.

Drake nodded. "I will be. I'm still angry. I don't understand why Gerald deceived my Aunt Millie like that, but there's one thing bein' with Mason has taught me. There's more goin' on than meets the eye."

"That's a healthy attitude to have."

We turned to find Gerald Wa standing behind us and the Conclave gathered in a line behind him.

"Is the secret meeting over?" Pierce asked.

He sighed and nodded, clearly exasperated. "Finally!" he said with a nod and an eye roll to the robed figures behind him. That was the man I remembered. Gerald had always been a unique wizard. While he could be as cold and logical as the rest of his species, he had a sense of humor I'd never found in another of his kind.

"If I'd known joining the Conclave would involve endless hours of meetings, I would have likely declined." He put his hand over his mouth in feigned embarrassment and grinned.

The gesture earned him smiles from all of us. Well, everyone except the rest of the Conclave. They were probably frowning beneath those hoods. But that didn't matter. Revealing who he was had gained everyone's trust.

That was what we'd needed to unite us.

"Are we going to get our answers now?" I asked.

He shook his head. "You're still a dog with a bone, aren't you?"

"Perhaps," I offered with a grin.

"I'll give you what answers I can," he said. "There are limits to what I can reveal, especially in mixed company." He eyed Drake and Ben.

"We can leave," Drake offered.

Ben's only reply was to cross his arms and snort.

"Not necessary," Gerald replied. He gathered his gray robes about him and gave a slight nod to Aiden. "Your Highness."

Aiden returned the gesture.

"I hear your realm is under siege," he said with a frown as he sat in the red wingback chair. "This is unacceptable."

"I agree," Aiden replied. An imperial tone settled over his words. "I'd appreciate assistance and whatever answers the Conclave possesses."

Gerald nodded and waved us closer. "Ask me your questions."

"You know who the shadow weaver is, don't you?" I asked.

"Yes," he replied without hesitation.

His answer caused a stir of voices.

"Why keep this from us?" Mr. Proctor asked.

"Because knowledge is power," he answered. "Once shared it is out of our control."

"And ignorance is a weakness," I replied. He arched a warning eyebrow at me. He might have revealed himself, but he was still a member of the Conclave. It would do me well to remember that. "I'm just saying you're a wizard. More than most, you understand the importance of facts and dealing with them logically."

The Stonewalls nodded in agreement.

I decided to push my luck anyway. "Why not simply tell us?"

He sat in silence for a minute. By the way his eyes darted back and forth, I could tell he was communicating with the rest of the Conclave. "To prevent panic."

"You're being all mysterious again," Mason said. If he were any more irritated, he'd be rolling his eyes. Thankfully, he had enough self-control not to do that in front of the Conclave.

"You are part of that reason," he said.

Mason surveyed the room. "Me?"

Gerald laced his aged fingers in his lap and sat back, regarding Mason carefully. "You are the first shadow weaver since Bartram Kane's time," he said with a sigh. "We sensed the power within you at Mabon, and it surprised us. The last time a shadow weaver walked our planet, he created the vampyren and almost killed us all."

"But I'm not Bartram Kane," Mason said.

He nodded. "Yet the potential for corruption exists. Every warlock in our long history who has ever tapped into the power of darkness has gone mad."

There was no use arguing that point. It was a fact, and it was something we had already discussed as a family.

"But what does that have to do with you keeping the identity of the shadow weaver from us?" Pierce asked. "That's apples and oranges."

"Perhaps, but we believe the shadow weaver is amassing power. To what end, we are uncertain. But now that he knows another shadow weaver exists, we have no doubt he will attempt to claim you as his own."

"He's already tried," Mason announced with a proud jut to his chin. "And failed."

"Yes," Gerald agreed. "But there is more than one way to collect the growing power within you."

"Like how?" Mason asked, clearly not buying what the old wizard was trying to sell.

"We can only speculate, and speculation isn't fact. Until we are certain, we will say no more on the subject." His tone was firm. The decision was final.

"Then can you clear something up for me?" I asked.

"I can try," he replied, studying me intently.

"What is the relationship between this shadow weaver and Bartram Kane?"

My question visibly startled him, and the Conclave stepped forward. There was a connection. I knew it.

"You're very careful with your word choice. I remember that about you, and you just told Mason 'he was the last shadow weaver since Bartram Kane's time.' That can only be true if *this* shadow weaver we're fighting hadn't come into his powers in the generations since then."

"Very astute observation," Mr. Stonewall said. Did he have to sound so impressed? "How is it possible this shadow weaver has been around since the Salem Witch Trials?"

"I will not answer. That knowledge cannot go beyond the Conclave." He studied the growing concern that filled the room. "However, I cannot stop you from finding out on your own."

Each member of the Conclave grew stiff. He probably was not supposed to say that. Why did I feel as if Gerald was not only giving us a clue but his blessing to dig deeper?

"I don't proclaim to understand the Conclave's annoying need for secrecy," Aiden said. "But as a member of the Royal Fae Court, I expect concrete answers to my questions, not ambiguity."

Gerald nodded. "And you will have them," he said. "The Conclave wishes to continue all cooperative measures with your kingdom."

While I knew much about the fae in terms of their powers and duties, their history was shrouded in secrecy. At one time, they'd resided on our plane, but something happened that led to the creation of and their move to Otherworld. Aiden's clenched jaw told me it hadn't been a joyous event, and that obvious tension still existed between his people and the Conclave.

"Why is this shadow weaver in Otherworld?" Aiden asked. "And what is he doing with the banshees?"

Gerald shook his head. "As you know, we cannot see into or visit your realm without the permission of the king." When Aiden nodded, I surveyed the expressions of the rest of the protector covens. This was evidently news to them as well. How was it possible the fae kept the Conclave from piercing the veil between the worlds? That told me Aiden and his people held far more power than anyone gave them credit for.

"And with your knowledge of the shadow weaver's identity, you can venture no guess as to his intentions?"

"Beyond what I've already revealed, no." Gerald punctuated this with a firm shake of his head.

Aiden's stare turned diamond hard. He either didn't like the answer or believed he was being lied to. But if Gerald was still the same wizard I'd known, he truly had no answers for Aiden.

I surprised myself when I took Aiden's hand in mine. I hadn't planned it, but when I saw he needed the comfort he had previously given to me, I automatically responded.

He gently squeezed my hand in thanks.

The gesture caught Gerald's attention. He stared for a moment at our joined hands before turning back to me. His wide eyes told me he was surprised, and it wasn't due to learning my sexual preference.

"We have to do something," I said. "We can't just sit around and wait. Let us go to Otherworld. Maybe then we can learn what the shadow weaver is after and find out why it's speaking in Greek."

Gerald grabbed my forearm with a firmness I hadn't expected in a man of his age. The force of his grip tore my hand from Aiden's. "What did you say?" he asked as he stood.

The Conclave drew closer until they stood directly behind him.

What had I said to produce this bizarre reaction? "We can't just stand here and do nothing. We have to go to Otherworld. The light fae most likely need our help."

"Not that," he said, waving my previous words away like a bad spell. "Did you say he spoke Greek?"

I nodded.

All the color drained from Gerald Wa's face. He turned to gape at the Conclave, and they nodded in unison. When he returned his attention to me, he licked his lips before speaking. "Greek is the language of blood magic."

I barely heard what anyone said after that. Their voices turned into background noise as I processed the revelation. Blood magic was an ancient power that hadn't been practiced for centuries. It predated the spells we cast today and was considered the most powerful type of all. With it, the practitioner could do almost anything, and it was why the Conclave had forbidden its use.

If the shadow weaver, who had already harnessed the power of darkness, also managed to learn how to cast blood magic, his power not only surpassed ours but rivaled the combined abilities of the Conclave.

"BLOOD MAGIC?" Pierce asked. "That's bad, right?"

I didn't possess the energy to respond to my brother's understatement. I was too upset at being escorted out of the library while the Conclave spoke with our parents.

"Well, it sure doesn't sound good," Mason answered.

Miranda leaned against the wall and glared at my brothers. "Did the two of you hit every branch of the stupid tree on your way down?"

"Miranda, please," Charlotte said to her sister. "You're not being helpful."

"Yeah, well, neither are Dumb Ass number one or number two," she said with a scowl.

"Fuck you, Miranda," Mason said. "If you're so damned smart, why don't you tell us what you know about blood magic?"

She waved Mason away as if he were a mosquito. "I don't have to tell you shit."

"That's what I thought," he said with a smirk. Drake held him from behind, trying to calm down his boyfriend with his touch. It seemed to work. "You have no clue either."

"I'm smart enough to realize whatever can spook the Conclave is not exactly rainbows and unicorns," Miranda replied with a slow eye roll.

"Will the two of you *ever* stop fighting?" Edith Stonewall asked. As always, she stood next to her twin, Elliot, and their younger siblings stood in front of them.

"Yeah," Kate said with a nod. "You fight more than Keaton and I do."

"You start it," Keaton replied.

"Nuh-uh," she retorted.

Keaton's rebuttal was to stick out his tongue and shout, "Yeah-huh!"

That's enough, Elliot said. Evidently, now that he'd used a wide telepathic link once, he felt comfortable enough to use it to broadcast his thoughts. Too bad it still hurt like hell.

"You've got to know somethin' about this, Thad," Drake said.

I didn't even know where to begin.

"It's an ancient and forbidden type of magic," Ben replied from where he leaned against the wall. "The Conclave forbade it because its power derived from blood sacrifices that were used to control others."

Everyone, including me, gaped at Ben. "How the hell do you know that?" I asked.

A grin stretched wide across his lips. He clearly enjoyed surprising me with his knowledge. "I read," he said, repeating the words he'd spoken to Hannah in Salem.

"Is he right?" Adam asked me. I'd clearly become the resident expert on all things magical for everyone.

"He is," I said with a nod.

"Sacrifices?" Aiden asked in disgust. "That's vile."

Ben shrugged. "At the dawn of our species, it wasn't. Human sacrifices were pretty common back then. Using blood magic from those rituals was one of the first ways our kind learned to protect ourselves from afar from the humans who wanted to kill us. Sure, we had access to our typical spells and active powers, but with blood magic, we were able to wipe out whole tribes without breaking a sweat."

Aiden's features hardened. He clearly didn't like Ben's comment. Truthfully, neither did I. "A cavalier attitude toward mass murder."

"Murder?" he asked. He chuckled at what he perceived to be Aiden's naïveté. "I'm sorry if our history offends your sensitive fairy feelings, but what we did back then wasn't murder. It was self-preservation."

"Perhaps," I replied. "But it went too far, and you know it."

"What do you mean?" Charlotte asked. Ever the peacemaker, she hoped to steer the conversation away from conflict.

"Blood magic was used to manipulate others without their knowledge. Fathers were made to slaughter their wives and children."

"That's awful," Adam said.

"And that's not even the worst of it," I replied. "Its potential remains fully untapped, and that's why it was stopped. With the proper training and spells, someone using blood magic could not only kill us with the proper enchantment but the Conclave as well. And the Gate?" I stopped. The full weight of the implication crashed down on my shoulders as if I were Atlas supporting the world. "Well, the Gate would be in grave danger."

"That's unacceptable," Edith said. For the first time since I'd known her, anger flashed in her eyes. "We must do something."

"And we will," Mr. Stonewall answered after he swung the library doors open. He motioned for us to enter the room.

As I crossed the threshold, our parents' solemn gazes greeted us. They eyed my father with eyes filled with regret.

"So?" I asked. "What's the plan?"

Dad sucked in a deep breath and said, "You and your brothers will accompany Aiden back to Otherworld. Alone."

A quick gush of air could have knocked over Adam, Charlotte, and Miranda, while Edith and Elliot's wide eyes communicated their shock. The Conclave was sending us into battle with a powerful enemy with no backup and little support.

My brothers reacted as they typically did—with anger.

"You've got to be fucking kidding," Pierce said. "*This* is your decision?"

Gerald Wa nodded. His downcast eyes told us he wasn't pleased either, but he'd clearly been outvoted. He took a deep breath and schooled his face, ready to toe the party line. "It is, and we expect you to comply."

"And what if we don't?" Mason asked. He clenched his fists, and the shadows within the library gathered around him in writhing tentacles. They slithered and tensed as if they were ready to strike.

Gerald's expression didn't betray his emotions. He regarded my brother kindly for a moment before Mason flew into the air and spun around in circles. Pierce and I stepped forward to intervene, but my father flicked his wrist in our direction, and we suddenly found ourselves immobile. The pain in his eyes communicated he was stopping us for our own good.

"Stop it!" Drake called from where Adam restrained him. "You're hurtin' him!"

"I'm doing no such thing," Gerald replied as my brother's spinning body slowly came to a halt. "I'm merely reminding him I'm *not* to be trifled with."

Without a gesture or a word, Mason slowly levitated toward Gerald Wa. He fixed his gaze upon Mason and sighed. "And you wonder why we are leery of your powers? At the first hint of disagreement, you summon your shadows with every intention of using them against us." A sudden frost flashed across his gray eyes. "Did you truly think we would allow it?"

"I wasn't going to attack," Mason answered. "It was a knee-jerk reaction because your decision pissed me off."

A few seconds later, his feet once again met the floor. "And that is why you must learn to control your temper," Gerald said.

"You're right," I said, finally finding my words. My voice trembled not in fear but in complete exasperation. "My brothers, like most warlocks, lack the restraint of the other magical orders. That is a well-documented fact."

The Conclave nodded in unison.

"But it's the nature of our species to react. It's what makes us formidable protectors of the Gate." I addressed the three members of the Conclave in black robes. As warlocks, they knew that better than anyone else. Their slow nods acknowledged my words. "When we fight, we fight to win, and your decision puts that in jeopardy."

"Our decision ensures that the Gate, which is our primary concern, remains protected," Gerald said as he once again took his spot with the other members of the Conclave. "You wanted answers and the means to find them, Thaddeus. You now have both. In the next few days, you and your brothers will find some way to infiltrate Otherworld with Prince Aiden. The other members of the protector covens remain here."

Without another word, the Conclave vanished.

The Proctors and the Stonewalls gathered together in their respective covens, and their combined gazes switched from our father, who'd turned around to face the wall, to my brothers and me. The emotion behind their expressions told me what my brothers and I had already concluded.

No one expected us to make it back alive.

AFTER EVERYONE left, my father quietly excused himself and shuffled up the stairs. He'd been unable to speak after the Conclave's decision. He was a strong warlock with power that could make the earth tremble, but when faced with a mission that might steal his sons from his life, all that power meant nothing if he couldn't use it to protect his children.

"I should go after him," Pierce said, glancing up the staircase after Dad shut the door to his room.

I shook my head. "He needs time to process this. We all do."

"I'll tell you what we need to do," Mason said, his face flushed with anger. "We need to summon the others back here and make them go with us."

"They won't disobey the Conclave," I reminded him.

"This is a fool's mission, and you know it!" Mason railed. "We'll be facing a shadow weaver wielding blood magic, banshees, possibly more vampyren, and who knows what fucking else."

Drake clutched Mason, as if his touch would somehow prevent what we all feared. "How can they do this?" he asked. "It doesn't make sense."

"The Conclave doesn't make sense," Aiden added. His scowl communicated his dislike of our governing body. "After all these years, they remain as foolish as ever."

"How old are you?" I asked.

A sly grin briefly spread across his lips as he rubbed his thumb across my chin. My brothers and Drake glanced sideways at each other in disbelief at the display of affection.

"Older than you might think," he finally answered. As quickly as the smile appeared, it vanished. "But I don't speak from personal experience. My father has told me stories that his father's father's father told him about our great migration to Otherworld. Only their pride can rival the power they possess."

What did that mean? What did Aiden know about the Conclave we didn't?

"We can stand here insulting the Conclave all night. I'm sure as hell game," Ben said. He sat back on one of the leather couches, extending his arms along the top of the cushions as if he had no care in the world. And really, he didn't. He wasn't the one being sent to his death. "But you guys need to spend less time bitching and more time coming up with a plan." A cocky grin spread across his lips. "Lucky for you, I'm good at strategy."

"You aren't a part of this," Pierce said. "I'd leave now while you've got the chance."

"Fat chance of that happening." Ben's gaze lingered on Aiden when he next spoke. "I'm ready to get my hands dirty."

Aiden replied to his comment with an arch of a bushy dark eyebrow. Why did I get the feeling Aiden had just told him to "bring it"?

"Strategizing is all well and good," I said, interrupting the stare-down between Ben and Aiden. "But we need to understand what we're up against first."

"The banshees obviously know somethin'," Drake said. "Or the shadow weaver wouldn't have killed them. Maybe all you have to do is capture one and get her to talk."

"That would likely get you nowhere," Ben said. "The shadow weaver would just kill her like he did the others. You need to break into Otherworld without alerting the dark fae or the shadow weaver. If you take them by surprise, you can get the answers you need."

Aiden chuffed. "That's impossible. Our land is protected by enchantments that would kill you if you tried to cross over uninvited. I can take us there through my portal."

Ben regarded Aiden as if he were a simpleton. While I didn't appreciate the look, I understood where Ben was coming from. The fae could obviously sense Aiden's magic, which was why they attacked him when he tried to get home. We'd lose the element of surprise if we went that route.

"How do you suggest we sneak in?" I asked. Ben clearly had an idea he was just waiting to lord over Aiden.

"I'm glad you asked," he replied. He sauntered over to me, making a big show of walking around Aiden. "It's Samhain. The veil between worlds is thin, right?"

Of course. Fae often stumbled into our world during this time of the year. Chances were we could do the same. If we could somehow find a weak spot between our planes, we could cross without alerting anyone on the other side what was happening, but we had to act fast. The barriers separating us from Otherworld grew stronger each day after Samhain. In a week's time, it would once again be impregnable.

"I'll start researching the Grimoire," I finally said. "There's got to be something in there to help us."

It was definitely a way into Otherworld without immediately getting us killed, and if it worked, we might even make it back alive.

CHAPTER 6

I WOKE with a start. I'd been poring through our Grimoire and every magical book I could find, looking for a solution after everyone else went to bed. As usual, they'd left everything up to me. The jerks!

All my research had gotten me nothing but a headache. I had closed my eyes for a few minutes, just to rest enough to continue, but I'd evidently slept through the night.

When I sat up, I winced. A huge knot had formed in my neck muscles and between my shoulder blades, most likely a combination of poor sleeping posture and tension from the impossible feat that awaited my brothers and me.

I rubbed the sleep from my eyes before once again focusing on the blurry lines of text that sprawled across the desk. The fruits of my previous labors had been disappointing.

I'd found spells that allowed the caster to open portals or teleport, which would potentially allow us safe passage to Otherworld, but without a means of detecting the weakened boundaries between worlds, they were useless.

The answer had to be in here somewhere.

"Good morning, Thaddeus."

Aiden stood from the couch where he must have fallen asleep, and stretched. He still wore the sweatpants I'd given him last night, and the waistband dipped as he worked out the kinks in his muscles. A dark brush of hair peeked out over the fabric as if inviting me for a closer look.

"Good morning," I finally said when I realized I'd been spending too much time staring at Aiden's crotch instead of the green eyes that greeted the world with a smile. "I didn't know you were here. You could have slept in my bed."

My cheeks immediately flushed at the unintentional suggestiveness of my comment. Under ordinary circumstances, a blunder like that wouldn't have affected me at all. I probably wouldn't even have realized what I had said, but when I was around Aiden, the emotions I tried to hide had no problem springing to the surface.

"But you weren't there," he said with a grin. "So I stayed here with you."

I didn't know how to respond. After my tantrum last night, I figured Aiden would stay as far away as possible, but my outburst hadn't affected him. Was that because he was a fire fairy? Emotions were their bread and butter, after all.

"I'm sorry about last night," I finally said, surprised that an apology slipped so easily from my lips. That had never happened to me before, either.

"You were tired," he replied. He stood beside me, looking at the books that had been my bedding. He smelled like cinnamon and musk. "That's nothing to be sorry about."

"Not about that. About the way I acted in the hallway last night. The things I said. They were uncalled for, and you were just trying to help." I took his hand in mine, rubbing my fingers across the smooth, creamy flesh. "I'm sorry."

He cupped my cheek in his big hand and smiled down at me. "That's very sweet of you to say, especially since I can tell apologizing is not something you often do. So while it's unnecessary, I thank you anyway."

"How do you do that?" I asked, leaning into his touch.

"Do what?"

"Read me the way you do. Is that your fairy magic?"

"It's part of who I am," he said with a nod. "But it's not the whole answer."

"Then what?"

He scrunched his lips, evidently uncertain if he should tell me.

"I really want to know," I said.

"My answer will likely make you uncomfortable."

I nudged him with my shoulder. "Tell me already."

He let out a long sigh before answering. "Like I was telling you last night, I can see you. The real you. Yes, that's part of being a fire fae. We can look into the hearts of humans and inspire the passion and creativity they might lack, but with you it's different."

"Why? Because I'm a warlock?"

He shook his head.

"Then what is it?"

"Well," he said before a long pause. "I like you."

I couldn't help the smile that turned me into a grinning idiot. "I think Charlotte already established that I like you too." I stood, stepping into the space that had previously separated us. "And that's pretty out of character for me. I don't typically allow myself to feel for others."

"Why is that?"

I glanced away, embarrassed by the words I was going to let free. "Emotions are deadly. You don't control them. They control you."

"They can," he admitted. "I have a temper. My father says it's because I'm an only child, who has been spoiled rotten. But that's not it. I've always felt things deeply. It's who I am, and I'm not going to change or apologize for it."

"And you shouldn't," I said. "But if that's who you are, isn't not expressing or liking emotion who I am too? I shouldn't have to change or apologize for it either, right?"

"If that was who you were, I would agree."

I cocked one eyebrow at him. "Are you trying to say you know me better than I know myself?"

"Not at all. I just don't believe that's truly who you are. I think you want to feel, to express what's in your heart, but for some reason, it terrifies you." He locked gazes with me. His eyes were wide and sympathetic. They told me he wanted to know why I was the way I was.

"I lost control once. When I was younger." I closed my eyes, trying to block out the memory of my youth that played in my mind. Pierce and Dad were screaming at me. My mother was trying to snap me out of my anger. And Mason. I opened my eyes and shook it off. He was too young to remember the afternoon that still haunted me to this day. "I can't ever allow that to happen again."

Aiden didn't push for specifics. He rubbed my shoulders. "But there's a difference between controlling your emotions and denying them. Should we all try harder to rein ourselves in? Yes. But if we stop feeling, we stop living."

Maybe that was what I had done. Losing control terrified me. It had almost cost me my brother. I had shut myself off from everyone except my mother. Now that she was gone, I had no one because I had let no one else in.

"Let yourself feel," he said, squeezing my shoulders. I didn't tense or attempt to shrug off the contact like I had done last night when the emotions got too real. "And never regret those emotions. They make us who we are."

Aiden was right. Perhaps it was time for me to experience the world the way everyone else did.

A sly grin hooked up the corners of my mouth. "Let's go," I said, grabbing his hand.

"Where?"

Instead of replying, I led him up the stairs.

AIDEN ARCHED his eyebrow as I shut my bedroom door behind us. "Why are we here?"

I responded by unbuttoning my shirt.

He grinned. "I enjoy it when you look at me like that."

"Like what?" I asked as I swept my gaze over the firm peaks of his chest down to the muscled ridges of his abdominals.

"Like you want to touch me." He slowly closed the gap between us, and the closer he got, the harder it was for me to breathe.

"I do," I admitted.

"You can," he said. His voice had dropped to just above a whisper. "I don't mind. I like being touched."

He caressed my cheeks. I closed my eyes and leaned into his touch. We hadn't known each other long, but Aiden's flesh against mine felt like home. It was the most bizarre feeling I'd ever experienced. I'd grown used to my solitary life, but being around Aiden had opened up a strange new world of feelings, which both excited and concerned me. It made me vulnerable, but it also fueled an untapped power within me. It grew like a seed, spreading its roots through my soul.

Was this what my father had felt for my mother? Or even what Mason had with Drake? My brother had told me he and Drake were spell bound, a rare, magical pairing of two linked souls.

But that wasn't what I felt for Aiden. There was no sudden clicking of parts, as if I'd finally found the one I'd forever been destined to meet. It was more primal than spiritual, as if my blood surged through my veins, not in search of my heart, but in an effort to reach the one that beat within Aiden's chest.

No. We weren't spell bound. In a strange way, my connection to Aiden reminded me more of my bond with my mother. She called it being blood tied. Since we were family, that meant we'd do anything for each other, love each other no matter what, and even give up our lives if necessary.

It sounded bizarre, but it was the only way I could make sense of what I felt for him. From the moment I'd seen Aiden, it was as if he were a missing part of my family, an unknown blood tie that had been left dangling, but once found, joined me to him completely.

"Do you feel it?" I asked, gazing up into the green field of Aiden's eyes.

A naughty grin slinked across his lips. "Not yet. But I hope to real soon."

His gleeful bawdiness made me laugh. "Well, me too, but that wasn't what I was talking about."

"I know," he said. "And I'm uncertain what it means."

I nodded. "Me too."

He shoved a stray dark lock from his eyes and bit his lip. "Can I be honest with you about something before we, well, you know?"

"Please do," I replied. I cherished honesty. Whether it was painful or not, it provided the data needed to make rational decisions.

"Fairies are free spirits, and the fire fae, well, we make the other fae look downright conservative." He grinned at me and laced his fingers in mine. "We take great pride in the fact that we don't take anything seriously. Except maybe keeping the hearths burning and the fires of creativity and passion roaring. It's what we do."

He wasn't telling me anything I didn't know already. "And?"

"Well," he began, gnawing on his bottom lip. It was an unusual tic for someone of royal fae blood. The Royal Fae Court projected only strength and unity. Right now, Aiden looked uncertain and lost. "For us, relationships are just, I guess, fluid is the right word. We drift on the current, following our passions from one set of arms to another. There's no rhyme or reason. No commitments are exchanged. We do what feels good when it feels good."

I didn't need a road map to tell me where this was going. "So you want me to know I'll just be another spot along the riverbank, right? That when the current moves you again, you're going to follow where it leads you."

"Well, yes and no."

"I don't understand."

He wrapped his arms around my neck and placed his forehead against mine. "What I feel for you is bizarre. Unique for someone like me. It's like you're in my blood, if that makes any sense."

It did.

"Perhaps it's the conflict we are facing together," he continued. "Battle has a way of heightening passions, but it's important for both of us to face the fact. I can't change my nature any more than you can change yours. I'm a fire fae, and I will always be one."

Although I didn't want to admit it, Aiden was right. There was no telling what the future would hold. What stirred my blood—no, our blood—might be a passing phase, and once satisfied, the same current that had brought us together might set us adrift from each other.

The logical course of action would be to not dip our toes in the water. They raged by too swiftly to be trusted, and my heart had already been shattered. Losing my mother, the only person on this planet I ever felt truly loved me or understood me, had ripped my insides to shreds. The pain had been unbearable, and if losing Aiden would come anywhere close to that, could I even chance it?

"I don't care," I said, surprising Aiden and myself.

He wrapped his arms tighter around my neck and squeezed. "Really? Because I don't want to hurt you. Ever."

I nodded. "I don't care if this ends tomorrow or two weeks from now. Well, that's not true. I do care, but tomorrow is tomorrow. We're here, and right now, here is pretty fantastic."

Aiden pressed his lips to mine, and I trembled. Although we'd kissed briefly before in the woods, it had been nothing like this. It was as if every cell in my body had come back to life. Had I been dead inside until this moment? It certainly felt like it.

The lingering iciness with which I greeted the world melted, and my blood boiled in response to the fire Aiden's kiss fanned within me. It rushed forward, filling me with the life energy I'd previously denied myself.

And for the first time in months, perhaps even years, life turned from one big question mark to a giant exclamation point.

I pushed harder into our kiss, exploring the sweet warmth of Aiden's mouth with my tongue, and I surfed my hands down his smooth, creamy back. I followed the curvature of his spine to the swell of his ass before taking his firm butt in my hands.

Aiden moaned and pressed against me. The fabric of the sweats he wore tented outward, and I eased the pants from his waist.

His gorgeous, seven-inch cock bobbed before me. It was the most beautiful prick I'd ever seen in my life, rooted in a thick nest of hair, out of which hung a pair of the most perfect balls in existence.

"I want you, Aiden. More than I've wanted anybody in my life." I brushed my lips against his, and the slow burn that had built in my body since the moment I first saw him in the woods came to a rapid boil.

"I feel the same way," he said, panting into our kiss.

And that was all I needed to hear. We melted against each other, his chest heaved against mine, his arms held me as tightly as I held him, and our erections ground between our sweaty bodies.

Aiden gasped as I palmed his ass, squeezing the muscled globes. He found the buttons of my pants and unfastened them before sliding down the zipper. He shoved his eager hand beneath the fabric and took my hard cock in his grasp.

"Fuck," I mumbled as the warmth of his grip sent ripples of pleasure coursing through me. He pulled on my dick, swabbing his thumb over the head while he worked the shaft with his strong fingers.

I slid my fingers from his hand to his cock. I jerked it between us, sliding my fingers up and down his length before trailing along the curve of his cockhead.

"Shit, that feels good."

I kissed my way from his lips to his chest, where I took one nipple into my mouth. I fluttered my tongue along the pebbling flesh while I continued to stroke his cock. Precum wept from the slit, and I dabbed my forefinger into the liquid before rising off his nipple and sucking the finger into my mouth.

I shoved my tongue between Aiden's parted lips, his juices making our kiss even sweeter. He moaned into the lip lock while I clutched at his back, massaging his slick flesh in my hands.

As we kissed, I guided him to the bed, where I gently lowered Aiden onto the mattress. I crawled between his legs, delivering soft kisses to his shuddering stomach. I licked a path through the treasure trail that tasted of sweat and precum before I swabbed along the base of his cock.

Aiden arched his back and cried out softly. He gripped my head with his hands, guiding me where he wanted me to go.

I took his prick in my hands, working my hand up and down as I slipped my tongue across the weeping opening and suckled. More precum flowed from his cock, and I drank it all down.

"Yes," he purred. "Like that."

"Like this?" I asked, wrapping my lips around the swollen head and sliding down to the base of his cock.

"Fuck yes," he muttered.

With his shaft lodged in my throat, I tightened my muscles before rising all the way back up to his head. I swirled my tongue along the shaft before swallowing his entire length.

I worked his prick that way for a few more moments, bobbing up and off his cock to lick the sensitive flesh. He was getting close. He tensed, and his panting grew ragged.

"Stop," he pleaded. "Not yet."

I rose. "What's wrong?"

His eyes were wild with passion, his pupils completely blown. "Nothing," he growled. He grabbed me by my shoulders and flipped me onto my back. "I want some too," he said before he turned around and dangled his stiff cock over my lips and placed his head above my dick.

"I like the way you think."

He grinned. "Less talking, more sucking."

I was just about to repeat myself before Aiden's wet mouth stole all breath from me. He fell upon my entire length in one motion. His tongue danced across my shaft as he worked my hardness in and out of his mouth. Saliva slid down my prick, and he used the lubrication to jack me at a furious pace.

I sucked Aiden's cock back into my mouth, his balls slapping against my nose. I grabbed hold of his ass, sliding my fingers along his crevice. When I found his center, I drew circles around the edge.

Aiden groaned in response. He increased the suction on my cock and tugged on my balls. The sensation almost became too much. My nerve endings were on overload.

We thrust into each other's mouths, our paces growing as labored as our breathing before Aiden tensed and grunted. His cock grew as hard as steel before erupting volleys of hot semen in my mouth. I greedily drank it down, and as the last shot of cum hit my tongue, Aiden's fingers and mouth brought me to my own climax.

I thrust upward one final time before I unloaded. I cursed and gasped as I released months, if not years, of pent-up frustration.

When we recovered and could finally breathe normally again, Aiden turned around and curled up on my chest. He wrapped his arms tightly around me, and I sighed.

I'd never felt more complete, more content in my life than I did right now.

"Are you okay?" he asked, rearranging himself so he could gaze up at me.

"No," I replied, craning my head down to kiss his nose. "I'm better than okay. I'm fucking fantastic."

He grinned and burrowed into my neck. "Good. That makes me happy."

And I was happy too, happier than I'd been in a long time. This might go nowhere. It might end badly, and the logical part of my brain screamed at me to cut bait and run like I had in every other relationship.

For once, I wasn't listening to my brain. My ears only heard my heart, and its rapid beating told me all I needed to know.

A FEW hours later, I woke to the sound of Aiden's low snores. He rested his head on my chest where he had fallen asleep. I hadn't planned on passing out. I'd intended to watch him sleep. The way he'd snuggled into my embrace and wrapped his bigger body around mine filled me with so many emotions I couldn't name them all.

I was happy, of course. That was easy to pinpoint, as was the passion that once again reared its head. I could spend the entire day naked in bed with Aiden if time and circumstances allowed it.

But among the positive emotions that made me smile crept the ones that made me uneasy.

There were so many unknowns ahead of us already that adding this relationship to it only complicated matters further. I couldn't afford to be distracted and neither could Aiden.

We had a job to perform, and even though no one expected us to survive it, I planned on making sure we did. That was what made this added wrinkle so potentially devastating. If I hesitated for one second to do what needed to be done, whatever that might be, because of Aiden, my family could pay the price.

I had to do everything in my power to make sure that didn't happen. "Why so serious?"

Aiden's smiling green eyes peeped up at me. "Just thinking," I said, resting my head against his and trailing my fingers across his naked body draped over mine.

"About everything we have to do?"

"Yeah. It's a lot and extremely overwhelming."

"It is." He rolled onto me, resting his big, sexy fairy body against me. The movement awoke my cock, which grew fat between us. He grinned at me before shoving his hand between us and squeezing my dick. "Someone's ready to go again."

I thrust into his grip before dragging my fingertips across the expanse of his back. "I'm game if you are."

A wicked grin slid across his lips. "I'm a fire fae. Our sexual appetites are legendary."

I found Aiden's lips, and his tongue came alive in my mouth. I squeezed his body to mine before turning him over on his back and resting between his legs. I'd never wanted to make love to someone more than I did right now.

The door to my room suddenly rattled, and someone knocked on the door. "What the fuck are you doing in there?" Pierce asked. He banged on the door, trying to open it, but I'd had the foresight to lock it when we came in.

"Go away!" I called over my shoulder. Pierce was lucky I couldn't see him right now, or he'd be made entirely of ice at the moment.

He snickered. "Well, hurry up and finish. We don't have all damn day, you know? You've got to find us a way into Otherworld, and fast."

I groaned and let my head fall against Aiden's shoulder.

"I'll be out in a minute," I replied.

"Damn, bro," he said, chuckling as his footsteps padded down the hall. "You need to work on your stamina."

If Aiden hadn't been holding me in his arms, I'd have leaped from the bed, thrown open the door, and made Jack Frost nip at Pierce's balls.

"Don't worry," Aiden said, forcing my gaze to his. "I'm sure we'll have more opportunities than this."

He was right, and so was my brother. The sooner we went to Otherworld and dealt with the shadow weaver, the sooner Aiden and I could spend more time in bed together naked. "All right," I said, lifting myself off Aiden. "I suppose we should get up and get dressed."

I rose from the bed and searched the floor for the clothes I had haphazardly discarded.

"We don't have to," he said. "I don't have a problem with nudity. It's you and your prudish warlocks who seem to take issue with it."

That was the first time my species has ever been called prudes, but maybe to the fae, who were far more liberal, that was exactly what we were. "If it was just you and me, I'd demand for us to remain clothes free, but with my father and brothers in the house"—I shivered—"that's just a little too close for my taste."

Aiden pulled the sweatpants I'd loaned him back on. I couldn't stop the frown that bent my lower lip when the sight of his gorgeous cock was once again hidden from sight.

"Don't forget Ben."

"Who?" I asked, not really paying attention to what he was saying. I was too busy remembering the weight of his warm cock in my mouth.

Aiden laughed and waved his finger at me as if he knew what I was thinking. "Focus, Thaddeus."

I stuck out my tongue at him before putting on my shirt. When was the last time I'd done anything that juvenile? "What were you saying?"

He scooped up my underwear and pants from the floor and padded over to where I stood. "I said you forgot about Ben."

I took the blue briefs from Aiden and pulled them on. I had forgotten about him, which was strange. Every time I was around him, he seemed to occupy more and more of my thoughts. Apparently not anymore. The last I remembered was Pierce taking him upstairs to the guest room while I researched in the library.

"Ben's a big boy," I replied. "He can take care of himself."

Aiden stood there in silence as I pulled up my pants, a look of confusion played across his expression.

"What's wrong?"

"Nothing's wrong," he said with a wave of his hand. "I just hope I haven't come between you and Ben. It's obvious that he likes you, and I know warlocks aren't as fluid with their emotions as the fae."

That was the understatement of the century. My kind tended to have only two emotions—anger and lust.

"Ben and I had a one-time thing," I said. I glanced at myself in the mirror, making sure I was somewhat presentable. "There's nothing more between us."

He darted his eyes away, skeptical. "Perhaps not for you."

Aiden definitely had Ben pegged.

I took his hands in mine and pulled him into a kiss. For a fire fae with fluid relationships, he sounded a bit possessive. "Are you jealous?" I asked with a playful waggle of my eyebrows.

Aiden started as if I'd just slapped him. "What? No." His eyes darted back and forth, as if he were unsure if that was the right answer or not.

I chuckled before molding my lips to his once again. The fervor of the kiss and the way he held me indicated that perhaps he was after all.

I CONTINUED my search through the Grimoire for the spell.

While I researched, the others were busily accomplishing the tasks I'd given them.

My father and brothers went into the family's ceremonial room, retrieving athames they would then spell. While we typically relied on our magic in fights, the daggers would add another level of offense that would catch our enemies off guard.

Drake and Ben were outside collecting stakes from the wooden fence out back. We'd need them in case we ran into another vampyre. Pierce didn't believe we'd run into any, but I wasn't so sure. There were too many unknown variables as it was, and we needed to be prepared for as many as possible.

Ben had surprisingly gone along with my suggestion to work out back with Drake. Ever since Aiden and I had come downstairs, he'd been withdrawn and sullen.

That wasn't anything I could control. I'd been attempting to control too much in my life already. It was time for me to let things simply be. I did feel bad for Ben, but the sooner he accepted that nothing was going to happen between us, the better it would be for everyone.

As for Aiden, he was attempting to do reconnaissance. He sat cross-legged in the backyard, completely impervious to the brisk weather that had settled over Massachusetts. He was using his fae magic to pierce the boundary separating our worlds. We needed to know exactly what we were getting ourselves into, and he was our only chance of getting that information if his senses could pierce the veil. It was a long shot. Since it was likely the shadow weaver was manipulating the energies on the other side, the chance of Aiden's success was minimal.

But we had to give it a try, especially since it became obvious I wasn't able to focus with him within arm's reach.

Truth be told, part of me wanted to chuck all this and start living the life I hadn't really been living before. I was so determined to separate myself from my emotions that now that I had finally embraced them, waiting a second longer didn't seem right.

But then again, neither did standing idly by and letting the shadow weaver follow through with his plans in Otherworld. We'd find out what they were and put a stop to them. When we were done, Aiden was all mine.

"I see you're finally alone."

I turned to find Ben leaning against the open door. He gazed at me with the same half grin he gave me when I'd finally let him into my dorm room. He was an attractive warlock, and if I hadn't felt the way I did about Aiden, we might have had a shot. Then again, it was Aiden who'd reminded me my heart was more than just an organ that kept me alive.

Ben hadn't stood a chance.

"You all done?" I asked.

He nodded and closed the door behind him. "Drake's taking point on making sure the stakes are extra sharp. Since he's killed one and all, he seems to think he's the expert in all things vampyre."

I smiled, but it was more for his benefit than any true amusement. We needed to have a talk. I just didn't know how to begin.

After a few moments of silence, he crossed to the chair beside me and sat down. "We should probably talk, huh?" He sat forward and gazed at the floor.

"Ben, I—"

"Can I go first?" he asked.

I nodded and turned to give him my full attention.

"I'm not blind. I can see what's happening between you and Aiden," he cracked his knuckles and grinned. "But I'm not going to throw in the towel just yet."

"Ben—"

"You and I have a connection," he said. He scooted the chair closer and placed his hand on my knee. I responded to his touch. My head swam, and my cock twitched. This wasn't right. If I wanted Aiden so much, why were my hormones kicking into overdrive for Ben? "I know you feel it. I can see it when I touch you. When I'm near you." He leaned closer, inhaling the air around me.

I pushed him back and stood up. "Ben, this isn't going to happen."

"But it can," he said, standing in front of me. The intensity of his eyes pushed down upon me like a weight suddenly lowering on my chest. I was having difficulty drawing breath. "I'm not saying you can't explore whatever you might feel for Aiden. Just explore what you feel for me too."

Could I really do that? Aiden had virtually said fire fae weren't monogamous and had multiple partners. If that was the way he lived, why couldn't I do the same thing? It was certainly logical.

Ben wrapped his arms around my waist, pulling me into him. I went slack in his embrace, unable to summon the will to fight him and the insistent desire his presence fueled within me.

An impish grin traveled along his lips as they drew closer to mine. I became lost in his persistent touch, in his alluring dark eyes, in the overwhelming copper scent that clung to the air around him. More than anything, even more than I'd previously wanted Aiden, I needed Ben to kiss me.

To own me, body and soul.

"I love you, Thad," he whispered before brushing his lips against mine.

He loved me? How was that even possible? Yes, we'd had sex, but he didn't know one thing about me. I hadn't shared with him my fears of opening up to others, and his advice hadn't helped me realize I'd been denying myself.

That was Aiden.

It was Aiden's touch that had given me comfort. It was in Aiden's big, green eyes where I'd seen the potential for a new home. It was Aiden's embrace I'd sought, his flesh I longed to press against, and his lips that would touch me again.

Not Ben's.

"*Demitte me*," I uttered after breaking free of the kiss.

Ben released me, and his big brown eyes regarded me in shock.

"*Sede*," I said, and Ben sat back down in the chair.

"What the fuck are you doing?" he asked. He was pissed and clearly not used to being overpowered.

"*Tace mehercle*." It was the first time I'd ever said an incantation with a curse word, but he needed to shut the fuck up. "I want you to listen to me. Actually hear the words that are coming out of my mouth. Okay?"

His lips curled in an angry snarl. He evidently had a few more choice words for me, but he was unable to give them voice.

"You and I are *never* going to happen." The conviction of my words gave me the steady legs I'd previously lacked in his presence. "I don't mean to be so cruel. That's not the warlock I am, but damn it, Ben! You've given me no other choice. You push and you push and you push. That's not love. That's some freakish obsession that has gotten way out of control, and it has to stop."

An arctic chill drifted across his gaze.

"You're angry. That's fine. I'm pretty fucking pissed off at the moment too, and you know what? That's okay. It's okay for me to be angry with you, and it's fine if you want to stay ticked off with me. You know why? Because for the first time in my life, I'm not running from what I feel. I'm not scared of what I might accidentally trigger by letting the real me free, and it's Aiden who has done that for me. He's given me the courage to face what I've been too terrified of embracing." I stood before him, my shoulders squared and my heart, not my brain, held on to the reins. I'd never felt more alive. "Do I make myself clear?"

Ben locked his gaze onto mine. He gave me one slow nod before staring straight ahead.

"*Te libero*," I said with a wave of my hand, releasing him from my spell.

He stood up, walked back the way he'd come, and shut the door behind him.

IT TOOK me a few moments to calm down after my confrontation with Ben. I was still upset that he would try to force himself on me, but I had to let it go. My attention was needed elsewhere, so I resumed my search in the Grimoire and found the spell.

We didn't need to find a weakness between the worlds. We could bring it to us.

If it worked, we'd be safely transported to Otherworld. With a whole lot of luck, we'd stop whatever the shadow weaver's plans were and get fairyland back on its feet.

"Your positivity does you well, Thaddeus."

I jumped at the sound of the voice and turned, a spell ready on my lips and a slow chill emanating from my hands. Evidently, my encounter with Ben had left my nerves frayed. But it wasn't Ben who stood in the room with me. It was Gerald Wa, and his friendly gray eyes lowered my defenses. "You really shouldn't sneak up on a warlock," I advised with a grin. It was nice to smile when I felt like it instead of looking constipated all the time.

"I think I can handle myself," he said. Although he spoke the words with a smile, his eyes held an absence of joy. Pain weighed heavily on him.

"Where is the rest of the Conclave?"

He snorted. "Where they have been the last few weeks, staring at the insides of their own asses."

I chuckled at his comment. The grave wizard who'd given us our marching orders had departed in favor of the man he had always been. It was a definite improvement. "You don't agree with them, do you?"

"Not entirely," he said with a sigh. "Don't get me wrong, I understand their decision. Our first duty, which is yours as well, is to the Gate. You know that."

I did. Or at least I had at one time. My priorities were no longer so black or white. Aiden had had something to do with that. "But?"

He shot me a mock grimace. "You think you're so smart. You always have."

"That's because I am," I replied with a jut of my chin. "There's obviously something you want to say. Otherwise you wouldn't be here right now."

He nodded. "I do. And I'm crossing a line by doing so. The Conclave doesn't believe in individual thought or action. Group mind think and decision making rule the day."

"It's what provides the balance," I added. "Without it, the witches would side with witches, the warlocks with the warlocks."

"And the wizards with the wizards," he said with a nod. "By ruling as one, we keep the natural pull of our orders from swaying us. The magical community would be in anarchy, and we cannot travel down that path again."

I couldn't argue with that. Before the three orders of magic decided to create a governing body, we'd caused more harm to ourselves than the humans had. Each order of magic thought it better than the other, and our history pages were filled with one bloody battle after another.

Until the Gate was first attacked by sorcerers, a result of our kind breeding with humans. "Are you trying to tell me sorcerers are the enemy we face?"

"I certainly hope not," he replied. The magical half-breeds had the ability to tap into the power of the Gate and completely circumvent the black, white, and gray magic that fueled the rest of us. While they siphoned impressive power in that manner, they couldn't sustain the connection. As they were only part magical, once the mana with which they were born had been exhausted, their link to the Gate was severed. Still, the untamed magic they'd been able to harness had almost destroyed us all. "But we haven't ruled out the possibility."

"Shadow weavers, vampyren, blood magic, and sorcerers," I whispered. "Our list of enemies continues to grow."

Gerald nodded.

"Is that why you're sending only me and my brothers? Because you fear this attack on Otherworld might be a diversion?"

The old wizard smiled. "I think you were born into the wrong order," he said. "That's the thinking of a wizard, not a warlock."

"Why not just tell us that?" I asked.

"The Conclave enjoys its secrets."

"But you told me just now."

He shook his head. "No. You guessed it on your own."

"You're splitting hairs, and you know it, which is more like a warlock than a wizard."

He snuffed. "Stick and stones, Thaddeus."

"Will you get in trouble for this?" I asked. Although I appreciated the information, Gerald Wa was our only real connection to answers. It wouldn't do us any good if the Conclave turned on him.

"Don't worry about me," he said. "I'm more than capable of handling those fuddy-duddies. Besides, you'd be surprised. I'm not alone in my thinking. There are other members of the Conclave who wish for a change in our practices as much as I do."

"Really? Why?"

"I've already shared too much."

He was right. Giving away even more secrets would make his return to the Conclave that much harder.

"But I do have one final piece of advice."

"What's that?"

"I know everyone believes this is a suicide mission, and I can certainly understand why," he said. "And our very specific orders were that the rest of the protector covens, including your father, must stay here."

I nodded and waved him on. "So?"

"Ben Crane is not a member of a protector coven."

I liked this wizard more by the second. He was crafty and sly, but the thought of Ben traveling with us to Otherworld left a bad taste in my mouth. "If he came with us, we wouldn't be breaking our orders, would we?"

He smiled in reply. "Don't forget young Drake Carpenter."

If my jaw had hit the floor any harder, all my teeth would have shattered. "You can't be serious. He has no magical abilities. He'd be a sitting duck, and Mason would never agree to it."

"You underestimate the boy," Gerald said. He gazed off in the distance as if he were trying to see past an impregnable barrier. "He's an enigma to us. We still don't understand why the sleeping potion you gave him or Camille Proctor's attempts to spell him failed. But that may just be the kind of weapon you need in Otherworld."

Drake? A weapon?

"I must go now," he said, gathering his robes. "I have been gone too long as it is."

"Thank you, Gerald."

"You're welcome, Thaddeus," he said with a smile. This time his gray eyes sparkled. A second later he was gone.

MASON TOOK the news about as well as I expected.

"Are you out of your fucking mind?" he railed. He stood toe-to-toe with me, poking my chest, a rage I'd never seen before blazing in his blue eyes. Aiden stepped forward, clearly wanting to intervene but uncertain what to do. "There's no way in hell I'm allowing Drake to go with us."

"Mason, please," Drake said, his tone as smooth as honey. It was his usual timbre whenever he was trying to talk Mason down from the rafters. "I'm a big boy, you know?"

My brother wheeled around. His eyes had gone mad. "I know that, but this is too dangerous. You have no powers, no magic. You'd be eaten alive."

Drake crossed his arms and blew his long blond locks out of his eyes. "I think I've done pretty good so far, haven't I? Which one of us killed that vampyre again?"

"This is different," Mason insisted. "We don't know what we're up against in Otherworld."

"I know it's a scary proposition," I said, hoping he would hear the logic of my argument. It was a long shot for someone who flew off the handle more than Faye Dunaway had in *Mommie Dearest*. "But Gerald's right. There's something special about Drake."

"I don't need you to tell me that," he seethed.

"And Gerald Wa came here to tell you that?" my father asked. He held three backpacks in his hand that were likely filled with the weapons we'd be taking with us. The weight of his fear about our mission still coiled about him like a python.

"Yes. The Conclave has been unable to determine why magic doesn't seem to work on him, and Gerald believes that may be useful to us."

"I'm not experimenting with the life of the man I love," Mason rumbled. "Besides, we can't miss school."

Mason was grasping at straws now. He never needed a reason to play hooky. Drake evidently realized that. He unwrapped Mason's crossed arms and placed them around his waist. The move quickly abated my younger brother's bluster. He could bitch and moan until the end of time, but whenever he held Drake, his belligerent nature faded.

"I love you too," Drake said. He kissed Mason's lips. "But if I can help, I want to."

Mason squeezed him hard. "I know you do, but my decision is still no."

Drake's cornflower blue eyes flashed steel. Mason was in for it now. "Your decision?" he asked. He pulled out of the embrace and took a step back. "I'm not some puppy you can keep on a leash, you know? I've got my own mind, and I'm fixin' to use it."

"But—"

Drake held up his hand, and Mason wisely shut up. He turned to face the rest of us. "I know this is dangerous, but you're all my family now, and if my goin' helps you to come back safely, well, then, dammit, I'm goin'." He glanced over his shoulder at Mason, whose pleading eyes begged him to reconsider. "My mind's made up, so quit with the puppy dog eyes, or I'll get a rolled-up newspaper and swat your behind."

"I'd do what he says," Pierce advised. "My money's on Drake kicking your ass if you don't."

Mason exhaled and threw his hands in the air. "Fine." He grabbed Drake and pulled him into an embrace. "But you're not leaving my side the whole time. Not. For. One. Second."

Drake's smile told us he agreed to the terms. "It's really hot when you get all protective."

"You like that, huh?" Mason asked. His voice grew husky.

"All right, that's enough," my father said. He eyed Mason and Drake until they released each other and the raging hormones that seemed to constantly hold them under their sway. He turned to me and said, "What else did Gerald tell you?"

After I'd revealed to them most of our conversation, it took a few moments for the information to sink in.

"Sorcerers?" my father asked. "Really?"

"The only thing Gerald said on the subject was that the Conclave hadn't ruled out their involvement."

"I thought they were virtually extinct," Ben said.

"Virtually means there are a few still out there," I said. From what I'd read, the sorcerers that did exist were either ignorant of the power they carried or in hiding. "We have to be prepared for anything."

Everyone nodded. But there was one final piece of the conversation I'd yet to relate. The part that involved Ben. While I understood why Gerald had suggested Ben go with us, I wasn't completely sold on the idea. Besides, after what had just happened between us, I doubted he would agree to go.

"And what about me?" Ben asked. For most of our talk, he'd stood there, tapping his foot as if waiting for me to reveal what he'd already guessed.

"This isn't your fight," my father said with a pat on his back. "You came to Havenbridge for business. To expect anything more from you isn't fair."

All light faded from Ben's eyes, turning them black. "Screw that!" he said. "I'm a warlock, and I don't run from a fight." Why did it seem as if he were addressing that statement to me?

"We could use his help," Pierce said. He gazed at me, obviously expecting me to agree. "The more firepower we have the better, right?"

There was no denying we would benefit from Ben's abilities, and our chances for success would increase. His hard gaze told me Ben was offering to go for reasons beyond wanting to fight the fight.

"Thad?" Pierce asked, repeating his previous question.

I finally nodded. "You would be a big help," I said.

"That's all I need to hear," Ben said, snatching one of the backpacks from my father. "So count me in."

Pierce pumped his fist in the air and hooted. The only thing he loved more than kicking ass was fucking it. "It's time to get this show on the road."

His attitude riled my father. He puffed out his chest and glared at his eldest son. "You're not going to a beach party, Pierce," he said. "You're being sent to—" He stopped and swallowed hard. He clearly couldn't give voice to his fears.

I crossed to him and rubbed his shoulders. Fear fueled the anger that played across his face. Like most of our kind, he didn't know how to process such a debilitating emotion, so he brandished the one that came more easily—fury. "We'll be back, Dad."

He locked eyes with me while a sneer curled his lip. "You don't know that," he said, his stern voice trembling.

"And you don't know that we won't."

Mason and Pierce suddenly appeared on either side of him. He switched his gaze back and forth among the three of us, as if he were memorizing every curve and blemish in case what he feared most came true.

"We'll be fine," Mason said. "That's a promise."

My father held Mason's cheek in his big hand and squeezed it. "What have I told you about promises?"

"Don't make them if you intend to break them," Pierce answered. "And we won't break this one, Dad. We might blow smoke up everyone else's asses, but not each other's." He hauled his big arm around my neck and my dad's. Mason copied the move, drawing both my father and me closer to him as well.

Before long, the four of us were embracing, giving each other the assurance the family needed that we would see each other again.

"I'm gonna hold the three of you to that," he said.

"Deal," I replied.

He looked at Drake, Aiden, and Ben. "You better look after my boys."

"I will, Mr. Blackmoor," Drake replied.

"I'd gladly lay down my life for theirs," Aiden said.

When Ben replied, he looked at me and not my father. "I've got it all covered."

CHAPTER 7

EVERYONE GATHERED around me in the library while I drew a door on the wall. This was how we were getting into Otherworld.

"With a piece of chalk?" Pierce asked. "Is that really going to work?"

I nodded. "It's a symbol to focus the spell, to call forth the weakened barriers between our worlds."

"And how do we get back?" Drake asked.

I glanced over at Aiden, who had traded in the sweats for a pair of my black jeans. He still refused to wear a shirt, and I wasn't about to complain. "I can get us back easy and quick if need be with my portal."

"Or we can just use this spell again," Ben said. He most likely didn't want to rely on Aiden to get us home.

Aiden understood the message. He arched one dark eyebrow at Ben before settling his gaze on me. When our eyes met, his lips hitched to the left. Ben might have quickly riled him up, but I just as easily calmed his hair-trigger temper. My stomach flip-flopped from the implications.

"Okay," I said, tossing the chalk onto the desk. "It's ready."

Mason walked over to the wall and knocked on it. "Nothing's happening."

"Probably because I haven't said the spell yet," I answered with a blank stare.

He flipped me off and returned to Drake's side.

"Is everyone ready?" I asked. Everyone except Pierce nodded. He gave me a thumb's up and a wicked grin. He was evidently ready to crack skulls and get some answers.

Drake's eagerness to go with us had turned into anxiety. He clutched Mason's hand while staring intently at the wall that would take us to fairyland. Mason placed his arm around Drake's waist in a lovingly supportive gesture. The changes I'd noticed in him since he'd fallen in love with Drake made me smile.

"Then let's get started," I said, taking two steps toward the wall. I placed my hands against the cool surface and closed my eyes, connecting to the magical energy that swarmed all around us. "*Aperi, porta ad mundum alternum,*" I began, sending forth my wishes for the portal to open into the land of the fae.

When I opened my eyes, I no longer saw the world as a human but as a warlock. Swirling bands of color twisted and knotted around me and converged upon the spot I touched. "*Furto noctis advenimus,*" I said, flexing my fingers against the wall. It was important for us to arrive under cover of night, and in response to my incantation, the swirling colors merged into one black thread that widened until it filled the chalk doorway with a swoosh of air. The wall disappeared, and a long dark tunnel stretched before us.

But there was one final phrase that needed to be spoken. We had to also arrive unseen. "*Et invisibilim.*"

Shadows within the portal sprung outward and surrounded the six of us before tugging us forward.

I glanced back over my shoulder at my father, who stood on the other side of the room. He bit his bottom lip, and after I offered him a thin smile and a nod that we'd return, the strings of energy pulled taut and tugged us through.

Once we pierced the barrier, our tethers sprang forward like a bungee cord and rocketed us through the dark tunnel.

Shimmering lights filled my vision as we zoomed through the void that connected my world to Aiden's. Despite the breakneck speed with which we traveled, I didn't register the velocity. My spell protected us from whirling forces. It gave us time to appreciate the surrounding vacuum, which reminded me of outer space. But this was inner space and it was beautiful and peaceful. As an added bonus, we had oxygen to breathe.

Pierce, who'd never been a fan of roller coasters, had turned an interesting shade of chartreuse and held on to the black tether that pulled us forward and toward our destination. Mason hooted and yelled like a dumb ass, while Drake spread his arms as if he were Superman.

On my right, Aiden reached out, trying to catch the glimmers of light that sped by. A gleeful smile spread across his cheeks.

Ben was an entirely different story. He looked around as if he were searching for something.

"What's wrong?" I asked.

He didn't respond. I wasn't sure if the low hum that surrounded us cancelled out my words or if he was ignoring me. I was about to repeat my question when his eyes grew wide, and he pointed behind me.

When I turned, my stomach sank to my feet.

Four vampyren flew straight for us, their talons extended. "We've been waiting for you," hissed the one in front. Its long tongue lolled between razor sharp teeth as its friends smacked their lips in anticipation of the meal they planned to drink from our torn open throats.

How was this possible? Where had they come from?

A bolt of electricity streaked through the darkness, but the vampyren scattered and easily dodged the attack. "Fuck!" Pierce yelled. The speed at which we were being pulled through the barrier upset his aim. He punched the bands of energy that held us, trying to break their hold.

"We have to get free," Ben called, pulling on the magical energy rope that bound him. "You have to release us."

Was he out of his mind? "*Propellit*," I uttered with a gesture at the vampyren. My spell worked and sent them tumbling backward. "If I do that, we might be lost between the worlds forever."

"If you don't," Mason said. "We might not make it to Otherworld alive. We're sitting ducks here."

"And what are you going to do?" I asked. "Fly? There's no place to stand."

The vampyren screeched as they righted themselves and dove toward us once again.

Aiden sent a volley of fireballs hurtling toward the monsters. It caused them to scatter and slowed their progress, but it wouldn't last. Before long, they'd be on us.

"You must do it," Aiden said. "I can use my fae magic to keep us afloat." His green eyes pleaded with me to trust him.

And I did. With one word in Latin, the black cords released us and disappeared, and for a few moments, we hung suspended in the air before the strange gravity that existed in the void exerted its influence. Ben, Mason, and Pierce fell down while Drake and I fell up.

In an explosion of light and heat, fiery wings sprouted from Aiden's back, and embers of flame burned in his eyes. He reached out with his magic and grasped us in his power. He screamed in agony as he struggled to bring us together. A ring of fire erupted around us, erecting a fiery dome for protection and a floor of solid red light that provided the stabilization we needed to fight.

How powerful was Aiden? None of us could have done that.

Sweat poured down Aiden's brow. "I can't hold this forever," he managed between gritted teeth. "I'd light a fire under your asses if I wasn't so busy."

"Attack!" I shouted to the others.

The words had no sooner left my mouth than blasts of electricity, darkness, sand, and ice were fired at the vampyren. They cackled and dodged the attack without breaking a sweat.

Their moves were so choreographed, it was like they knew what we were going to do. But how?

"Such pitiful creatures," one of the vampyren said. This one was a female with long black-and-gray hair that slithered as if it were snakes. "Too blind to see the truth."

What truth?

They broke their dive, banking left and wide before splitting in four different directions. With a hiss as a rallying cry, they plunged toward us like heat-seeking missiles.

"*Desinite!*" Mason yelled, obviously hoping his spell might slow them down. Instead of barreling toward us, they dropped like stones for a few seconds before regaining their speed and momentum.

At the rate they recovered, our incantations would no longer be useful. Vampyren built up immunity by prolonging exposure to magic. It was one of their abilities that made them so deadly.

That was when I remembered the backpacks my father had packed for us. Drake, Mason, and Pierce each had one, and inside them were the stakes we could use to end this. My gaze caught Ben's, who nodded. He'd guessed my plan.

But before I could react, the world around me spun.

The vampyren crashed through Aiden's magical fire barrier, shattering the invisible dome that protected us. Within moments, they were on my brothers and Drake. They ripped the backpacks from their shoulders and tossed the bags into the sprawling void.

They'd known we had stakes, but how?

"What are you going to do now, nephew?" one of the female vampyren asked Drake.

She clutched him and brought him to her snapping jaws.

"Who are you?" he asked in terror as her tongue slid over his face.

"You don't recognize your Aunt Millie?" she asked before letting out a cackle that shook the air around us.

Drake cried in protest before Pierce punched her in the face. The vampyre claiming to be Drake's Aunt Millie dropped Drake and lunged at my older brother.

Pierce punched her in the gut, but it did no good. She smacked Pierce in the face and landed on top of him, clawing at his flesh with her talons. The others quickly subdued Mason and Drake, yet they completely ignored me.

Ben, who stood a few feet away, raised his arms to unleash a sandstorm, but the other female vampyren snapped around, her tongue shooting out of her mouth. It wrapped around Ben's neck, strangling him. He choked and gasped for air as she reeled him in.

"Thad!" Aiden shouted. He kneeled on the cracked remains of the magic that still supported us. It took all his remaining strength to speak and maintain our foundation. "Do something."

I couldn't. My muscles had grown rigid and wouldn't obey. It was like I had lost control of my body. All I could do was watch as the vampyre's tongue squeezed tightly around Ben. His eyes caught mine, desperately pleading for me to do something. *Anything.* But I stood there as she separated Ben's head from his shoulders. In a squeal of delight, she sprang upon his corpse and drank his blood.

"No," I muttered.

Drake's eyes went wide when he witnessed Ben die. He yelled something, but I couldn't make out what he said. Anger had clouded my vision. All I could see and hear was red. It was as if the color had come to life. It throbbed and pulsed around me, setting my blood on fire. This had happened to me once before, when I'd first tapped into my powers. The day I'd almost killed Mason.

The final remnants of my restraint snapped free and let loose what I'd been attempting to suppress.

"You fucking bitch!" I screamed. A torrent of emotion flew out of me, and a column of ice suddenly appeared. It slammed into the vampyre that had killed Ben and sent her sprawling off Aiden's magical floor.

The others sprang to their feet, blood dripping from their teeth. Had they killed my brothers and Drake? Their bodies hid my loved ones from me, so I couldn't tell. The lack of knowledge was like throwing gasoline onto my blaze of fury.

But before I could react, Aiden wrapped his arm around my waist, and he leaped with me into the darkness.

"No!" I yelled, reaching back up to the floating base where my family remained.

We fell a few feet before a flaming pinwheel formed underneath us. Its blazing wheels spun rapidly and opened a portal just wide enough for the two of us to pass through before reversing its rotation and closing behind us.

WE LANDED with a thud amid a sea of fuchsia and lavender.

I quickly rose to my feet, searching the golden sky above for the vampyren I was sure had followed us through Aiden's portal. Instead of snarling teeth and elongated, prehensile tongues, white, billowy clouds danced across the firmament.

I surveyed our surroundings, preparing for banshee, shadow weaver, or whatever hellish nightmare might be lying in wait, but only a field of pink flowers and purplish blooms stretched all around us. We'd landed in the middle of a clearing and along its edges stood majestic trees, their broad, cone-shaped canopies soaring into the heavens.

There was no one for me to fight, and the rage in my blood demanded payment.

"Thad."

I spun around to the voice behind me. "*Propellit*," I uttered with a wave of my hand. Aiden flew backward six feet. He landed hard on his back with a loud grunt. The current of anger ebbed once I realized what I had done.

I dashed over to his side and kneeled next to him as he lay among the colorful blooms. "Are you okay?"

He nodded but didn't respond. He'd had the air knocked out of his lungs and needed a moment. He closed his eyes for a few seconds and took several deep breaths. When he had recovered, he stared up at me, his bottle-green eyes slits of concern. "What happened?"

I couldn't answer because I had no idea. What the hell *was* wrong with me? It wasn't like me to shoot first and ask questions later, but it also wasn't like me to stand around and watch someone die. I had done nothing to save Ben, though his eyes had begged me for help. I'd just stood there, statue-still, until that damned vampyre beheaded him with her tongue.

"Thad," he whispered. He sat up and rubbed my cheeks. "You're crying."

I was? I wiped the tears I hadn't even realized I wept from my cheeks and sat back on the cool grass. More emotions than I knew what to do with churned within me like a whirlpool. I couldn't think. I couldn't speak. If I tried to stand, I'd likely fall on my ass.

Was this the result of finally letting myself feel? Was I now at the mercy of my emotions?

"Thad?"

"I didn't do anything," I finally mumbled. "I stood there while Ben was killed. And my brothers?" I swallowed hard. "I did nothing to save them."

The ferocity I'd unleashed earlier bubbled up from my soul. It slithered around inside me, looking for a place to gain purchase before springing out of me once again.

Aiden scooted closer to me in the grass and wrapped his arms around me. The coiled rattlesnake within me shook its tail in warning. It wanted out. It needed release. Nothing was going to stop it.

But Aiden wasn't nothing.

He nuzzled my neck and delivered gentle kisses that eased the anger and pain, but they couldn't erase my guilt. Nothing would be able to do that.

"First of all, we don't know what happened to your family," he said. "The vampyren might have taken them hostage."

I snorted. "Yeah, because that's what those bloodsuckers do. Take hostages." The idea was ridiculous, and my anger coiled tightly inside my gut.

"Don't give up hope," he said. He squinted his eyes and looked deep into my soul. If I'd been a book, he would have opened me up and started reading. "I can sense the fury in you. It's overwhelming."

"And why wouldn't it be?" I asked. "I wish I could be all fairy optimistic like you, but I can't. I'm a realist, and your hostage idea is laughable at best."

Aiden's gaze sharpened, and his lips cut into a thin line. I was being an ass. I knew it, but all my buttons seemed to have been pressed at once. I was too angry to be reasonable. He pulled away from me and stood. "Your tone and your attitude need to change," he said in a low warning.

"Why? Because you say so?" I asked as I rose to stand toe-to-toe with him. It was like I'd boarded a crazy train and couldn't hop off. My emotions barreled full steam ahead. "Chances are Pierce, Mason, and Drake are dead. Just like Ben."

The mention of Ben's name sent my wrath into overdrive. My chest heaved, and I clenched my hands at my side. If a vampyre showed up now, it would be dead in ten seconds flat.

"You need to calm down," Aiden said. He grasped my shoulders and shook me.

A snarl curled my upper lip, and I growled. If Aiden wanted a fight, I was ready.

But instead of throwing a fist, he pulled me into his arms and crushed his lips to mine. His tongue dove inside my mouth, and the kick of his cinnamon kisses acted like a dam against the rising tide of anger. His hands on my shoulders, clutching my back and sliding down to my ass, massaged the tension from my muscles.

"Think of me," he whispered. The soothing aroma of honeysuckle and cedar filled the air between us, quickly displacing the rage that still swelled within. "Let me be your anchor. Don't get swept away."

Even though I had no fucking clue what he was talking about, I latched on to him. I clutched his waist, sliding my fingers up his smooth sides. I wrapped my arms around him, pressing his hard body against mine. I inhaled the sweetness that followed him wherever he went. His scent filled my lungs, exorcizing the demon that still wailed inside, refusing to be defeated.

When I returned Aiden's kisses, when my lips molded to his and I slipped my tongue into the warmth of his mouth, the screaming became a dull roar.

"Stay with me, Thad," he pleaded.

"Where else would I go?" I asked.

Aiden smiled, placed his forehead against my cheek, and sighed. After that, the rage that had gained brief control turned into a whisper before falling completely silent.

"That was close."

I didn't understand. "What was?"

He stepped back and eyed me apprehensively. "Really?"

"What?"

"Look around," he said.

I shifted my gaze from his gorgeous green eyes to the ground and gasped. We stood at the center of a twelve-foot ice patch. "What the hell?"

Aiden hooked my chin with his thumb and brought my gaze back to him. "You really didn't know you did that?"

I shook my head. It was news to me. I didn't even remember summoning my powers. How the hell was this even possible?

"You were caught up in a rage I've never experienced before," he said. He held on to me tightly as if he was terrified if he let me go, the angry waters might return in a flash flood and reclaim me. "It came on so suddenly, I didn't know what else to do but hold you and get you to focus on me."

I exhaled. This wasn't the first time something like this had happened to me, and it was why I'd done my best to control my emotions. "This is what I was afraid of," I admitted.

"Is that what you were telling me about at your house?" he asked. "About why emotions are dangerous for you?"

I nodded.

"Tell me what happened," he said.

I'd long since blocked that afternoon out. It had been so terrifying and traumatic I'd promised myself I would never experience such a loss of control again. I'd failed. "My brothers and I were never really close, especially as children. Pierce was Dad's favorite. The golden boy who'd tapped into his active power before he even became a teenager."

"That's pretty early," Aiden added. "I've heard most of your kind inherit their powers around sixteen."

"But not Pierce," I said with a shake of my head. "When he let loose his first electrical burst, I pretty much disappeared in my father's eyes. It became all about teaching Pierce the ways of a warlock. My father spent hours with him practicing magic and reading the Grimoire to him. Whenever I asked to join in, he told me I was too young. That I wasn't ready."

"Well, you weren't, right?"

"No, I wasn't. But it was his attention I wanted. I never really got that again."

Aiden ran his fingertips across my lips, urging me with his eyes to continue.

"Then Mason came. I got even less attention after he was born, and I was pissed. I was born first. I deserved some recognition for existing before him, but no. My dad either practiced magic with Pierce or took care of Mason. The only one who gave me the time of day was my mother." I rested my forehead against Aiden's and closed my eyes. Memories of our play dates and mother-son outings filled my mind. It had been the only time I'd ever felt special.

"I can sense how much you love her," he said. "And how much your heart breaks in her absence."

I nodded, a stray tear slipping down my cheek. Aiden brushed it away with his thumb before I continued.

"She would teach me spells in secret, and she was the first one to talk to me about magic. I remember watching her levitate or using her mist powers. The things she could do with vapor astounded me. Although my parents never discussed it, I think my mother was far more powerful than my father."

"Did she help you tap into your power?"

"She tried," I said. "Especially when I turned sixteen. That whole year we worked together to turn my powers on, but it never worked. And then one summer afternoon, Pierce was teasing me about it. Calling me a loser and a momma's boy. Saying I'd never be as good or as powerful as him. The bastard."

"What did you do?"

"What I always did," I answered with a shrug. "I ignored him. If you give Pierce attention, he never drops it. It's best to pretend he doesn't exist because he tends to go away. But on that day, Mason started in on me. He copied everything Pierce did because Pierce was his favorite. And it pissed me off. I was used to being teased by Pierce. He was my older brother, and that's what they do. But when my younger brother started taunting me, I lost it. I got so angry, I shook and started screaming, and the next thing I remember, Mason was encased in solid ice, and it grew thicker by the moment. Pierce yelled at me, trying to get me to stop, but I didn't even hear him."

Aiden kissed my trembling lips. Reliving that day brought back all the guilt I'd held on to since that moment.

"It was Mother who stopped me," I said after regaining my composure. "She appeared in front of me, her eyes calm and filled with love. She kissed my forehead and called me her Thaddy. That was her nickname for me, and when she held me and stroked my hair, I stopped encasing Mason in ice while my father saved my little brother."

I nuzzled my head into the crook of Aiden's neck, sobbing. I hadn't spoken about that day since it happened. It had been one of the worst days of my life, and it was because of what I'd almost done that I had sworn to never feel anything again.

"You need to stop beating yourself up about it," he said as he ran his long fingers through my hair. "It happened long before you knew how to control your powers. You didn't do it on purpose."

"But I just did the same thing to you," I said. I pulled myself out of his embrace and took a step back. "I could have killed you, and there would have been no one here to stop me."

He spanned the distance between us. He grabbed my hands and wrapped them around his waist before settling the weight of his body against mine. "No one had to stop you," he said. "You stopped yourself."

"Only with your help," I said, staring back into green eyes that smiled back at me.

"There's nothing wrong with getting a little bit of help every now and then," he said. His gaze locked on mine, and his face turned serious. "But this *isn't* your fault."

I rolled my eyes. "Who else is there to blame? The vampyren?"

He shrugged. "Maybe."

I didn't like assigning blame that was mine to others. "I'm not some puppet dancing to the strings of some puppeteer. I'm a big enough warlock to accept when I've screwed up, and I screwed up."

Aiden crossed his arms and sighed. I'd come to know him just enough to realize this was his pissy stance. "Will you shut up and listen to me?"

I zipped my mouth.

"I'm a fire fae, remember? Emotions are what I do. We help stir passion in humans, and anger is one of our stocks in trade."

I arched my eyebrows. It was my way of asking "And?" without speaking.

"What I sensed from you wasn't natural," he said. "It was magical."

"A spell?"

"Not quite," he replied with a shake of his head. "More powerful."

My breath caught in my throat. "Like blood magic?" I asked.

Aiden shuffled back a step. He'd obviously not considered that possibility, but now that he had, it was clear to both of us that was potentially what we were dealing with.

Trying to wrap my mind around this latest revelation was impossible. From what I knew about these types of spells, my blood would be needed during the casting. When had the shadow weaver gotten my blood?

"How did this happen?" Aiden asked.

"I'm not sure," I replied. Had he stolen some of it during my battle with the vampyre shortly after Mabon? That damned thing had beaten the hell out of and almost killed me. It would have succeeded if Mason hadn't intervened. Perhaps that was when the shadow weaver had taken it, and he'd been plotting to use it against me ever since. That would explain why the pumpkin-headed shade had said *you will be mine* after it killed the banshees in the library. "But he obviously has plans for me."

Aiden's eyes narrowed. "They will fail," he said with the certainty he was used to inspiring as a prince in this realm. I appreciated his protective nature, but the situation required logic, not emotion, if we were going to make it out of this alive.

"I can't guarantee that," I said. "And neither can you."

My answer didn't sit well. Aiden wrapped his arms around me and rested his head against mine. "We will fight it. Together."

I liked the sound of that. It meant there was more potential for the two of us than Aiden had led me to believe. "And I'll fight it like hell," I said. I rubbed my hands up and down his bare back before I settled my grip on his shoulders. I moved us out of the embrace far enough for our eyes to meet. "But we have to prepare for the worst. I'm obviously a liability. That shadow weaver could cast another spell and attempt to force me to do something I don't want to do. Like hurt you."

"He can try," he replied. Complete trust was in his emerald eyes. "But I know you would never hurt me."

Aiden was right. Under normal circumstances, I wouldn't, but these were as far beyond normal circumstances as we could get. I cupped his fair cheeks. It was important he accept the truth. "But we have to be ready if the moment ever comes when I try. You have to do everything and anything to stop me. Can you promise me you will?"

His nostrils flared. "I will not," he replied before breaking contact. He crossed his arms and gave me his back. The fire fae who'd been swayed by his passions gave way to the royal prince who was not accustomed to acting against his will.

"You have to," I said, sidling over to where he stood. I embraced him from behind, molding his back to my chest, and I marveled at how perfectly we fit together. "I'm not important in the grand scheme of things. We both know that."

"Not true," he said, his voice hard and distant. "You've become important. To me."

I kissed his ear and then his neck. The regal indifference he attempted to hide behind faltered against my touch. "And you're important to me too. That's why you have to be ready. And you have to remember there are more things to consider than me. There's my home to think about and yours. Don't forget your family and mine. Not to mention the Gate. If worse comes to worst, you need to do what's necessary to make sure all that is safe."

"Do you realize what you're asking me to do?" he asked. His words were as sharp as an athame.

I inhaled the woody scent of his hair and nodded. "I do."

He turned in my arms, his eyes wide with fear and wet with anticipated grief. "I don't know if I can."

I grinned down at him and brushed my lips against his. "I know you can," I said. "You're Prince Aiden of the Royal Fae Court. You've taken on banshees, vampyren, and even the Grumpy Wizards of Havenbridge. I have faith you will do what needs to be done to protect Otherworld."

He went slack in resignation. He slumped into my embrace and let loose a long exhalation. "I will," he finally said. He stood up straight. His regal bearing had returned, but the distant gaze and tone had faded. "*If* I have to. We just have to make sure I don't have to."

I could agree to those terms. "Seems reasonable enough."

"Good," he said. "Now there's something you must do for me."

"What's that?"

He grabbed my hand and led me across the clearing and farther into Otherworld.

DESPITE MY repeated questions on what he wanted me to do, Aiden refused to answer.

He led me into the forest, which he called the Arbor, and through a maze of massive trunks, each of which was about twenty inches in diameter. The thick green canopy above let through only minimal light from a sun that was already retreating toward the horizon.

We found a path made by whatever woodland creatures dwelled in the forest and followed the snaking trail through the trees.

"Are you going to answer me?"

Aiden glanced over his shoulder and grinned. The mischievous glint in his eyes told me he was clearly enjoying this. "Soon," he responded as a warm breeze whipped around us. It sent his dark hair fluttering, and if it was possible, a full head of hair in disarray made him even more stunning.

Not that he needed any help with that.

Everything about him was beautiful.

The pronounced dimples on his cheeks when he smiled, the flexing of his back muscles as he swung his arms, the sensual curve of his lower back as he navigated the trail, and the contracting of his butt muscles as he walked.

He was absolutely stunning.

The path ended at a gathering of rocks. He scrambled to the top and gazed down at me. "What are you waiting for?"

"An answer," I mumbled before scaling up to where he waited.

Past the rocks was a dense thicket of brush, and beyond that a brook babbled. Its topaz water flowed languidly through the woods, in no great hurry to get to its final destination. A huge, mossy trunk had fallen across the brook, providing a natural bridge across the water. On the other side, the dense brush gave way to flat, green grass and more trees that extended into another dense section of the forest.

On the horizon stood a cliff, its sheer face looking directly at us. Patches of green grass grew along its rocky sides, but on its top was what appeared to be a castle composed of red brick.

That had to be Aiden's kingdom, what he'd referred to as the Hearth.

"It's beautiful," I said.

He nodded at the palace, which sported a tall brick tower with smaller structures of similar material surrounding it. "It is," he said with a nod. "But we're not going there just yet."

I tore my gaze from the natural splendor around me to Aiden. "Then where?"

Fiery wings sprouted from his back in a heated whoosh. He grabbed my hand, and seconds later we were floating over the water and landing on the other side.

"Give a guy a warning next time," I said. The unexpected liftoff had made me queasy. "I think we left my stomach on the other side."

Aiden's wings disappeared in a puff of smoke, and he rubbed his strong hand across my stomach. "I'll make it better."

I was intrigued. "And how are you going to do that?"

A grin slid across his lips as he massaged his way from my stomach to my waist. He tugged the fabric of my shirt up and over my head before pressing his body against me. He wrapped his arms around me, gripping my muscles as he followed a steady path to the small of my back, where they rested.

"What are you doing?" I asked.

He didn't answer. He rubbed his face against my chest, licking a trail across my pecs and up to my neck. I gasped when he lightly nipped at my flesh. I dug my fingers into his waist and held him tightly, pressing my fattening cock against the bulge in his jeans.

"Aiden, I—"

"Shhh," he whispered, trailing his fingertips along my jawline before scratching his way through the reddish stubble. He drew slow, lazy circles around my lips, which trembled in response.

Aiden's touch communicated something greater than words could hope to convey. The gentle brushes of his fingers on my skin revealed I *had* become special, and the lingering of his lips upon mine offered a promise far sweeter than the honeysuckle that filled the distance between us.

I inhaled deeply, taking the scent and the unspoken emotions into my soul, where they worked to untangle the darkness that crouched within me.

How we'd gotten here was a mystery to me. We hadn't gone out on a date or even spent much time together that hadn't been dominated by constant threats, yet here we were, our arms around each other, and our hearts beating in synch to the rhythm our bodies created.

"We've got a lot going on right now, and it might not be the right time considering everything, but we need this and I want you to remember this moment," Aiden said as he pressed his lips to mine. His tongue came alive in my mouth while he unfastened my jeans. "If you feel yourself losing control again, remember my touch. Nothing is more powerful. Not blood magic. Not some shadow weaver. Just you and me."

And he was right. The moment he undid the zipper and pushed my jeans past my hips, he created a weakness in my knees. My seven-inch prick stood out from my body, throbbing in want. He took my hard cock in his hands, and my knees practically buckled. He gripped the shaft and began a leisurely tug that made me moan. "Can you remember that for me?"

I nodded. I couldn't form intelligible words. I could only mumble and groan as he jacked my dick to full mast.

Aiden continued the hand job while I fumbled with the button and zipper on his jeans. There was no way I was going to be denied the pleasure of holding his hardness in my palm.

I shoved my hand underneath the denim, grabbing hold of the prize I'd first seen in the woods. The hot, hard flesh throbbed in my grip as I pulled the sensitive skin up and down with my right hand while my left sent his jeans fluttering to his ankles. "I've never wanted anyone like this before," I finally managed. "Whenever I'm around you, it's like some wonderful spell has been cast on me. It's magic I've never experienced before."

"I know," he said. He gazed into my eyes, the fires of his passion raging within. "We have blood magic of our own."

I tangled my fingers through his dark hair before kissing a trail from his lips to his neck. I lapped at the sweat-slick skin and then his nipples. I flicked my tongue around the taut flesh and gently sucked on each one until they pebbled.

Aiden cooed in appreciation. He fluttered his fingers along my neck and shoulders as I followed the lines of his abdominal muscles with my tongue, licking up the perspiration that had collected in the ridges before kneeling in front of him.

I grabbed his hard cock at the base, slowly jacking it until a tiny pearl collected at the slit. I lapped the sweet nectar before slipping the head of his thick cock in my mouth.

"Damn, Thad," Aiden moaned. He pumped his hips, forcing his prick past my lips and into my throat. "You feel so good."

I could only mumble in reply. The saltiness of his cock, combined with the musk from his nest of dark pubic hair, intoxicated me. I greedily slurped up and down his dick, swirling my tongue around the shaft before swallowing the entire length.

Aiden continued to pummel my face, working his hardness in and out of my mouth as he moaned and gave himself over to the pleasure I gave him. "It's too good," he said. "I'm not going to last much longer."

I pulled off his prick and grinned up at him. Sweat poured down his forehead and dripped onto his heaving chest as he lovingly caressed my cheek and chin.

"Can you do something for me? Something that will make me remember right now for the rest of my life?"

He nodded. "Of course."

"I want you to make love to me," I said. I'd never uttered those words to another man in my life. I was the top. I was always in control. I didn't want that with Aiden. No, I didn't need that with Aiden. For us, there were no limits, no boundaries, no need for reins.

I gave myself freely to him, and I wanted him to take it. I wanted to be his.

Aiden bent down and took me by my neck before delivering his yes with a long, electric kiss. I let go of every reservation, every shred of control, and it left me breathless. I tingled with the anticipation of Aiden's body on top of me, within me, and the world around me spun by in a dizzying euphoria.

Aiden gently lowered me onto the grass. The coolness of the soil pressed against my flushed flesh caused shivers to run up and down my body. Aiden rested on top of me, grinding his erection against mine. The weight of his throbbing prick nestled against my hardness, and Aiden's pumping hips created a flash fire across my skin.

I whimpered in approval, moving my hands wildly across his body as my lips once again found their mate. I clutched at his muscled shoulders, his hard ass, trying to force as much of Aiden against me as I could. It wasn't enough. I needed more, and Aiden evidently read the mad desire in my eyes.

He crawled down my body, kissing and licking a fiery path down my chest and through the reddish nest that surrounded my weeping cock. He grabbed my prick, pumping it slowly before lapping up the shaft. I grabbed a handful of dirt when his hot mouth slid down to the root of my dick, lodging it down his throat.

"Fuck," I whispered.

Aiden's throat muscles and tongue massaged my cock in alternating pulses of pleasure. I grabbed the back of his head and forced myself farther down inside him.

"Feel good?" he asked, rising off my prick just long enough to grin up at me.

"Fuck yes," I replied. A red haze settled over my vision, my mind completely lost to the passion that coursed through my blood.

Aiden continued bobbing up and down my cock, this time running his fingertips through the saliva that coated my shaft. His moistened fingers found their way to my crevice, and I parted my legs without a second thought. He rubbed the moisture across my opening while he used his mouth to work me toward a mind-blowing orgasm.

When he slipped his finger inside me, I bit my lip and clawed the earth underneath me. His digit wiggled, opening me up for the moment when my body became Aiden's.

A second finger and then a third penetrated me, and I practically jumped out of my skin. Aiden pushed farther inside me at the same time he increased suction on my cock. I bucked my hips, forcing more of my dick in Aiden and his fingers in my ass.

When he pulled off my cock and out of my ass, I'd never felt emptier in my life. "What's wrong? Why did you stop?" I asked. The tremor in my voice was unmistakable.

"I'm not stopping," he said, positioning himself between my legs. "You're ready."

I nodded. "Yes," I said, practically panting. "I am."

He grabbed his cock and pointed it at my center.

If this had been anyone but Aiden, I'd be reminding him to put on a condom, but fae were creatures of pure magic, immune to the diseases of man. "I've never been more certain about anything in my life."

I spread my legs wider, giving him the access he needed. Aiden spit into the palm of his hand, coating his throbbing cock with more lubrication before he pressed the tip of his engorged head against my opening. With one thrust, he parted the first ring of muscle, and perspiration immediately erupted across my body.

He massaged my chest and legs, urging me to relax. A few seconds later, he pushed inside. I opened up and drew him in until his groin rested against my ass. The red haze that had enveloped my world lifted, and I saw Aiden with crystal clarity.

His green eyes were wide with want, his lips parted in silent ecstasy as I squeezed his girth within me. I brought his face closer, needing to feel his lips on mine, but before we kissed, I muttered one final request. "Harder."

Our kiss intensified our lovemaking. Our tongues dove in and out of each other's mouths as I slid my hand down to Aiden's thrusting ass. I grabbed hold of him, forcing him in and out of me harder and faster.

Aiden clutched my shoulders, using the leverage to increase the strength of his thrusts. He nibbled on my lip before biting a trail to my neck, where he nipped and licked. I dragged my fingernails across his back, digging into hard muscle and silky flesh.

"Shit," Aiden mumbled. He took my earlobe in his mouth and sucked, thrusting wildly against me. He was no doubt reaching the point of no return, and I wanted to join him.

I shoved my hand between our sweat-soaked bodies, palming my cock. I jacked myself to the same frenzied rhythm with which Aiden pounded my ass. My moans became louder and more fitful as I barreled toward the same precipice where Aiden floated.

"F-f-fuck," I groaned as my orgasm released, launching five volleys of spunk across both our stomachs.

Aiden pushed forward in response to my contracting muscles milking his cock. He let out a growl as his dick throbbed within me, filling me not only with his semen but with something far more potent.

An unspoken promise and the power it ignited within me.

WE LAY naked in the grass, my head on Aiden's chest and his arms wrapped around me. Our rapid breathing finally returned to normal. Everything was different. Having Aiden inside me, surrendering myself to him, had changed me profoundly.

I'd been terrified of emotion, of letting go, for fear I might unleash the monster that almost killed my brother. What happened instead proved far more surprising. Released from the iron fist of control, I hadn't tumbled into a sea of churning emotion. I wasn't swept away, lost to the dark depths.

By letting go, I'd found firm ground beneath my feet instead of the shifting sands of uncertainty. I'd always believed my family to be idiotic for reveling in their emotions, for giving in to them so wholeheartedly. For me it had only led to disaster.

Now I saw the truth.

Emotion didn't make us weaker. It amped up our powers. Perhaps that was why Mason had finally tapped into darkness. Because he'd fallen in love with Drake.

Was that what had happened to me?

I gazed up at Aiden. His eyes were closed, but he wasn't asleep. A thin smile stretched across his lips. He was still basking in the afterglow.

I mentally traced every line on his face, the curve of his strong jaw, the dip of the dimple on his chin, the swell of his cheeks, and my heart fluttered inside my chest. It was like hundreds of butterflies flitted around within me. It tickled and made me smile.

What I felt for Aiden wasn't love. At least not yet. The potential was there. It swelled within me like the ocean responding to the pull of the moon, but only time and the tide would fill our hearts with love's waters.

"You're staring again," Aiden said, gazing at me through one partially opened eyelid.

"Tough," I replied. I rolled on top of him and leered down at him. "Get used to it."

He grinned broadly. "Too late," he admitted, resting his hands on my ass. "I already am."

"Good," I replied, brushing my lips against his.

He strummed his fingertips up my back and down toward my ass in light, feathery strokes. "Being with you was amazing. It's never been like that for me before."

He didn't have to tell me. The pleasure had been so intense, I'd almost crawled out of my skin. "For me either. You touched places inside me I didn't know existed."

"That's because I've got a pretty big cock," he said with an eyebrow wiggle. "It's a curse the Teine fae must live with."

I rolled my eyes. "Although your dick is pretty amazing, I don't think that was it."

"Are you doubting the power of my family's vigor?" he asked with a fake scowl.

"How do you know it wasn't the supremacy of the Blackmoor ass?" I asked in return.

He grinned. "How about it was both?"

"Now *that* makes sense," I said with a smile.

Neither of us wanted to lose the bubble we'd created around us, keeping the crazy that awaited us at bay. Our silly banter allowed for the illusion of normalcy to linger instead of drift away like smoke on the wind.

"It's time to go, isn't it?" he asked, his eyes filled with regret.

"Not yet," I answered. "Like you said earlier, we need this. I think we should stay here tonight. Sleep in each other's arms. Tomorrow, we'll face what comes together."

The width of his smile told me he wholeheartedly agreed. He squeezed me tight and let out a long, contented sigh.

"I can't thank you enough for what you did for me."

He pulled out of the embrace and turned over. I fell off him and onto the warm grass. "I didn't do it for you," he said. The playfulness disappeared, and a stern severity settled in his gaze. "I did it for us."

I liked the way that sounded. Us. I could certainly get used to an "us."

"Do you think it worked?" he asked.

"I believe it did." Together, Aiden and I created magic that only our bodies could cast. It swirled within me, empowering me and giving me the defenses I needed to stave off whatever blood magic the shadow weaver intended to use against us. "But I think it did more than we expected," I said after rising. I stood naked, glancing around. The colors were brighter than I remembered, and a hum of energy I hadn't heard before whispered in my ears, as if it were calling to me and letting me know it was here.

"What do you mean?" he asked.

I closed my eyes and opened up my soul to the powerful thrum. It poured into me, through me, before settling down within. "Your touch gave me more than a shield. It gave me a battering ram."

"Really?" Aiden asked. He rose and took my hands in his. "Do you feel your powers growing?"

"I do," I answered. "It reminds me of that afternoon as a teenager, when I froze Mason. All these things were going on inside me I couldn't explain. All I knew was I had to let them out, and I did. And it terrified me. It made me afraid of what I could do. That's kind of what I'm feeling now. Like the power I've held inside me not only doubled but quadrupled. But there's also something else." I couldn't quite put my finger on it, so I didn't even try.

"Is it scaring you?"

"No," I answered without hesitation. "It's exhilarating. It makes me feel alive, and whatever it is, it's just dying to be released."

Aiden led me back to the spot where we'd made love, under a huge tree that was most likely at least a century old. He lay down and pulled me into his arms. When we were settled in and firmly in each other's grip, he said, "Then let's get some sleep. Tomorrow, we'll find that shadow weaver and set you loose. That bastard won't know what hit him."

No, he wouldn't. I would make him pay. For my brothers. For Drake. And even for Ben.

CHAPTER 8

THE NEXT morning we ate berries and nuts Aiden had gathered for our breakfast before getting dressed. A few hours later, we emerged from the Arbor. It existed between the four kingdoms of the light fae. The Sylphs, or air sprites, lived to the east of the Arbor, while the water fae known as the Undines lived to the west, along the Gulf of Mist. To the north, the Gnomes dwelled among the rocky crags of Mount Matakin.

We were headed south along the grasslands and up to the Hearth, the place the fire fairies called home.

"That's the Shade," Aiden said as we made our way up the hill toward his home. A patch of land dominated by shadows stretched beyond the northern boundaries of Mount Matakin. Unlike the golden sky above us, dark, purplish clouds, which resembled huge bruises across the heavens, tumultuously roiled over the dark patch of land. "That's where the dark fae live."

"And your father is king over all fairies?" I asked. The politics of this land had always confused me. Each tribe had their own leaders, and they made up the Royal Fae Court, but they all answered to one king. It had never made sense to me why that was.

Aiden nodded as he led me farther up the hill. "He's ruled Otherworld for nearly a century now."

Damn. How old *was* Aiden?

"I'm old enough not to answer that question," he said, giving me a smirk.

"How'd you know that's what I was thinking?"

"Because I know your kind," he said, pretending to be disgusted with my need to know his age. "Always concerned with numbers instead of just letting someone be."

I stopped. "Let me make one thing clear. I don't care if you're sixty years old. It wouldn't change one damn thing."

"That's good to know," he said before kissing my lips. He grabbed my hand and tugged me forward. "But I haven't been sixty in years."

I let fly a low whistle, to which Aiden responded by slamming into me with his shoulder.

I decided it was best to change the subject. "I don't understand why the other fae don't follow a leader from their own tribes."

"We used to. Many generations ago." His face grew dark and serious. "That was before my time, but my father told me stories about a civil war between the fae."

I couldn't hide my shock. Everything I knew about the fairies indicated they were a peaceful species who abhorred violence. And hadn't Aiden told us the fae had always lived in peace? "Really? But that's not what you said back in Havenbridge."

"I know," he said. "We have lived in peace my entire life. That point in our history wasn't one of the better moments, and it's not information I freely share. It was fueled by discontent with our removal from your world."

So I'd been right. The fae hadn't come here by choice. They had been forced. "Because of the Conclave?"

"Yes." His muscles tensed. "Your kind had just fought an uprising of sorcerers, and they beat them with our help. But after our victory, more humans became aware of magic, and more witch hunters were born. They tracked down all magical creatures, killing whomever they could, and it was learned these hunters could sense magic, follow it like a homing beacon. Since we were beings of pure magical energy, they could easily pinpoint the fae and through us find your kind."

"So it wasn't animosity that caused the Conclave to make this decision, but concern for the safety of all?" That didn't sound too bad.

Aiden snorted. "That was what they claimed, but you merely tap into magic. We are comprised of it. The Conclave perceived us as a threat, and after the sorcerers, they were taking no chances. They wanted us out, so they cast a spell that blocked the energy of the Gate. Without it, we would die. They promised only to release the spell once we had left their world to create our own."

"I don't understand. Why go to such extreme measure? Why not negotiate?"

"Because the Conclave concerns themselves with being the strongest forces of magic in existence. They didn't care that we were their allies. Their desire to remain the strongest in all the land prompted them to turn against us and force us here. If we had not come, we would no longer exist."

Something was missing from this story. While I didn't think Aiden was lying to me, he had only the fae's version of the truth. The real answer had to lie somewhere in between. "How did this lead to a civil war?"

"The dark fae wanted to return to your world."

I stopped. The banshees we had captured back home had been telling the truth. They were motivated by an ancient desire to reclaim the land that had once been theirs. "But you stopped them?"

"We did," he said, pointing to the Shade. "And they have resided there ever since. It was decided after their defeat all fae, light and dark, needed a voice to avoid further dissension, and the Royal Fae Court was born. But the leaders could never agree. They constantly argued until it was decided we needed a ruler, one who would be in charge of protecting our species from threats within and outside the fae."

"And your tribe was chosen to lead?"

"It was the decision of the court that only a light fae would lead since the dark fairies had been responsible for our conflict," he answered. "The Sylphs expressed no desire to take on the responsibility. The air sprites prefer to dance on the wind than concern themselves with the everyday problems of our world. The Gnomes seek only solitude and also withdrew from the running. That left only the Undines and the Salamanders."

The Undines consisted of merfolk and river spirits that were charged with the protection of every body of water on the planet, and their kingdom had become legendary on earth. They had been the residents of Atlantis.

"How was it decided?"

"One battle between the most powerful Salamander and Undine. The stories tell of an epic battle that lasted for days, until at last, my father's great-great-grandsire won. Ever since then, my family has been charged with protecting and leading our people."

I didn't know what to say. I had a whole lot of information to process.

The fae weren't as everyone believed them to be, so why did the books written about them portray them as staunch pacifists? Was it done to downplay their threat?

And if peace had reigned so long here, why stir up the banshees now? What could be gained from that?

I glanced over my shoulder at the Shade. The dark, menacing land stretched far beyond what I could see, but as I swept my gaze across their kingdom, a question I hadn't previously considered sprang to mind.

Where were the dark fae now? We'd been in Otherworld for a day and hadn't been attacked once. They had been lying in wait for Aiden the moment he'd tried to come home, after I met him in the forest.

Something was going on.

"What's the matter?"

Aiden's question snapped me out of my thoughts. I tore my gaze from our surroundings, where I was searching for an unseen threat and focused on him. "Just wondering where the banshees are."

He nodded with a sigh. "I've been wondering that too." He surveyed the landscape. "And how did the vampyren get into the tunnel connecting our worlds?" Aiden added.

"I'd place my money on the shadow weaver," I answered.

"But how did he know we'd be there?" he asked. "Was he listening to us from the shadows?"

That was a safe bet. The shadow weaver had obviously been eavesdropping while we interrogated the banshees in the library. He'd killed them before we could get our answers. It made sense, yet my gut told me that wasn't the answer. I was missing a piece of the puzzle.

"You don't think so, right?"

I shook my head. "How did you know?"

"You get this faraway look in your eyes whenever someone says something you disagree with. You also gnaw on your bottom lip while you search for the right answer."

I released my lip from my teeth. I hadn't realized I did that. My mother had chewed her lips raw whenever she was about to offer an opinion that countered my father's. Knowing I'd inherited her habit made me smile. "I have no doubt he was there in the room with us. We were fools not to consider the possibility, but something tells me he wasn't hiding in the shadows."

Aiden's arched eyebrows almost joined his hairline. "I don't understand."

"Neither do I," I answered. "It's just a gut feeling I have."

He nodded as if that made complete sense, and to a fire fae it probably did. They trusted what they felt far more than anything else.

"What else do you have a gut feeling about?"

Where did I begin? "This shadow weaver obviously has an agenda. We thought it was Mason at first. We believed he had sensed the power of darkness in my brother and saw the potential to either recruit him or somehow steal his powers, but that wasn't the case. He'd been surprised by my brother's abilities."

"Which means it wasn't your brother he was after. He was after something else," Aiden said.

"Right. I think that's why he's here in Otherworld. There has to be something here he wants too."

Aiden pondered the question in silence before speaking. "I have no clue what that could be. We don't have anything of value to anyone else. We are simple folk."

"I know," I said. "So it must be something so unordinary it's easily overlooked. And I think we've all been guilty of looking past the obvious."

"What do you mean?"

"If he's here to further his plans, then it makes logical sense that when he was in Havenbridge during Mabon, he was after something while he was there. And I bet he got it." What would that have been? All he'd managed to accomplish was to order the vampyre doing his dirty work to murder four innocent people, who had been turned into vampyren.

My heart broke again at the memory of Drake's surprise when that vampyre had claimed to be his Aunt Millie. Had she been telling the truth? And if it was Aunt Millie, how would Drake deal with that knowledge if he was still alive? Or Gerald Wa? He had been in love with Millicent Carpenter.

"The Conclave thinks he's amassing an army," Aiden said. "Maybe that was what the shadow weaver was after. That might have been phase one of his plan."

I bit my lip.

"Okay," he said. "You obviously disagree."

I did. But why?

The only answer I had was the tightening in my gut.

ONCE WE crested the hilltop, the Hearth was a few hundred feet away, nestled on the edge of the cliff visible from the Arbor. Curtain walls, constructed from red brick, formed a protective rectangle around the perimeter, making the kingdom impregnable. The raised drawbridge appeared to be the only way inside.

"It's beautiful," I said. Roofs that appeared to be made from gold covered the main building and the conical spires that topped the turrets. Hadn't Aiden said the fae were simple folk? The structure seemed to disprove that. The sheer opulence of their kingdom put Blackmoor Manor to shame. "Must be nice being a prince."

"Says the man with a sprawling estate," he replied with a wink. "Don't be fooled, though. It's not what you think. We didn't build the castle for the sake of ceremony. It's mainly for protection."

"From the dark fae?"

"No. The Hearth was built long before the civil war."

My gaze swept over the castle keep, which rose at least thirty feet into the sky. From the round arched windows at the very top, any approaching enemy would be spotted. "Then what's it all for?"

Aiden glanced at me out of the corners of his eyes, uncertain if he should reveal the information he possessed.

"What's the big secret?" I asked.

He stared straight ahead in silence instead of answering my question.

"Aiden?"

He blew out a lungful of air before finally settling his emerald gaze on mine. "It's not something we talk about with outsiders," he said.

Since when had I been relegated to outsider status? "You don't trust me?"

He shook his head and grabbed my hand. He squeezed it tightly before letting go. "It's not that. I promise."

"Then what?"

We continued on for a few more minutes. Only the wind, which whistled around us, broke the silence. Threatening clouds gathered in towering thunderheads above us, signaling the onset of a powerful storm.

Aiden stopped walking, his eyes fixed on me. He either was oblivious to the encroaching darkness or choosing to ignore it. "If warlocks had a weakness, would you go around telling people what that was?"

We did have a weakness, and Aiden, and every magical creature that existed, knew what that was. "But we do," I answered. "It's called the Gate. Why do you think we protect it?"

"Because it's the source of all magic," he replied. Why did he suddenly seem irritated?

"Well, yes," I said. If we didn't protect the Gate and it was destroyed, well, I couldn't even fathom the consequences. "So you're saying the fire fae have their own version of the Gate?"

"In a way," he replied but didn't elaborate.

As much as it irritated me, I understood Aiden's reluctance. While the existence of the Gate was a well-known fact in the magical community, its location was not. The Gate had existed in various spots throughout the ages. Right now, it opened up in Havenbridge, but only the Conclave possessed knowledge of its precise location.

Whatever the fire fae protected did not move. It rested somewhere within the kingdom, and remaining unidentified kept it more secure than the castle walls that surrounded it and the fire fae who guarded it.

"Okay, so you're not going to tell me what it is," I said. The clouds eclipsed more light from the previously golden sky, and thunder rumbled in the distance. "But can you at least tell me why you're protecting it?"

He mulled it over for a few second before reluctantly nodding. "It's the bedrock of Otherworld. We call it the Hearthstone."

His answer shocked me. In everything I'd ever read about the land of the fae, I never once came across information on such a powerful talisman. I'd been told Otherworld was created for those composed of pure magic, who couldn't reside among humans without revealing our existence. Of course, that hadn't been the complete truth. I'd never once considered that the survival of this place depended upon a magical token.

"Do you see why I'm reluctant to share much more about it?"

I did, and the knot that wound in my stomach told me something far more important. "I have a feeling that's what the shadow weaver is after."

Aiden's eyes grew wide as he glanced over his shoulder in a panic. He started toward his kingdom, but I held him back. "We have to think this through," I said. "We can't go charging in there without a plan."

"I have one," he growled. He strained against my embrace. "I'm going to kill him before he lays one hand on our most precious relic."

I turned him around in my arms, caressing his cheeks. I cupped his chin in my palm and forced his panicked eyes to mine. I hoped my gentle strokes and soothing voice would calm him as he used his touch to center me. "That's not good enough, and you know it."

His eyes smoldered in green flame. "I'm not going to stand here one minute longer, debating the issue," he said. Fiery wings sprouted from his back, and he hovered a few inches off the ground. As usual, whenever Aiden grew angry, he spoke as a prince. "I'm heading into the Hearth, where I will guard its contents with my life."

"And what if he's already there?" I asked.

His gaze snapped back to mine. "No," he said, shaking his head. Fear doused the anger in his eyes, and instead of flying away, his wings disappeared. He landed beside me, clutching my arms as if I'd become a lifeline in the ocean of turmoil that churned around him. "I can't be too late."

"I don't think you are," I replied. Gloom dominated the sky, and lightning streaked overhead. "If you were, Otherworld would already be feeling its effects."

My words offered some relief. He visibly relaxed and took several deep breaths.

"But he's getting close," I said. "Look around, Aiden. Do you see what's happening?"

Aiden tore his gaze from me and focused on the long shadows that crept across the landscape. Dark clouds, resembling the skies that hung over the Shade, roiled overhead. "I thought it was just a storm," he whispered. "But it isn't, is it?"

I shook my head.

"We must do something," he said. He squared his shoulders. Determination had replaced his fear and impulsive anger.

"We will," I said. "I even have a plan."

WE STOOD before the raised drawbridge. No scuttling feet on the inside or calls welcoming Aiden home greeted us from the interior. The parapet walkway above remained free of guards, and eerie silence enveloped the castle.

"This isn't good," Aiden said.

"But we were prepared for this."

Aiden craned his neck upward, trying to detect any movement on the walkway. "And you still don't think we should fly over the wall?" he asked. "I can penetrate the spell that protects the castle from above."

We'd already debated how to infiltrate the Hearth on our walk here. It was too dangerous to attempt a flyover. While Aiden believed it would be more expedient, we'd be vulnerable to attack. He hadn't been pleased with my more cautious approach. Rage fueled by anxiety roared within him.

I understood the emotion. It was how I'd felt after the vampyren attack and Ben's murder, but the red haze of rage, which had briefly colored my perceptions, was gone. For the moment at least. "It's safer to go through the front door," I replied. "Where we have some protection from the walls of the castle."

"The drawbridge is enchanted," he reminded me. "Only a fire fae inside the castle walls can open it."

Aiden had already told me about this additional safety feature for the Hearth. It ensured that only those who needed to get in were allowed entrance, but the enchanted drawbridge and the protection spell had obviously been unsuccessful at repelling the shadow weaver.

He was inside. His presence tugged at my blood like the moon pulls upon the tide.

"How are you going to open it?"

"With magic," I answered.

He crossed his arms. Irritation twisted his lips and scrunched his eyes into slits. "It won't work. I've told you that."

"And I told you I can feel my power growing." I ran my hands down his arms and squeezed his biceps. "Trust me."

"I do," he said. A teasing smile hitched the right corner of his mouth. "But I won't believe it until I see it."

"Then stand back," I said, extending my hands in front of me. "Because I'm about to get us in."

I closed my eyes, hoping Aiden couldn't sense I wasn't as confident as I pretended to be. I had no knowledge of any spell that could cancel out fae magic, which was more powerful than I'd realized. I'd need to research the Grimoire to find one or piece together a spell from others in the book that might work. That was obviously out of the question.

The only option left was to improvise, do something only the most powerful warlocks could hope to do—cast my own incantation and hope it worked.

I opened my senses to the magic, and the bands of swirling colors almost blinded me. I'd never seen magic this alive or vibrant before. Blues and yellows and greens I'd never realized existed twined up to the sky, connected the trees to each other, and shot out in different directions, creating a latticework of energy that linked everything together.

All I had to do was find the words that would strike the right chords around me, and the best place to start was with the pure essence of the realm, what had likely filled my soul back in the Arbor.

"*Magia fairia*," I said with my hands raised over my head, "*ad me veni*."

Strings of yellow, red, and orange energy shot out of the sky, the ground, and from all around me in response to my summons. They pierced my flesh, snaking paths through every muscle and bone in my body. The pain was excruciating, but I couldn't stop. Now that I had the attention of the magic in Otherworld, I had to do something with it.

"*Solve vinculum*," I chanted, lowering my hands to point at the drawbridge. The cords of power within me flew out of my fingertips and struck the drawbridge in one loud thunderclap. The magic I'd summoned did as I asked, breaking the seal that kept the entrance to the Hearth closed. "*Et ianuam mihi aperi*."

And with my final command, the chains holding the counterweights snapped, and the drawbridge fell open with a crash.

Drained, I sank to my knees. Sweat poured off my face, and my body exploded in pain.

"Thad!" Aiden said at my side. He kneeled beside me, glancing back and forth from me to the open drawbridge. "You did it," he said in disbelief.

"I told you I would," I replied through ragged breaths. I tried to stand, but my knees refused to lock. Aiden had to wrap his arm around my waist and lift me.

"Take it easy," he said.

Being in Aiden's arms once again worked its miracle on me. His touch and his words replenished my reserves, and my wobbly legs finally supported my weight. "Thanks."

"I've never seen anything like that before," he said. "You actually used fae magic to open the door. How'd you do that?"

I didn't have an answer. In all my studies, I'd never encountered any inscription that said tapping into another type of magic was possible. Black magic belonged to warlocks, white magic stayed with witches, and fairy magic responded to the fae. How had I been able to manipulate energy I'd never harnessed before? "I really don't know," I answered.

"Well, it was badass," Aiden said, clearly impressed. "Think you can do that again?"

I glanced through the open entry way and into the inner courtyard. No banshees or vampyren flew out at us. The deserted interior filled me with dread. Whatever waited for us inside was not going to be pleasant. "Let's hope so," I said, grabbing Aiden's hand in mine and walking into the castle.

HAND IN hand, we made our way to the main building in the far right corner. According to Aiden, this structure housed the throne room and living quarters for the fae. As he explained the layout of the interior, I sensed unseen eyes studying our movements. I attempted to discern their location with my supernatural senses, but a shadowy rampart shielded most of the area. The only section of the kingdom that wasn't protected was the building we now stood in front of.

This was obviously where we were supposed to go.

"We're walking into a trap," Aiden whispered. "I can sense others around us. The hatred emanating off them is making me nauseous."

I couldn't feel their anger the way Aiden could, but different types of magic coalesced around us. What other creatures had the shadow weaver amassed? "But they're standing their ground," I said. "If they wanted us dead, they would have attacked by now."

"Why doesn't that make me feel better?" Aiden asked.

It didn't make me exactly want to jump for joy either. There was still some purpose either Aiden or I served, and not knowing what that was made me uneasy. If it was only me, I could handle whatever the bastard threw at me, but if it was Aiden he was after, I'd rip him apart before he laid one hand on him. He was my fairy, and no one but me was going to touch him.

"Wow!" Aiden said, coming to an abrupt halt. "I felt that."

I glanced around, drawing him into my protective embrace. "What?"

"You," he answered, brushing his lips against mine.

"I don't understand."

"Your passion for me, to protect me, exploded from you like a solar flare." He leaned his entire body against mine. "It was beautiful."

"And I mean it," I said, pressing my body to his. "I won't let anything happen to you."

"I know you won't," he said. "That's why I'm not as scared or as angry anymore. Because of you."

I smiled at Aiden before glancing at the huge red door before us. "Should we?"

He nodded. "Allow me." He waved his hand at the door, and it flew open, slamming back against the wall inside. He cocked one eyebrow at me and grinned. "You're not the only one who can be badass, you know?"

I laced his fingers with mine before replying, "I had no doubt."

We walked up the steps and crossed the threshold as one.

Our footfalls echoed off the marble floors, where each tile had been buffed to a reflective shine. Exquisite paintings of various landscapes adorned the walls of the foyer. A set of double staircases, one on the right and one on the left, spiraled to the second floor, which appeared to be as abandoned as the rest of the castle. The wooden railings of the staircases had been engraved with vines and flower blooms that trailed all the way to the top.

Six large, evenly spaced stone pillars kept the second floor from crashing down upon the first. The stone columns had been intricately carved in a style more Renaissance than fae.

"That leads to the library," Aiden said as we passed a grand red door to the right. "The one on the left leads to my mother's greenhouse."

But I kept my gaze focused straight ahead. A magical blind spot had erected itself within the room at the end of the twenty-foot long hall. That was where we'd find the shadow weaver. "What's up there?" I asked.

"The throne room."

It made sense.

"That's where he is, isn't he?"

I nodded.

Aiden tensed, and his grip around my hand tightened. He was clearly doing his best not to fly into the throne room, hurling fireballs at everyone within. Thankfully, our joined hands allowed him to draw from my strength as easily as I drew from his.

As we approached the double golden doors that opened to the throne room, I saw scorch marks had been etched into the cold marble floor, and the acrid scent of smoke clung to the air. There had been a battle, and judging from the lack of devastation, the fire fae had been taken off guard and easily dispatched.

"Thad!" Aiden said, pointing to the evidence of a struggle.

"I know," I said, rubbing my thumb along the back of his hand. "Stay focused and whatever you do, don't let go of my hand."

"Why?"

I had no clue. I just knew it was important. "Ready?"

He nodded.

"*Aperite*," I muttered, and the double doors slowly swung inward.

THE WALLS inside were decorated with bas-relief, depicting the various kingdoms of Otherworld as Aiden had described them to me earlier: the whispering fields of the Sylphs, the kingdom of Atlantis belonging to the Undines, and Mount Matakin, where the Gnomes lived.

On the left, the room opened up. Tapestries and long, narrow windows decorated either side, which was bisected by a red-carpeted walkway. At the end, a three-stepped platform led up to a high-backed chair constructed from a dark, red wood.

On the throne sat a man who looked familiar but whom I didn't recognize. He had a full head of white hair and sparkling green eyes.

"Dad!" Aiden shouted. He released my hand and ran toward his father.

"Aiden, wait!" I yelled.

Shadows quickly engulfed the room, forming a barrier between Aiden and me. He snapped around, cursing his impulsiveness. He hurled fireball after fireball at the opaque ebon wall, but it caused no damage.

"Enough!" King Oberon commanded.

Aiden quickly obeyed, but his eyes lingered upon me. "I'm sorry," he whispered.

"You apologize to that warlock and not to me?" his father asked. "You bring black magic to Otherworld, you lie with one not of our kind, and you have the gall to offer *him* contrition? You should be on bent knee, seeking forgiveness from your father and your liege."

Aiden offered immediate supplication. "Father, there is danger here. We must protect—."

"Do not tell me what we must do," he said. His silver eyebrows knitted together in parental consternation. "I'm well aware of the violence you have brought to our peaceful land, but do not worry your brash little head. I have rectified what you have wrought."

"What do you mean?"

Fire fae, dressed in black pants and with bare chests, stepped out of the shadows, carrying swords of flame in their hands. Their fiery wings spread wide as they regarded me with hatred and contempt.

Their anger made no sense, so I opened up to the magic around us and searched for an answer. The magic in the throne room vibrated with a strange crimson energy, which coiled around every fire fae in the room, including the king.

Only Aiden remained untouched by the snaking bands of magic that filled the room.

When I looked down at myself, I noted thin threads of ruby dangling from me. They clung to my hands, my chest, and my heart. How had I not noticed this before?

"I have made a pact with the shadow weaver," the king announced. As he rose from his throne, the red cords around him pulled taut, as if they were controlling his actions. "All he requires for peace is your warlock."

Aiden rose, crossing to his father, but armed guards quickly blocked his path. They pointed their burning swords at Aiden's chest, ready to eviscerate him upon command. "You can't!" he said to his father. "You don't know what you're doing."

King Oberon glared down at his son. "It is *you* who knows nothing. As you always have." He turned to address the shadows over his shoulder. "He's yours. Take him and leave."

A man made entirely of shadows stepped forward. He nodded at the king before turning his attention to Aiden. "You have complicated my plans, young prince," he said. The voice was rough and gravelly, but it sounded familiar.

"It's always a pleasure to be a pain in your ass," Aiden spat. His hands clenched, and fire engulfed his fists. The swords of the guards encircling him drew ever closer, singing his flesh.

The shadow weaver laughed. "But I'm sure it was infinitely more fun being a pain in our Thad's ass, wasn't it?" The dark holes that were his eyes locked onto me. A devilish grin parted his inky lips as he approached Aiden.

"Stay away from him!" I yelled, striking the shadow wall that refused to give.

"Or what?" he teased. With a gesture, chains made from shadows shot out of the corners of the room and wrapped around Aiden's neck, wrist, and ankles. They pulled tight and forced him to his knees.

King Oberon made no move to protect his son. His eyes had glassed over.

"Aiden!" I unleashed a barrage of ice upon the wall, but the shadowy projection absorbed the attack.

"You'll never break through," the shadow weaver said as he wound the chains around his hand and yanked. Aiden sprawled onto the marble in a grumble of pain. "I've been around a lot longer than you, and my magic is far more formidable than yours."

"That's the blood magic," I said. "I can see you manipulating everyone in this room with it."

That made him pause. "An interesting development," he said with a slow nod. "Your powers are growing, Thad, but then again I always sensed great power in you. It was why I wanted you. With the power I have, and what remains untapped within you, we could have done anything together." He glared down at Aiden. "But you chose the fae."

Without even a gesture, the chains whipped Aiden into the wall, which exploded outward in a cloud of white plaster. Again the chains pulled, and Aiden flew back first into one of the stone columns and then into the ceiling before slamming onto the marbled floor.

"And your fairy will pay!"

Aiden moaned on the floor, bleeding. He tried to stand, to fight, but the shadow weaver stepped on his back and forced him flat against the marble.

"What the hell are you talking about?" I asked, trying to distract him with conversation rather than having him continue his attempts to kill Aiden. "What choice?"

"Have you forgotten me already, Red?"

My gaze crept back to the shadow weaver, who mocked me in laughter. Only one person had recently called me by that name, and I'd stood by and watched while he was killed. "Ben?"

With a gesture, the shadows flew off him, revealing the cold, dark eyes and mischievous slanted grin of Ben Crane. "Took you long enough," he said.

My vision swam, and it took every ounce of willpower at my command to keep me upright. How was this possible? How could Ben be the shadow weaver?

"This would have gone much easier had you just given in," Ben said. "I wove a powerful blood magic spell on you after taking your blood that first night. You do remember that, don't you?"

So that was how he had done it. When my guard was down, and he was seducing me with magic, he had taken what he needed to further his plans.

He grinned at me before continuing. "And it was working. The vise-like control with which you led your life was slipping, and every time we were together, the blood tie I created between us drew you closer and closer to me. And it would've worked too." He ground his foot on Aiden's back. "But I hadn't counted on the fire fae or his charms. Being with him somehow canceled out my spell, severing *our* blood tie and forming an unseen tether to him. And I intend to find out how that happened."

He made a rising gesture, and the shadow chains pulled Aiden until he was dangling in the air. Blood spilled from pale lips, splattering his bare chest with drops of crimson. He wasn't moving, and his chest didn't rise and fall. Was he dead?

If he was, Ben would soon follow.

"Don't get ahead of yourself," Ben said, shooting me a fake smile. "He's still alive."

"I'll kill you," I said through clenched teeth.

He chuckled as if I'd told the funniest joke in the world. "Your power is nothing compared to mine." He played with the emerald pendent that hung on the chain around his neck. What was the deal with that damn stone? Was it a talisman that somehow kept us from discerning who he was?

"I was able to avoid detection from the protector covens, your High Priests, and even the Conclave themselves. And you think you're going to somehow fare any better?"

I clenched my hands into fists, forming sharp icicles in my palms. "I've changed since we last met," I said. "You'd be surprised what I can do now."

"Like what?" he asked. "Make popsicles?"

I smirked and threw them at the wall. "*Penetrate per murum*," I chanted as they struck the obsidian barrier. My icy missiles pierced the shroud and flew straight at Ben, who caught them in his hand.

He crushed them before clapping. "I'm impressed. Your gifts are growing, and that is cause for further investigation as well." He motioned to the shadows. In reply to his summons, a horde of banshees stepped forward, as well as the four vampyren that had attacked us on our way to Otherworld—one of these unrecognizable monsters was Drake's aunt Millie. He gestured toward the chains that held Aiden, and the chains holding Aiden followed him as he walked away.

"Where the hell do you think you're going?" I asked.

He paused at the rear door of the throne room. "I have something to collect before I depart," he said. "But don't worry, I'm not leaving you empty-handed."

The shadow wall fell. The banshees, vampyren, and fire fae stepped forward, ready to fight.

I glanced at Aiden, who gazed at me between half-closed eyelids. "I'll be coming for you," I said before the door slammed and my enemies descended.

"*PROTEGE ME*," I said with a flurry of hands. A dome of crystal light surrounded me. The vampyren squawked as they bounced off the protective shield. The banshees flew high above, concentrating their sonic screams on my barrier while the fire fae assaulted the wall of light with their flaming swords.

I gritted my teeth as the combined attacks threatened to collapse my protective sphere. I wasn't going to last much longer, and I needed a plan.

"Get him!" King Oberon commanded, spittle flying from his lips. He resembled a rabid dog more than the leader of the fae. He rose from his throne and stood in the center of the room. The crimson energy Ben had used to control the king coiled around him as if a hidden marionette guided his actions.

If he was being controlled, that meant he and the other fire fairies were acting against their will, unlike the banshees and the vampyren. No crimson energy emanated from them. I had to somehow sever the blood tie Ben had created with the king. If I could do that, he might be able to snap his people out of Ben's power and help me fight the others.

It was a long shot, but it was the only one I had.

But first, I had to get to him.

I centered myself like I had outside the drawbridge of the Hearth and called to the fairy magic once again. The snaking chords of light found me, easily penetrating my shield and once again filling me with the raw power of Otherworld.

"What's this?" the king asked. "He's using the magic of the fae."

That pissed off the banshees and the fire fairies. They redoubled their efforts to break through and kill me, but their struggle was no longer necessary.

"*Propellit*," I uttered with a wave of my hand as I lowered my shield. The majority of the enemies around me flew backward, crashing through the walls and out into the courtyard below.

A second wave of fire fae converged, raining fireballs down upon me. I pointed at the onslaught before flicking my hand at them and reciting a spell. My words halted their flaming missiles in midflight before returning them to their casters. The fireballs struck their mark, and the fae cried out in pain as they crashed to the marble floor.

I still had no idea how I had managed to tap into the magic of this world and overpower their abilities or knew what to do. It was like some instinct within me had been turned on.

As long as it continued to work, I'd follow the lead of the magic that somehow wielded me.

A shrill cry filled the air, causing every windowpane in the room to explode outward. I covered my ears as a group of banshees prepared to attack. They inhaled big breaths to summon screams that would no doubt shatter my eardrums. "*Sin aere este*," I chanted, stealing all air from where they had gathered. Their yellow eyes grew wide, and they clasped their throats.

"Die!"

Claws grasped me from behind and threw me into one of the stone columns. I landed with a thud just in time to see the return of the vampyren and the others I had knocked outside the castle.

While spells might continue to work against the fae and the banshees, the vampyren built up an immunity that would eventually make them invulnerable. I had to switch things up and use the other weapons in my arsenal.

I tapped into my ice powers and let them loose. A flash freeze covered the entire room in ice, instantly freezing everyone who touched the ground. Dozens of ice statues stood around me, trapped within my icy grip. The only parts of their bodies that could move were their eyes, and their hatred burned hotter than the sun.

Gathering my breath, I kneeled on the ground, eying my prisoners. The low hum of the banshees' powers caught my attention. They were attempting to shatter their prisons, while the ice around the fire fae began to melt.

I had only a few minutes to do what needed to be done.

I was sprinting over to the king, concocting a spell I hoped would free him from Ben's sway, when the ice around him exploded outward. I tumbled across the floor from the force of the explosion and shielded my face from the shards that bit into my flesh.

"You have bastardized our magic," King Oberon said. A fiery broadsword formed in his hand as he walked toward me. "I will not allow this perversion to last one moment longer."

Flaming wings, bigger and grander than Aiden's, sprouted from his back as he lunged at me. I managed to roll out of the way seconds before his sword struck.

Out of nowhere, a storm of blazing arrows headed toward me. "You must listen," I said, dodging the fiery onslaught. The power I sensed from him was immense. If he managed to land even one blow, I would be dead. I hid behind one of the pillars as the arrows rained down, melting everything they touched. "You're being controlled by blood magic."

"I'm the king of the fae," he announced, slicing through the column where I'd taken shelter. "No one controls me." The stone fractured and crumbled, falling into a rocky heap. With one of the supports now gone, the ceiling above creaked, and cracks formed in the plaster overhead.

The angry crimson lines wrapped tightly around him. Perhaps that was what I needed to attack. With my index and middle finger, I formed a makeshift pair of scissors. "*Inseco*," I said while snapping them closed.

The lines around King Oberon shuddered but did not break. I repeated the spell again with the same result. The increase in my power still wasn't strong enough to break Ben's enchantment.

With surprising speed, the king crashed into me. I slammed against the wall and before I could summon forth any of my powers, he wrapped his flaming hands around my forearm. I screamed in pain as my flesh sizzled and he tossed me across the room where I landed in a heap.

He gestured at the others, and a heat wave spread across the room, instantly melting the ice that held them captive. Freed, they advanced toward me, each of them ready to end my threat.

There were too many of them. I couldn't take them all on by myself, but if I didn't, Aiden would pay the price for my failure. I couldn't allow that to happen. I had to focus on him, use the memory of the strength his touch gave me.

I'd made a promise I wouldn't let anything happen to him, and it was a promise I intended to keep.

The only way I would be able to do that was if I relied on my brains, which had always served me well before, instead of my brawn.

I collapsed onto my knees, pretending defeat.

"You surrender?" King Oberon asked.

I nodded. "I'm no match for all of you."

The banshees cackled, and the vampyren responded by snapping their jaws shut. Their tongues slithered between their razor-sharp teeth, obviously itching to tear into my flesh and drink my blood.

"Kill him," said the Aunt Millie vampyre. Black saliva dripped from her jaws.

"Yes," agreed one of the banshees. "Those were your orders."

Interesting. The banshees and the vampyren were going to allow King Oberon to kill me. That wasn't like them. Their perverted natures insisted on drawing blood, so why the change? How did my death at the king's hands play into Ben's plan?

"Hold him," King Oberon commanded. The fire fae restrained my hands behind my back and forced me to my feet. Two of them held their fiery weapons poised at my neck while the king approached with his sword and murder in his eyes. "It's time for you to die, warlock."

Time was running out. I had to find some way to break the spell that controlled the fae, but everything I'd tried had failed. How had Aiden severed my blood ties with Ben? He hadn't cast a spell or known what he was doing. All it took was the warmth of his flesh and the sweetness of his kisses to bring me around.

Was it because of the feelings we had for each other? Had the attraction that had grown to so much more been the cause?

"Where's the queen?" I asked.

He hesitated. His eyes darted back and forth as if he were searching for an answer. This was what I needed. From everything Aiden had told me, King Oberon doted on Queen Una.

"Is she safe?"

"Kill him," commanded one of the male vampyren. He dug his claws into the king's shoulder, snapping him from his thoughts. "Do it. Now."

"The Queen is of no consequence to you," the king answered, but the conviction in his voice faltered slightly. The memory of his wife swirled from the depths of his soul, and the red tethers around him grew slack.

"But she is to you," I said.

The other female vampyren charged through the crowd, knocking back the fire fae that restrained me. She grabbed me by my shirt and lifted me in the air. "Shut up! If you say one more word, I'll bite off your tongue." She punctuated her threat with a snap of her jaws.

"And what will your master do to you if you do that?" I asked, briefly switching my gaze to where the king stood slack. The sword disappeared from his hands. The blood ties that held him grew looser and threatened to slip free. "That wouldn't be following orders, would it? You can't kill me, or did I get that wrong?"

She glanced over her shoulder at the other vampyren, who hissed in reply. She let me go, and I fell to the ground.

"Wise choice," I said, struggling to my feet. "You don't want to piss him off. He killed the banshees he sent after Aiden."

"He what?" asked one of the banshees. She glided over to where I stood and got in my face. An angry snarl curled her withered lips. This was news to her.

"You didn't know?" I asked. "I figured he told you he snapped them in two for disobeying him."

The banshees behind her wailed in anger.

"Was that not part of your deal?"

"You lie," she said, wrapping her hands around my throat. "The shadow weaver promised us freedom from Otherworld if we followed him."

So that *was* the carrot Ben dangled in front of the banshees. The dark fae had never appreciated being forced to live here. If they had their way, they'd tear down the barrier that separated them from Earth. "Well, he did free your three sisters," I said matter-of-factly. "From their lives."

She let go of me and turned to the vampyren. "Is this true?" she shrieked. "Has the shadow weaver betrayed us?"

In response, the two female vampyren sprang on her, tearing out her throat. The banshees struck back, bringing the remaining vampyren into the fray. While they fought, I inched over to King Oberon, who stood still. The faraway look in his eyes told me he wasn't seeing the events unfolding around him. He was lost in the memory of his wife.

"You've got to find Queen Una," I said. "She's in danger."

The fire fae, who had been distracted by the eruption of the vampyren-banshee war, grabbed me, pulling me away from their king.

"*Memento amoris*," I said, casting a simple spell that would allow the king to remember his love. A second later, the red vines of magic around him snapped, and he fell to his knees.

When he looked up, anger had turned his green eyes into twin flames of emerald fire. Except this time, it wasn't directed at me. He balled his fists, and a flaming hand appeared in the throne room.

Its sudden presence stopped the fighting.

"That is *enough*!" he commanded. The hand closed around the red strings of magic still clutching the assembled fire fae and set them on fire, freeing his people from Ben's power.

"No!" shouted the female vampyre that wasn't Aunt Millie. She leaped at King Oberon, but the fiery hand reached out and grabbed her. When the hand opened up, a pile of ash fell to the ground.

Evidently, wooden stakes weren't the only way to kill a vampyre. The fire of the fae worked just as efficiently, and the others realized the danger. They took to the air and flew through the broken windows.

"After them!" King Oberon commanded, and his subjects immediately pursued. He turned his gaze to the banshees, who snarled and hissed. They were ready for a fight. He nodded at the remaining fae, who had their fiery swords already in hand, and they attacked.

"King Oberon," I said, staring at the exit beyond his throne.

"We will handle the dark fae and find my wife," he said. A smile spread across his wizened face. It reminded me of Aiden's. "Go get my son."

I ran out the same door Ben had had used.

I *would* get Aiden back, no matter what I had to do.

CHAPTER 9

I STOOD in the middle of the courtyard where the door led, unsure where to go. Ben could have taken Aiden anywhere, and I didn't have time to search every inch of the Hearth to find him. Ben was obviously after whatever relic kept Otherworld and my world separate. That was most likely why he'd taken Aiden and why I needed to get to them fast.

Once Ben had what he'd come here for, Aiden became disposable.

I took several deep breaths and closed my eyes before opening them to the vibrant web of magical energy that wove through every inch of fairyland. *"Duc me ad Aiden,"* I said, asking for the lines of power to lead me where I needed to go.

One of the red strings grew rigid and pulsed like a neon sign. It traveled through the archway about twenty feet away before ending at the door of the castle keep.

I ran, uttering a spell that would increase my speed. Within seconds, I was throwing open the doors.

A huge rectangular room opened up beyond the entrance. Arched doorways with chevrons carved along the top lined the forty-foot area, with a gallery running along each of the four floors.

The band of energy I had followed traveled up the spiral staircase on the right, so I dashed up the steps to the top floor. It continued down a six-foot long hallway before disappearing through the only door on this level.

I charged forward, a spell on my lips. In response, the mahogany door exploded inward, sending splinters of wood across the marble floor. While careful thought had saved me from certain death before, I didn't have time to formulate a plan. Aiden's life hung in the balance.

Along the far wall stood a fireplace constructed from faded red bricks. It spanned the entire length of the room, and the hearth was so wide at least two vehicles could have parallel parked inside with plenty of room to spare.

A fire roared at its core, sending out immense waves of heat that seared my skin from where I stood some thirty feet away.

Who had built this? Giants?

"It's stunning, isn't it?"

The shadows in the room parted, revealing Ben standing to the right of the fireplace. Aiden still dangled in midair from the chains. His eyes were closed, and the shifting glow of the fire made it impossible to tell if he was breathing or not.

"Let Aiden go," I said, taking a step into the room.

Ben didn't reply. He turned to gaze into the fire. "It's truly a remarkable piece of masonry." He ran his fingers along the brick. The suggestive way he bit his lip made it seem as if he was caressing a lover's flesh instead of brick and mortar. "A true testament to fire fae construction, wouldn't you say?"

Anger once again built up inside me. Its currents churned deep in my soul, and it longed for release. "Let. Him. Go."

Ben glanced over his shoulder at me, a wry smile twisting his lips. "I'm pleased to see you're still alive," he said. "I'm not surprised though. You've managed to tap into the magic of this place. How did you do that?"

I had no clue, but I wasn't going to tell him that. "If you don't let Aiden go, I'll show you."

He chuckled. "You're not powerful enough to be a threat to me," he said, wagging his finger. "Don't go thinking you're all that, Thad. You've never encountered someone like me." He paused for a moment, a gleeful smile spreading across his lips. "No one has, in fact."

"And once you're dead, no one else will. Ever again."

"I agree," he said. He clasped his hands behind his back and strolled the length of the hearth. Like an obedient dog, the chains keeping Aiden suspended followed close behind.

Why was he talking to me instead of fighting? What was he waiting for?

"I'm rather unique," he finally said. "But I won't be dying any time soon. I can pretty much guarantee that."

His cockiness stoked my fury. I had to restrain myself from lunging at him and shoving him into the fire, but that was what he wanted. He was goading me into acting rashly. He was counting on my newly found emotions taking over, as they had before, and leading me into whatever trap Ben waited to spring.

I held on tightly to my restraints. I wouldn't make a move until he revealed his hand.

"Let me tell you a story," he said. He motioned toward two chairs across the room. One slid over to him, and the other crossed the room to me. He sat down and gestured for me to join him. When I didn't move, he shrugged. "Suit yourself.

"Did you know that centuries ago the Conclave forced all the fae here?" He waited for me to respond, but I'd already heard all this from Aiden. When I didn't, he continued, "The fae didn't want to leave our world. They loved it, but the Conclave insisted. Do you know why?"

"Because they are made of pure magic," I answered. It wasn't the whole truth, but I wasn't going to share what I knew with Ben. It was better to let him talk while I figured out how to save Aiden and get us out of here. "Had they stayed, it would have been impossible to keep our existence a secret."

He shook his head as if he were disappointed with me. "And here I thought you were the smart one. What you've been told is a lie fabricated by nine robed figures with more secrets than you can imagine."

Aiden had implied the same thing, but what did Ben know about the Conclave's secrets? More importantly, how could he know *anything* about them? They only associated with the protector covens, and our contact with them was minimal at best.

"They herded the fire fae here for their own selfish reasons," he said. "None of which had anything to do with keeping magic a secret. Unlike the rest of us, the fae are creatures of pure magic. Their link to the Gate is even stronger than ours, and the Conclave feared that power. The only way to solve their little dilemma was to make the fae depart our world, thereby removing their immediate threat. They will do anything to keep their stranglehold of power, anything at all. That's why I am here. To release the fae from their imprisonment." He studied the floor with great sadness and pain. "I know what it's like to live apart from everything and everyone else. Being kept in a jail of the Conclave's making."

I didn't trust every word that came out of his mouth, but the emotions behind his words told me part of his story was undoubtedly true. He had been the Conclave's prisoner. That must have been how the Conclave had known who the shadow weaver was, and if they were harboring secrets, it would even explain why they hadn't told us.

"I know you don't trust them," he said. "And you shouldn't. They aren't what you think they are."

"Yes, well, neither are you," I said. "You pretended to be a friend to my family. You were just using them. And me."

He jutted out his lower lip, pretending to pout. "Don't be upset with me," he said. He leaned back in his chair, shining his crooked smile in my direction. "I may have had ulterior motives, but believe it or not, I wanted you from the first moment I saw you. That's why I didn't let that vampyre kill you during Mabon. He wanted to. Very badly. But I saved you."

I scoffed. "You didn't save me. Mason did."

"You can't really believe that?" he asked with a laugh. "Your brother might be a burgeoning shadow weaver, but he's not exactly an experienced warlock. He'd just come into his powers, for fuck's sake! Do you really think someone with virtually no experience with his magic would have been capable of saving you?" He stared at me as if the answer was obvious. "It was me. Not Mason. I ordered the vampyre not to kill you when it had you in its grasp. That's what gave Mason the time to run in and save the day."

Was he telling the truth? I recalled the vampyre hesitating for a moment before Mason ran into the backyard. That was what had given me the time to freeze it and for Mason to use his shadow powers and send it packing.

My knees unlocked, and I fell back into the chair.

Ben stood up, slowly traipsing the distance between us. "There was something about you. The defiance in your eyes as you fought. The coldness with which you viewed the world. It reminded me a lot of myself when I was younger."

"I'm nothing like you," I mumbled. My eyes threatened to close, but I forced them open. Why was I so tired all of a sudden?

"But you are," he said, standing only a few feet away. "The way you viewed the world was the way I used to. Because I had no choice. My father demanded restraint. He forced me to control myself, much the same way you had lived your life in emotional shackles. I had no choice but to obey, to be what he wanted me to be. But I rebelled. I finally did what I wanted, and I paid the price for disobedience. My father stood by and watched as I was punished. He could have saved me, but he didn't. And because of him, I am what I am now."

"And what are you?" I asked. Only a foot separated Ben and me. He gazed down at where I sat, his brown eyes regarding me with the same overpowering desire I'd seen when we first met.

"I'm everything you could be too." He cupped my cheek in his hand, and my skin crawled upon contact. "All you have to do is let me in."

I stood, crossing the remaining space that separated us. "Is it that easy?"

A smile spread wide across his face. "It is," he said, reaching out to me. "Just take my hand, and neither of us will be lonely ever again."

I took his hand in mine, and when I did, he let loose a scream so loud, it echoed off the rafters.

BEN'S EYES grew wide as I poured all the gathered energy I had collected from Otherworld into him. He shuddered and convulsed before falling to his knees.

The idea had struck me when King Oberon incinerated the vampyre with his power. If the purity of fairy magic could kill a vampyre, then chances were good its natural radiance could do the same to someone whose power was darkness.

As if on cue, the shadows that clung about Ben were flung away as I dumped wave after wave of pure fae magic into him.

"What have you done?" he asked, attempting to pull his hand from my grasp. He glowed in a kaleidoscope of colors, as if a rainbow was attempting to force its way out of his skin.

"Giving you power," I replied before whispering a spell that turned my grip into steel. He wasn't going to get away from me. "Isn't that what you've been after all along?"

"I've been after you," he said.

His answer unleashed a hurricane of fury. It grew and swirled until I had no choice but to give it release before it shredded me from within. I increased the pressure of my grip and forced the remaining dregs of power into Ben in one concentrated burst. It crashed into him so hard, he flew backward out of my grip. He slammed into the brick fireplace and slid down its side.

"You played me for a fool," he mumbled. "I thought you were really considering choosing me at last."

"Are you fucking kidding me?" I asked. The winds of my anger howled. "Did you forget I can see the lines of your blood magic? *You* were trying to manipulate *me*! I could see you tugging on the strings, trying to get me to dance to whatever tune you happened to be singing."

He chuckled and winced at the same time. I'd inflicted some damage. It wasn't as much as I hoped, but it was a start. "You continue to surprise me," he muttered. "I won't underestimate you again."

"Good," I said, strolling over to the chains that clung to Aiden. If Ben was weak enough, my magic might break the restraints. I uttered a spell, and the chains shuddered before disappearing. Aiden fell into my arms, and I lowered him to the floor.

Dried blood caked his neck, and his breathing was extremely shallow. His already pallid flesh had grown even whiter. What had Ben done to him? "Aiden, can you hear me?"

His eyes fluttered open. He attempted to move, but he grimaced in pain. "Thad… you have to… get… away."

I wasn't going anywhere. "Not without you."

"You shouldn't underestimate me, either," Ben said behind me.

I turned to see Ben standing. He leaned against the fireplace. His brown eyes had gone black. Whatever emotions Ben may have felt for me, whether they were genuine or not, were gone. I'd attempted to kill him, and he was never going to forgive that.

"You can barely stand," I said. "You're in no shape to fight."

"I heal quickly," he said with a grin. "But until I'm up to snuff, I have others who will fight for me." He gestured to the shadows, and three figures emerged from the inky shroud.

It was my brothers and Drake. They were alive. I wanted to run to them, throw my arms around them and give them the biggest hugs I'd ever given them in my life, but red ropes of energy clung to them. They were being controlled by Ben's blood magic.

"It's time for your family reunion," he said, turning to my family. "Kill your brother."

I erected an ice wall as Pierce's electricity slammed into it. Blue sparks crackled all around me as he and Mason charged. I froze the ground around them, encasing their feet in ice. They cursed and fired volley after volley of electricity and shadow at my rampart. I had only a few minutes at most to get Aiden out of here and find a way to break the spell my brothers were under.

"Aiden, we have to go."

He waved me off, clutching his neck and stomach. "No," he said. His voice cracked like a whip, and his green eyes grew emerald hard. "Get out of here. Now!"

A huge arm wrapped around my neck and placed me in a stranglehold. It was Pierce. I kicked and flailed, trying to free myself from his grip, but he was too strong.

"Hold him still," Mason said. Shadows folded in front of him, weaving into a giant stake. "I want to look him in the eye while I kill him."

"I want to do it!" Pierce argued. Arcs of energy sizzled off his free hand. "He always thought he was better than me. It's time I proved him wrong."

"No," Drake said with his usual southern accent. He ambled over to us, a sly grin slanting his lips. "Let me do it."

"Fuck that!" Pierce said. "You're not even a warlock."

"That's right," Drake replied. "How humiliatin' would it be to know a human ended his life?"

My brothers laughed.

"Holy shit!" Pierce said. "That's perfect!"

Mason nodded. The darkness of his power infected his gaze.

As Drake drew closer, he winked at me, and that was when I noticed the red threads of energy hung slack around him. Blood magic had been cast on him, but it wasn't working. Just like when I'd given him that sleeping potion or when Mrs. Proctor tried to spell him.

He was somehow immune. Gerald Wa had been right. He was exactly the type of weapon we needed.

Drake raised the stake high. "You ready?"

"Yeah," Pierce replied, but Drake had been talking to me, not my brother.

I had no clue what he was planning on doing, but I had to be ready to act when he did.

He brought the stake down into Pierce's forearm. My brother hollered in pain, releasing me.

Although it pained me to do it, I froze Pierce solid. He was too powerful not to be taken out of commission.

Mason glared at Drake before lunging at me. "*Desine*," I uttered, and Mason stopped in his tracks, unable to move one muscle.

"Impossible!" Ben muttered. He didn't look as ragged as he had earlier. The color had come back into his cheeks, and he was able to stand without leaning against the brick wall for support. "How?"

"Your lame-ass magic don't work on me," Drake said. He pulled an athame out of his back pocket. When I saw the blade that had been blessed by my father, I smiled. Drake had had enough time to pull it from the backpack before the vampyren tossed them into the void between the two worlds.

"*Hupakoue moi,*" Ben said, grasping the red bands of energy that draped Drake.

"I will not obey you," Drake replied. His gift with language astounded me. The ropes of magic Ben tried to pull taut with his Greek incantation slid completely off Drake.

Ben's eyes grew wide, and he smacked his lips in hunger. "There's power in you," he said, inching his way closer. "I couldn't sense it before, but I can feel it now. I must have it."

"No, you won't," I said. I took a deep breath and exhaled a snowstorm. Wind and ice blinded Ben. He held his arms in front of his face, trying to block out the stinging barrage. Eventually, it became too much. He flew off his feet and crashed into the wall fifteen feet away.

Drake's blue eyes grew twice their size. "How the hell did you do that?"

I had no clue. "The idea popped into my head, so I did it," I replied. "Find a way to free my brothers. I've got a feeling you're the only one who can."

Drake nodded and darted over to Mason while I headed over to where Ben had fallen.

As I approached, he wiped the ice and snow from his face and laughed. "Your powers are growing rather quickly," he said. "You've *got* to tell me how that happened."

"You want to know?" I asked. "It was meeting Aiden."

His gaze grew sharp enough to cut me.

I laughed. "Yeah, I didn't think you'd like that answer. The moment I met him, something inside me changed. My life had been one frozen tundra of indifference. I didn't care about anything but my magic, my power, myself. But when I met Aiden, I thawed. I began to feel things again, like I used to when my mother was alive. He showed me it was safe to feel. It was okay to experience life and all the good and bad that came with it. And when I gave myself to him, I opened up a door that had frozen shut, and with each new emotion I've experienced since then, I've been able to do things I've never been able to do before."

A huge smile spread across Ben's expression.

"Do you find what I've said amusing?" I asked.

"I do," he said, sitting up against the wall in no apparent hurry to defend himself.

"Why?"

"I wonder what will happen to that newfound power when Aiden betrays you."

I snorted. "He's not like you."

"He's more like me than you realize," he said, pointing behind me. "Why don't you turn around and see for yourself?"

I glanced over my shoulder. Aiden walked toward me, dragging Drake's unconscious body behind him.

"Aiden?"

"I told you to get out of here," he said, his usually cheery voice turned stern and sour. His face contorted in pain as he underwent a complete metamorphosis. His strong, beautiful hands grew into talons, his full head of jet-black hair lengthened into long ratted locks, and his pretty pink lips turned chalk-white. When he opened his mouth, jagged rows of razor-sharp teeth snapped, and his tongue darted in the air as if it were alive.

"Yes," Ben said, suddenly standing by Aiden's side. "Isn't he beautiful? The first vampyre fae to ever exist. I don't know about you, but I can't wait to see what he can do."

For a few seconds, the Aiden I knew gazed at me. Regret filled his eyes, but he blinked it away. Anger sparked, and his tongue darted toward me, eager to satisfy his insatiable hunger.

AIDEN SLAMMED me against the wall. He wrapped his right hand around my neck, cutting off my oxygen. He dragged the talons on his left hand across my chest, ripping my shirt. "I can smell your blood," he said, towering over me. His tongue slithered toward me like a snake's. "I'm so hungry."

If I didn't do something fast, I'd end up being his first meal. I struggled against his grip and kicked his legs, groin, anything my feet could connect with, but he didn't flinch.

"Stop moving," he complained, shaking me like a rag doll before dangling me off the floor. The arms that had held me close as he made love to me last night threatened to choke the life out of me today.

His face drew closer, viscous, black liquid dripping from his lips. His eyes were mad with hunger, but deep within his bottle-green eyes, I could see Aiden. My Aiden. He fought his compulsion to kill me, the same instinct that had forced him to see me not just as the warlock he made love to in the Arbor but as the meal he couldn't wait to eat.

I had to reach out to the fae within the monster somehow. If I could get him to remember, to fight what Ben had turned him in to, we might still have a chance.

"Aiden," I choked out. I stroked his arm. I didn't see the white, withered flesh. In my eyes, the arms that restrained me were the same ones that had wrapped around me in the Arbor. The fingers that dug into my flesh were the same ones that had clutched me as he came inside me. The Celtic tattoo still circled his lean, muscled bicep. His lips were still pink and full of life. If I could see it, he had to as well. "Remember me. Remember us."

"Give it your best shot," Ben said, strolling away from us and over to the fireplace. "He'll eventually kill you, but watching you attempt otherwise amuses me. There's no stopping what will happen, though. A newborn vampyre only wants to feed. Nothing can prevent that."

I couldn't accept that. No, I *wouldn't* accept that. "It's me, Aiden. See me."

"No!" he shouted and flung me away.

I crashed into the opposite wall to the sounds of Ben's laughter. My head hit with such force, the world immediately went black. The waters of unconsciousness rushed through me, and I swam against the riptide. If I slipped beneath its surface, all would be lost.

I fought my drooping eyelids, and when I finally managed to get them open, Aiden stood above me, gnashing his teeth together.

"We can fight this," I mumbled. My vision spun, and it was difficult to focus. "Together. Just like we said we would."

"Oh, please," Ben said from across the room. He stood directly in front of the hearth, chanting some spell. "If I didn't have something more important to do than kill you, you'd be dead right now." The roaring fire inside the fireplace flickered before blazing to life once again. Whatever he was doing, the magical flame was fighting back. "Just kill him already and be done with it," he said, glancing over his shoulder at us.

Aiden reached down and yanked me to my feet. The intoxicating aroma of honeysuckle and cinnamon had been replaced by the acrid stench of rot.

I wrapped my arms around his neck, holding him tight. I pressed our foreheads together and leaned against him. Just like I had yesterday, I surrendered to his touch and to the emotions that lived within both of us.

Our connection was strong enough for Aiden to break Ben's blood tie. I only hoped I could awaken the fae I saw fighting within.

"I'm falling for you, Aiden," I said, clutching his back and nuzzling my cheek against his. "And you've fallen for me too. I know it's soon. Far too damn soon. But I don't care. I'm done with being careful. I'm finished thinking things through. For the first time in my life, I'm making decisions my heart wants me to make, and damn it, it wants you. Whether you're a fire fairy or a vampyre. It's you, Aiden. Only you."

I did the only thing left to do. I pressed my lips to his.

He went rigid as I delivered every feeling, every emotion I'd ever denied myself into our kiss. Magic purer than the fairy energy I'd briefly wielded flowed out of my trembling lips in wave after burning wave.

I cast aside every reservation, every fear I'd held on to like the scared little kid I was, and I became the warlock I'd always intended to be.

Aiden let go of my shoulders and pushed me away.

His chest heaved, and though the desire to cut my throat open still crouched at the edge of his vision, the Aiden I'd come to know stepped forth. "I can't fight this," he whispered. Guilt strangled his words as he continued to battle his newfound instincts. He closed the distance and placed his hands on my waist. His touch was gentle and loving. Whatever I'd done was working. "You've got to do what you made me promise to do."

I shook my head. There was no way I was going to kill him.

"You... must," he said through gritted teeth. He gripped my sides, not in anger or as a threat, but in pain.

I hooked his chin in my thumb and forced his gaze to mine. "No. We can fight this together. The way we have since the first moment we met."

"This is more powerful than either of us," he admitted. The tone of his voice changed. It grew harder, more like sandpaper than the usual lyrical quality of his pitch. The vampyre within surged forward again.

"Nothing is more powerful than us," I said. "I'm betting my life on it."

Aiden's eyes grew wide, and black liquid gushed out of his mouth and splattered all over me. What the hell was going on now?

"Oh shut the fuck up already," Ben said from behind Aiden.

I glanced down and noticed a shadowy stake jutting from Aiden's chest. He clutched it as Ben slowly withdrew it from Aiden's body.

"Aiden!" I shouted. He fell to his knees as black pools of blood sprayed my clothes and the marble floor.

The advancing monster that had almost overcome him drifted away, and his form returned to the fire fairy I'd first seen in the woods in Havenbridge. Except the black blood had reverted to fairy red, and a gaping hole now existed where I'd once laid my head.

Even though he had to be in tremendous pain, a smile wider than I'd ever seen before stretched across his lips. "And I've fallen for you too," he said collapsing onto his knees and then over onto his back.

I rushed to his side, tears blurring my vision. "No, Aiden. Don't go. Please don't leave me."

"I won't," he said. "I promise." His expression went slack, and his gorgeous green eyes closed.

"Not exactly what I wanted," Ben said, wiping Aiden's blood from the weapon he'd formed. "But I couldn't listen to that shit one moment longer."

His lips cracked into a satisfied smirk.

After that, the world turned white.

A BLIZZARD I didn't remember summoning filled the room. Ice and wind whipped around us, creating a whiteout. Though I stood only a few feet in front of Ben, he obviously couldn't see me. He squinted, scanning the area and holding up his hands to block the icy barrage.

I had no trouble seeing. This was my storm, and it responded to my will.

I commanded the ice to form into sharp needles and sent them barreling toward Ben. When they struck at thirty-five miles per hour, he howled in pain as salvo after salvo of tiny frozen daggers pierced his skin.

I would make him suffer for what he did to Aiden. Then I would kill him.

"Don't hide behind your storm," Ben screamed, trying to be heard above the roaring gusts. "Face me like a warlock."

"I am," I replied, making sure the wind whipped my voice around the room. That would make it difficult for him to find me. He swung his arms madly, sending shadowy tendrils blindly out into the room. They struck open air, not coming any closer than a few feet from where I stood. "I'm using your tactics. Letting my magic do the dirty work."

Ice formed along his skin and stung his eyes. As quickly as he wiped it from his face and mouth, more gathered on his flesh, working its way up his nose, where I hoped it would suffocate him. I wasn't just going to encase him. I planned on freezing him to the bone.

I wouldn't stop until his blood crystallized and his skin split and cracked. All I would have to do after that was punch him once and shatter him into a million pieces.

"You're just as pathetic as your fire fairy," he spat.

"Fuck you!" I screamed, and the fury of my storm intensified. The winds blew well past forty miles per hour, creating snowdrifts around him. He stumbled over them and slipped on the ice that covered the floor. He had no solid ground on which to fight.

Now was the time to strike.

With one upward gesture, the ice upon which Ben stood exploded in a bloom of sharp icicles. One pierced his right forearm and another tore through his left thigh. Two more ripped through his right foot, but the most damaging of them all was the largest one, which was at least six foot high and one foot wide. It impaled him from the back and jutted out of his chest.

Blood poured down his body and turned the ice around him scarlet.

I drew in a deep breath and called off the storm.

"There you are," he said, a gurgle of blood escaping his mouth. "Impressive."

I made a looping gesture with my hand, and the icicle embedded in his chest twisted forty-five degrees.

Ben wrapped his hands around the icy blade and screamed.

"Holy shit!" someone said to my right.

It was Mason. He and Pierce were awake, and the red bands of energy no longer coiled around them. They had been freed from Ben's blood magic.

Drake brushed away the snow that had collected on my younger brother's face as he gaped at Ben's mangled body. "That's fuckin' badass."

"I know," I said with a nod.

"How the hell did you do that?" Pierce asked. He stood up, using the wall for support.

I locked my gaze on Ben's. Even though he had been mortally wounded, it hadn't wiped the shit-eating grin from his lips. Why did my gut tell me this wasn't over? "It was Aiden," I finally answered.

My brothers glanced at each other before staring back at me. Before I could explain, the ground violently trembled.

"What's goin' on now?" Drake asked.

Another earthquake shook the world. Pierce fell onto his back while Mason and Drake were brought to their knees. They clutched each other as the walls of the castle keep swayed.

As if my feet were anchored to the floor, I stood my ground, glaring at Ben. Even though he continued to cough up blood, his smile never faltered.

"What have you done?" I asked.

He didn't answer. Instead he shot me a big grin as another tremor grabbed hold of the land and thrashed it.

Pieces of the roof crashed to the floor as the marble tile cracked and buckled. From the courtyard down below, the screams of the fire fae echoed off the walls.

"Still two steps behind me," Ben uttered.

I gestured again. Two more icicles sprouted from the patch of ice. One pierced his right hand while the other penetrated his armpit before tearing out of his shoulder. "Tell me," I commanded. "What have you done?"

He shook his head in disappointment. "Look around," he said. "What do you see? Or maybe I should ask, what do you *not* see?"

My gaze immediately shot to the hearth. The roaring fire had been snuffed out. Only the charred furnace remained.

"No!" I said. I ran to the fireplace, placing my hand along the bricks that had once been too hot to touch. They were as cold as the ice I'd created. The Hearthstone had been inside the flame. "Where is it?"

"Where's what?" Mason asked, straining to be heard over the death throes of fairyland.

"It's gone," Ben said. "The Hearthstone is mine."

I stormed back to Ben, an icicle forming in my hand. I raised it to his throat and pressed the sharp point into his flesh. A trickle of blood coursed down his neck, coating the emerald pendant he always wore on the chain around his neck. "Give it to me. Now!"

He blew a kiss at me. "Kinky," he said with a wink. "But no."

"I'll kill you right now if you don't."

"You can try," he replied.

I shoved my weapon into his throat, and his eyes went wide in surprise. He hadn't thought I would do it.

"What's happenin'?" Drake asked. The fear and uncertainty was evident by the tremor in his voice and the exaggerated drawl.

"He's destroyed Otherworld," I answered.

As if to verify my statement, another violent quake rattled the land. The far wall of the keep crumbled, sending tons of brick to the courtyard below. The columns supporting the roof groaned and split. In a few minutes, the entire structure would crash to the ground.

"We have to get out of here!" I gestured toward where the wall used to be and created a huge ice slide to the ground below. "Go now!"

Drake, Mason, and Pierce sprinted toward the exit while I headed back to Aiden. I scooped up his limp body and cradled him in my arms. I couldn't believe he was gone.

"You'll never make it out of here alive."

I stopped in my tracks and glanced over my shoulder. I watched in disbelief as Ben pulled out the icicle I'd jammed into his throat without flinching.

"What the hell are you?" I asked.

My brothers surrounded me, abandoning their escape in order to stay and fight.

"Did you really think any of this would kill me?" he asked, motioning to his body, which resembled a pincushion. "This hurts like a bitch, but it can't kill me." He snapped the end off the ice jutting from his chest before sliding off the projectile with a sharp inhalation. With a wave of his hands, shadowy tentacles shot from the corners of the room. They wrapped around the icy skewers and pulled them free at once. Ben let out a cry that rivaled the rumble of the quaking ground.

"You're not just a shadow weaver," I said. "You're a vampyre too."

My family gasped while Ben clapped. The wounds I'd inflicted began to close. "About time!"

As Otherworld convulsed around me, the last pieces of the puzzle slipped into place. He wasn't Ben Crane at all.

He was a warlock who was a vampyre. He'd been imprisoned by the Conclave. He had the power of darkness. He held his father responsible for what had become of him.

There was only one individual in the entire history of warlocks who fit that description.

"You're Ebenezer Kane," I said.

"At last!" he shouted. Shadows exploded around him as his form changed. Chocolate brown eyes turned as black as those of a great white. His flesh grew chalky. His fingers sharpened into talons, and when his lips parted in his cocky smile, black saliva dripped from razor-sharp teeth and a long gray tongue whipped around in search of blood. "It's so good to finally be noticed."

This wasn't good. Ebenezer Kane was the very first vampyre created through the *immortalitas* spell his father had cast to bring him back from the dead. That meant he'd been in existence for over three hundred years. Compared to him, we were in our magical infancy.

"We have to kill him," Pierce said.

Mason nodded. "Now, while he is weak."

Ben laughed. He lunged at my brothers. With one swipe of his claws, he sent them flailing backward. They tumbled over the ledge, landed on my ice slide, and slid to the courtyard below.

"Mason!" Drake screamed.

Before Ben could react, I uttered a spell that sent Drake floating off the floor and over the ledge, where he'd join my brothers.

"It's just you and me," I said, placing Aiden's body on the floor.

"Finally," Ben said. With the speed that his kind possessed, Ben leaped upon me and pinned me to the ground. He wrapped his hands around my neck as he lapped my cheek with his tongue. "I've been waiting for this moment for too long."

"Why are you doing this?" I asked as Ben kneeled on my wrists, preventing me from forming any more icicles that would damage him.

"Are you fucking kidding me?" he asked. Spit rained down on me as the anger that roiled inside him came spilling out. "I'm going to bring the world the Conclave has built down around their heads, piece by piece. And when it's been destroyed, when they are crawling through the rubble, I'm going to get drunk on their bloated bodies." He caressed my cheek, the anger briefly replaced by what appeared to be genuine affection. "And you could have been spared. No, you *would* have been spared had you embraced what I offered you."

"I'm going to kill you," I said through gritted teeth.

"You're not strong enough to kill me," he said, patting my cheek as if I were an errant child.

"No, but I am."

Fire slammed into Ben. He squealed and rolled off me, trying to put out the flames that scorched his body.

Aiden was behind us. He'd abandoned his fairy form and shifted into a vampyre. His tongue, which had once snaked its way to me, darted in the air toward Ben, and the hole in his chest had closed. "I can smell your weakness," he said. He positioned himself between Ben and me.

When the flames were snuffed, Ben rose and growled. "How are you alive? I ran a stake through your heart."

"A shadow stake, not a wooden one," Aiden replied.

The grin on Ben's face revealed he wouldn't make that mistake again. "Still, you're a baby vamp. You have no chance against me."

Aiden grinned as fire erupted in the palms of his hands. "Guess again."

Ben backed up, wrapping the shadows around him as armor. True terror shone in the depths of his cold eyes.

"We both know vampyren have a weakness to the fire of the fae," Aiden said.

"But you're a vampyre," he uttered. "How can you harness the flame?"

"Like you said, I'm the first vampyre fae. Not even I know what I can do." He paused, letting the information sink in. "Yet."

The encroaching shadows swirled around Ben before swallowing him whole. When they disappeared, Ben was gone.

Aiden turned to face me, reverting to the man I knew, the man I was falling in love with. "Are you okay?" he asked, helping me to my feet.

I fell into his arms, clutching onto him and fearing I'd never be able to let him go. I thought I'd lost him forever, that I'd never feel his skin against mine again. "Of course I am," I said between tears of joy. "You're alive."

He pulled out of the embrace and held me at arm's length, regarding me with sad, wet eyes. "But I'm not," he said. "Ben killed me and turned me into a vampyre."

"What's your point?" I asked, fighting against the muscled grip that refused to allow me into the embrace I required. "You're here. That's all that matters."

"No, Thad. It's not." He squeezed my shoulders once before letting go and stepping back. "I'm a danger to you."

"That's ridiculous," I said. I pushed my way past his protesting arms and pressed my body against his.

He tensed and refused to hold me. His arms remained slack at his side. He was pushing me away, trying to save me from the threat he believed he now posed. I didn't buy it. No matter what Ben might have done to him, he was still Aiden. That would never change.

"I'm a monster now," he whispered.

"No, you're not," I said, pulling out of the one-sided hug. I cupped his cheek, flitting my fingertips across the creamy flesh that brought love, not fear. "I see only the man who took my breath away. The one who made me feel again." I grabbed his hand and placed it on my chest. "The one my heart beats for."

He withdrew his hand from me and averted his gaze. He swallowed hard and shuddered as if he were fighting an inner conflict I knew nothing about. "You can't see me that way anymore. That's who I was." He shifted in form and stood before me as a vampyre. "This is who I am now."

I didn't see the talons, the razor-sharp teeth, or the tongue that searched the air for blood. All I saw were the rich, emerald eyes that had entranced me from the first moment I'd seen him. That was where the true Aiden resided.

"How you look on the outside doesn't matter to me," I said, spanning the distance he had created between us. I stood impervious to the nightmare he clearly believed he was. And to anyone else, that might be what they saw. I wasn't anyone else.

I was Thad Blackmoor, and I was in love with Aiden Teine.

Aiden used his vampyre speed to sprint to the other side of the room. "Stay away from me!" he warned as he sniffed the air and moaned. "I haven't eaten, and I'm starving. It's taking every ounce of control I have not to rip open your throat." He threw his hands in front of his face, mortified by the impulses that threatened to take over.

"But you are controlling yourself," I said. I uttered a spell that sped me to his side before Aiden could move. He jumped in surprise when I wrapped my arms around him and held him tight.

"Are you crazy?"

"Yes," I said. "For you." Though he tried to step back, I didn't let him. I clung to him, refusing to let go.

He gripped my waist as his urge to hold me won out against his need to feed from me.

"I trust you," I said, nuzzling him into the crook of my neck.

He jumped back and pulled away. "What are you doing?" He sniffed the air and groaned. "I told you I haven't eaten, and you smell delicious. I could kill you."

"You could, but you won't." I'd never been more certain about anything in my life, and that was more than wishful thinking. That was pure logic talking.

"How do you know?" he asked.

"Because I know you."

"That's not good enough."

"Fair enough," I said. "So how about this? Ben said there has never been a vampyre fae before, and no one knows what you're capable of, right?"

"I know what I'm capable of," he said, shutting his eyes. "Because everything inside me is telling me to slash open your neck and eat."

"Not everything," I replied, stroking his cheek.

He opened one eye and glared at me, clearly unconvinced.

"If everything inside you was telling you to kill me, you would have done it by now. I've had enough experience with vampyren to know that. But that's not what you're doing. You're not only controlling yourself, but you fought against Ben. Other vampyren wouldn't have been able to do that. He created them the same way he created you, yet you resisted that urge to join him in favor of protecting me."

"I had to," he said. His defenses were falling. "I couldn't let him hurt you."

"Exactly. That tells me your fae nature is just as strong as your new vampyren instincts."

As he mulled over the possibility, the vampyre gave way to the fire fae as he changed forms once again.

"See what I mean?" I said.

Aiden glanced down at hands that were no longer talons. "I'm me again," he said, surprised.

"You've always been you," I replied. "I never doubted that for a moment."

This time he pulled me into his arms and held me tight. "You're not afraid?" he asked. "Because I still want to eat you real bad."

I leaned back and grinned. "Oh, you can eat me if you want."

He laughed. "Sex jokes? Really? At a time like this."

I pressed my forehead against his. "We'll figure this out. I promise. And we'll do it together."

"Are you sure you want to risk it?"

I molded my lips to his as my answer.

AIDEN FLEW us out of the castle keep when another tremor shook the land. The towers and walls of the kingdom collapsed in on themselves, turning the once-glorious kingdom into a mound of red brick. We spotted the fire fae a few feet beyond the castle walls, where they had gathered. They wept at the sight of their destroyed beloved home, but as we drew closer, their gazes snapped to us.

Their keen abilities no doubt had already sensed the change in Aiden.

When we landed, we were met with drawn fire swords.

"He's a vampyre!" one of them shouted, inching forward.

Aiden hissed at the threat. He drew me closer, putting himself between the weapon and me. My brothers, who were clearly confused, regarded Aiden before settling their gazes on me. Their arched eyebrows asked if what they'd heard was true.

I patted Aiden on the shoulder, motioning for him to put me down. When he did, I stepped in front of him and the angry faces. "No matter what he is now, he's still Aiden."

My brothers' jaws hit the ground, and if Drake's eyes could have grown any wider, they would have popped out of his head.

"It can't be," King Oberon muttered. He inched forward, gazing into the green eyes that resembled his own. A woman who I guessed was Queen Una stood behind her husband. She had hair as thick and black as Aiden's.

"It's true, Dad," Aiden replied. He shimmered, taking on his vampyren form.

"Holy shit!" Pierce mumbled.

Everyone else shared my brother's sentiment. The flaming swords they had drawn were quickly snuffed out, and tears fell from their eyes. What further atrocities would their kind suffer today?

The queen strolled up to her son. She cupped Aiden's cheeks in her hands. "How is this possible?"

After I told them what happened, no one spoke. King Oberon stood in silence as the fae waited to see how their liege would react.

Queen Una couldn't hide behind the veil of nobility. She was a mother first and a queen second. Tears poured down her cheeks as she took her son in her arms. The only thing that obviously mattered to her was that her son had been hurt, and she gave Aiden what he needed—a mother's love.

Aiden wept in her arms, reverting back to his normal form. He clutched her as his grief fled him in violent spasms.

I had hoped for the rest of his kind to follow suit, but they did not. His people eyed him suspiciously. They trusted him about as much as my brothers did. From the looks on Pierce and Mason's faces, they were clearly planning the most effective way to kill the man I loved.

"What's the matter with you people?" I asked. My tone was sharp, and I intended it to cut deep.

The fire fae flinched in response while King Oberon regarded me with regal indifference.

"This is your prince, not some deranged killer you've come across. The real bad guy, the one responsible for all this mess," I said, gesturing to the shattered landscape before taking Aiden's hand in mine. "That guy is gone because Aiden fought him off. He almost killed the shadow weaver, who forced each and every one of you to do his bidding. It's because of him you are all still alive, and you dare to look at him as if *he's* evil."

I turned my anger on my brothers and Drake, who still weren't convinced. "You should all be ashamed of yourselves."

"You can't be serious," Mason said. "We both know what his kind can do."

"And what about you, Shadow Weaver?" I asked. "I think we all know what your kind can do too, don't we?"

That shut Mason up. His only comeback was a scowl.

"You know what Mason's tryin' to say," Drake said, coming to his boyfriend's rescue. "The vampyren have been tryin' to kill us for weeks now. Hell, they killed my aunt Millie and turned her into a vampyre. She loved me before she turned, but she tried to kill me. Why is Aiden any different?"

I blew out a lungful of air and calmed myself down. This wasn't easy for anyone, and I wasn't making it any easier by getting upset. When I'd gotten control over my emotions, I continued, "Because Aiden's not human. Your Aunt Millie was," I finally answered. "Fae aren't like humans or even warlocks. They are beings of pure magical energy, given life by the Gate to fulfill the duties of nature. Their bodies don't expire like ours do."

King Oberon reluctantly agreed. "When a fae passes, his energy returns to the Gate. We don't wither and decay."

"That's what makes Aiden different. When a human or a warlock is turned, he dies and is reborn as a mindless, bloodthirsty vampyre, but that's not what happens to fae. The curse of the *immortalitas* spell obviously works differently for them."

"I have heard enough," the king said. He was aware of the distrust still spreading among the fire fae. He moved his wife and me aside. "The warlock is right. I don't know what any of this means. I'm your father, and I accept you with open arms. I always will."

Aiden flung himself into his father's arms. Tears streamed down his face, and a relieved smile replaced the fear he'd previously worn.

"But I'm not just your father," he said, pulling out of the embrace. He took a step back, pain etched into each aged line of his face. "I'm also a king, responsible for the safety and welfare of my people."

The fire fae murmured their approval while Aiden glanced back and forth from his subjects to his father. "I don't understand."

I did. I stepped around the king and took Aiden's hand in mine.

"I have to make decisions for our tribe and all the fae who look to the Royal Fae Court to keep them safe."

Queen Una grasped her husband in grief.

"You must leave," he said. He swallowed hard, the words sticking in his throat. "And you should never return."

I could practically hear Aiden's heart break. He gaped at his father, unable to process the words.

"Are you stupid?" I asked. My question drew the sneers of the fae, and their swords once again returned. Even though my brothers didn't trust Aiden, they sprinted to my side, ready to protect me. "You can't stay here, either. The Hearthstone is gone. If you stay, you will die."

The king waved away my concerns. "Your kind has always underestimated mine," he said. "I would thank you for your assistance, but our world lies in ruins because of you and your Conclave." He gestured, and a ring of fire completely surrounded us.

"What the hell?" Pierce asked. Blue lightning streaked from his clenched fists.

"Go home," he said. The ground beneath us disappeared and for a moment we hung, suspended in the air.

"Good-bye, Dad," Aiden managed to choke out before the five of us fell through the portal and into the void between worlds.

THE PORTAL opened up in the middle of the living room of Blackmoor Manor, and we fell to the ground in a heap.

"Fuck!" Pierce cursed. He landed on his back, and Mason landed on top of him.

"Thanks for breaking my fall," Mason said. Pierce cursed and shoved him off.

"Boys!" my father yelled. He charged into the room, wearing his stone armor. Our thunderous entrance had no doubt made him think the house was under attack. When he saw us on the floor, his rock form disappeared, and he sprinted to our sides. "You're finally back. It's been almost a week."

I returned the confused gazes of everyone in the room. "We've only been gone two days."

"All that matters is you're safe," he repeated over and over as he inspected each of us from head to toe.

"We're alive," I said without much enthusiasm. I was too busy watching Aiden. He sat up and pulled his legs to his chest, looking like a lost child.

Dad was too caught up by our return to notice my mood. He pulled Mason up from where he sat and gave him a big bear hug.

"Aw, man! Cut it out." Mason grimaced when Dad grabbed him and delivered a huge peck to the top of his head. "I'm not broken."

"Speak for yourself," Drake said.

Dad pulled Drake into a giant embrace. "At least someone enjoys my fatherly concern."

Drake hugged him back while Pierce groaned. "When did you turn into a witch?" Pierce asked.

Instead of shooting my brother a warning glance, Dad released Drake and tugged Pierce into his arms, kissing his cheek. "You're not going to rile my temper tonight. I'm just glad you're back in one piece." He smacked my brother on the back of his head. A devious grin lit up his face. "But tomorrow, you'll pay for that."

Pierce smiled, clearly accepting the consequences.

He arched an eyebrow at Aiden, who had yet to move or say a word. "Where's Ben?" Concern quickly replaced his delight over seeing his sons alive when everyone believed we wouldn't return.

Instead of answering, my brothers and Drake exchanged glances. They then turned to me, expecting me to do the honors.

Dad followed their gazes. "Thad?" he asked. "What happened to Ben?"

I let out a long exhalation before filling my father in.

"Ebenezer Kane has been alive all this time? And he was here? In *my* house?"

When we all nodded, he fell back on the sofa. "You're going to have to give me a minute," he mumbled.

He could take as long as he wanted. Aiden needed me.

"Are you okay?" I asked, kneeling by him. He stared at the wall, but that wasn't what he was seeing. His eyes had glassed over. He was most likely replaying the last few moments we'd spent in Otherworld.

"No," he said.

I sat behind him and pulled him to me. His back rested against my chest as I squeezed him tight, attempting to fill the huge hole being banished from his home by his father had caused. "I know," I finally said. "And I'm here. For whatever you need."

"What happened?" My father stood over us. He rested his hands on his hips and studied us with the eyes of a parent. He could tell something was wrong. "Are your people okay, Aiden?"

"They're not my people anymore," he muttered.

Dad cocked one eyebrow at Aiden before gazing at me. "Care to explain?"

"It's complicated," I answered.

He turned to my brothers and Drake. "Well, someone needs to answer me. Just what the hell happened?"

A voice echoed around us. "We're interested in hearing what transpired as well."

The Conclave blinked into existence in the middle of our living room. Gerald Wa stepped forward and lowered his hood. "I'm glad to see you've returned."

"Don't you mean surprised?" Mason asked. He hadn't trusted the Conclave since Mabon, and the latest turn of events had me right there with him.

Gerald shot him a glance before he covered his irritation with a thin smile. "No," he said. "I had faith you would succeed and return."

"You're only half right," Pierce said.

Gerald gathered his gray robes and studied Aiden. He tilted his head to one side and a strange expression played across his face. It was a mixture of surprise and curiosity. He then sat down on the wingback chair. "Tell us what happened."

"What would you like to hear first?" I asked. "That someone we knew turned out to be our enemy? That we couldn't stop him from stealing the Hearthstone and possibly destroying Otherworld? Or do you want the really juicy stuff? Like the fact that Aiden has been turned into a vampyre and cast out of fairyland?" My chest heaved, and the temperature inside the room dropped.

All the anger I still harbored since Ben's betrayal surged forth. My breath plumed out of my mouth while snow flurries fell from the ceiling. Ice formed along the windows, sending crystallized trails snaking across the panes.

"Aiden's been turned into a what?" my father asked.

"A vampyre," I said, speaking to Gerald instead of my father. I clenched my hands as the ground underneath me froze.

"We can discuss all those things in a moment," Gerald answered. He wiggled his fingers, and my advancing freeze halted before completely reversing. The frozen patch of ground retreated, the ice melted on the windows, and snow stopped falling on the wooden floor. "First, we need to discuss your anger."

"Do you think that's wise?" I asked. The Conclave was responsible for everything we'd been through. Their lies and secrets covered an agenda.

My father tried to calm me down, but I pulled away. So what if I pissed off the Conclave? They might turn my bones to powder with a single thought, but they were the ones who needed to answer questions. Not me.

"Speak your mind," Gerald said, lacing his fingers in front of his face. "You have much to say."

"Why didn't you tell us Ebenezer Kane was still alive?" I asked.

He sighed. His eyes darted back and forth in that infuriating way when he was magically communicating with the Conclave. Why couldn't they for once just speak out loud? "Because his continued existence has been a much guarded secret. How do you think the magical community would have responded had it known such a powerful creature was still alive?"

"Why was he?" Dad asked. The distrust Mason had started and that I helped fan had begun to burn in my father. It pleased me to see he was no longer acting the part of a soldier. "We'd all been led to believe the Conclave of his time had eliminated him."

Gerald nodded as he studied us. He and the rest of the Conclave could no doubt sense our suspicions. Only Pierce gazed at them as he always had, with respect and reverence, while Aiden still sat on the floor, not really paying attention to the world around him. "And that is what they wanted everyone to believe," he finally said. "They instead kept him prisoner."

As I suspected, lies compounded by cover-ups. And we were supposed to trust them? "Why the hell did they do that?" I asked. "That makes no sense whatsoever."

"I won't disagree," Gerald replied. "But that was not *this* Conclave's decision. That choice was made by those who came long before us."

That didn't get them off the hook. *That* Conclave might have spared him, but *this* Conclave and every Conclave since that time had kept him alive. "You allowed him to live."

"Because we needed him in case the *immortalitas* spell was ever uttered again," he said. He realized only the truth would turn this around. The Conclave might be the most powerful of us all, but they needed us as much as we needed them. "Though steps were taken to eradicate the knowledge of that incantation from every book of spells in existence, we couldn't guarantee it would not somehow be unearthed. If it ever was, we could use our studies of Ebenezer Kane through the years to find a way to combat a new horde of vampyren. Or at the very least use blood magic to make him do our bidding to even the odds."

I couldn't believe my ears, and neither could the rest of my family. My father's lips moved but no sound issued forth. Mason shook his head in disbelief. Even Pierce clued in on the magnitude of what Gerald had just revealed.

The Conclave had broken their laws by using blood magic on Ben.

"You were the ones who taught him blood magic." I pronounced every word as an indictment. "That explains why Ben knew how to cast it. By using it on him all these years, you inadvertently taught him everything he needed to know to cast it himself, and you made him even more powerful than he was."

"We realize that," Gerald admitted. "Now."

Pierce finally found his voice. "You're the ones who forbade blood magic to begin with."

"And we still do," he said, rising from the chair. He crossed to me, his gray eyes wide with friendship. His gaze pleaded with me to remember he was my friend, not my enemy, and I did my best. While Gerald had kept secrets, he'd most likely done it at the will of the majority. He'd proven to me he was willing to help when he could.

I had to give him the benefit of the doubt.

"I know you think our decisions foolish, and perhaps they are." The eight robed figures behind him mumbled. He shushed them, then gripped my hands in his and held them tight. "But we were doing what we thought best to protect our kind. That was our only motive."

I could buy that. Sometimes those in charge had to act against the principles they'd established to protect the greater good. That was what Aiden's father had just done. It was true of any government, and like human politics, the Conclave was flawed. They knew that, and now they knew we knew that. It was a start.

"Did you know Ben was Ebenezer Kane?" I asked.

"Goodness, no!" he said. His eyes grew wide, and he seemed offended that the thought had crossed my mind. Either he was a good actor, or he was telling the truth. I had to believe it was the latter and not the former. "Had we known, we would have immediately taken care of it. We had no clue where Ebenezer Kane was once we discovered his empty cell. We could only hope his whereabouts and plans would be stopped. That was why we sent only you and your brothers to Otherworld. If he attacked while you were gone, and there were no protector covens around, the Gate would have been too easy a target for him."

"But he was with us," I said. "And what he wanted was there. Why did he take the Hearthstone? What can he do with it?"

Gerald scanned the air for several minutes. The rest of the Conclave didn't want him to answer. "I can't say," he said after glaring over his shoulder at his brethren. "But I will tell you that by itself, the Hearthstone is useless to him."

"So what does he need to make it useful?" my father asked.

"That is a discussion for another time," he quickly answered. That meant he would say no more, no matter how much we pushed. I had to accept that. For now. "Our present goal will be to locate Ebenezer and take back the Hearthstone. That will eliminate any threat and prevent whatever he might be planning."

"And what about the fae?" Aiden asked. He approached us, his shoulders slumped and misery etched onto his face. I took his hand, lacing his fingers with mine. He straightened in response to my touch. Gloom still held him in its tenacious grip.

"The fae will not perish, but Otherworld will continue to die without the Hearthstone," he answered. Gerald glanced at our joined hands, and a strange smile spread across his lips. "If we can find it and return it, your world will rebuild itself."

"And if we don't?" Pierce asked.

Gerald didn't answer right away, and he wasn't magically talking to the Conclave either. He was looking for the best way to phrase his answer. "We will have to find an alternative place for them to live. One that is *not* here."

His tone, not his answer, piqued my curiosity. The idea of the fae returning to our plane troubled Gerald and most likely the rest of the Conclave. Had Ben been telling the truth? Did the fae somehow threaten the power of the Conclave, or was there another reason?

Gerald threw me a cautionary glance and shook his head. He had read my thoughts, and for some reason, he didn't want my musings to reach the rest of the Conclave.

"What about me?" Aiden asked. While the pain of being kicked out of Otherworld continued to sting, he met Gerald's gaze with his usual confidence.

"I'm uncertain, young prince," Gerald answered.

"I'm no longer a prince," he admitted, devoid of any emotion.

Gerald nodded in understanding before he studied Aiden from head to toe. "During our conversation, there has been much discussion taking place regarding you. It's been quite annoying listening to the constant buzzing in my head." He snapped around to glare at the Conclave.

"And?" I asked.

"Ah, silence at last," Gerald said with a smile. The internal communication link had evidently been severed. He addressed Aiden and shook his head. "I just don't have an answer. There's never been a vampyre fae before. We will need to study you more closely. Figure out what your presence means."

"You will not experiment on him or imprison him," my father said. His voice turned low and gravelly. He was in protective papa mode, and he stepped between Aiden and the Conclave. I couldn't love him more than I did at that moment. "He's a victim. He didn't ask to be turned, and he sure as hell doesn't deserve to be treated the way he has been."

Gerald regarded my father carefully. "What do you recommend?"

Dad placed his hands on Aiden's shoulders. "He can stay here with us."

"What?" Pierce asked. He didn't agree.

Mason practically jumped out of his skin. "You can't be serious."

The disappointment in Dad's eyes as he glared at my brothers couldn't have been more obvious.

"Thank you, Mr. Blackmoor," Aiden said. "But I'm too dangerous. Too unstable to live with your family."

"You're not any more dangerous than the rest of us," he replied.

And he was right. Mason was a shadow weaver who had yet to reach his full potential, my powers were growing, and Drake had immunity to magic no one had quite figured out yet. And Pierce? Well, he was often a dumbass. With his power, that alone made him a threat.

"Then it's decided," Gerald replied quickly. I was expecting more of a fight. He held up his hand to the rest of the Conclave, cutting off their protests before they started. He then plucked a book bound in gray leather from the sleeve of his robe. "Take this," he said, handing it to me.

"What is it?"

"It's what we've learned about vampyren over the years," he answered. "It will hopefully help you and Aiden navigate the rough waters ahead and perhaps even provide you with answers."

Was there hidden meaning in his comment? But I couldn't pursue that now, not after what was a rather magnanimous gesture that would no doubt cause him some problems with the rest of the Conclave. "Thank you," I said.

Gerald Wa winked at me before rejoining the Conclave. "We will be in touch," he said, pulling the hood up over his head.

A second later they were gone.

CHAPTER 10

THANKS TO the book Gerald gave us, we were able to use the information the Conclave had learned over the years to understand the vampyre curse and help Aiden.

For one, his ability to remain in his fae form wasn't a fluke.

It was a common belief that once a person turned into a vampyre the individual he was disappeared and was replaced by the monster he had become.

We knew from experience that wasn't entirely true.

Ben had been able to pass as a warlock, and when he was in his vampyre form, he hadn't lost control to the bloodthirsty haze. We'd originally believed that to be impossible, that the ferocious nature of the vampyre established dominance.

But that wasn't always the case, especially for those of us blessed with magic.

Over the years, it had been documented that Ben had learned how to temper the base vampyre instinct, and with practice Aiden's already astounding control would only grow. This meant he wouldn't be a danger to me or anyone else. Well, at least to anyone who didn't deserve a vampyre ripping into them.

That had eased Aiden's burden regarding his new existence. He wasn't quite the monster he thought he was, but he wasn't the fae he had previously been either.

The vampyre curse was more like a magical virus.

Once someone was infected, it destroyed life before resurrecting it in a new form. That was what Bartram Kane had done to his son.

Ben came back as an undead monster who created others just like him.

While it had a similar effect on Aiden, the process differed since he was fae.

What that fully meant remained to be seen, but at least we now had information, and with facts, I could do just about anything.

A positive side effect of the gained knowledge meant my brothers and Drake could relax the constant vigil they kept, waiting for Aiden to snap and kill us all in our sleep.

"Where's your bloodsucking boyfriend?" Pierce nudged me in the shoulder on his way past, where I made a late-night snack.

"Resting," I replied. It had been a long couple of weeks. Although Aiden didn't need to feed constantly due to his fae nature, he had to drink blood every few days. He'd hunt in the woods behind Blackmoor Manor, preying upon the deer and other animals he came across. Drinking blood kept him alive, but the guilt weighed heavily upon him.

The fae were vegetarians, and he'd never harmed an animal for food before. He'd been almost completely distraught after his first hunt. It hadn't gotten much better since then.

With what I'd been gathering in my research, though, I might just have an alternative.

"Have you bought him a coffin yet?" Mason asked from the kitchen table. He crunched an apple with a satisfied smirk while Drake read through some of the books from the library. It appeared I wasn't the only one who was having trouble sleeping.

Drake looked up from the one he was currently reading and smacked his boyfriend's shoulder. "Be nice," he said before resuming his studies. Since returning from Otherworld, he'd taken an even stronger interest in magic. His immunity no doubt intrigued him, and like me, he was trying to figure out what it all meant, but that wasn't the only subject that interested him.

He hoped to find some way to help his aunt Millie.

Unlike us, humans infected with the vampyre curse lost themselves to the virus that seized their systems. It was what made them so deadly and also easy to control. A vampyre who didn't lose himself to the savagery could manipulate the simple needs of those who did.

Whether he'd find anything useful, I couldn't say.

Plus, we didn't even know if Aunt Millie was still alive after being chased away by the fire fae. Drake continued to hold out hope that what we learned from Aiden could somehow transfer to her.

"Listen to your boyfriend," I told Mason, who shot Drake a pretend scowl. "You'll live longer."

Drake agreed, and Mason replied with a raspberry.

"I'm not afraid of you, Thad," Mason said with a proud jut of his chin. "I'm a fucking shadow weaver."

I stared blankly at him before cutting my gaze to Pierce. My older brother apparently found Mason's bravado as irritating as I did. He needed to be brought down a couple of rungs and reminded he was still our little brother.

Pierce's big grin told me he agreed.

"What the hell are you two up to?" Mason asked, standing up from the table. "Don't make me hurt you."

"As if you could," Pierce sneered. A spark of electricity flew out of his index finger and zapped Mason in the groin.

"Fuck!" he howled. He covered his junk and winced. "That hurt." The shadows that slept in the corners of the kitchen came to life, inching their way toward Pierce.

I flicked my wrist in Mason's direction, and the shadows retreated. His eyes grew wide, and he hopped up and down, howling. Drake peeked over his book to see what the fuss was, and when Mason pulled down his pants and emptied the ice I'd formed in his briefs, he giggled.

"Nice," Drake replied with a drawl and a grin.

"Whose side are you on, you traitor?" Mason asked.

Drake blew him a kiss before continuing to scan the pages before him.

Mason hissed and grumbled. He wiped the frozen crystals off his junk and glared at me. "You're so gonna pay for that."

I wasn't worried. My abilities had grown since meeting Aiden. My love for him had unlocked power I'd no clue I possessed. If Mason tried to exact revenge, his balls would never recover from the frostbite.

"Are you three done screwing around?" my father asked as he walked into the room. He eyed the half-naked Mason and rolled his eyes. "Let's keep the little general in the bunker if you don't mind."

"Little's right," Pierce snickered.

Mason tucked himself back into his pants and zipped up. He rubbed his hands together, concocting revenge. "Just you two wait."

"Bring it," I said, taking a big bite of my sandwich.

"How's Aiden today?" my father asked. He stole the protein shake Pierce had just made and joined Drake at the table.

"He's okay," I replied while my brother grumbled about his stolen drink.

"We haven't seen him much the past few days."

Pierce and Mason nodded at my father's statement, waiting for me to fill them in. Drake even put down his book to hear what I had to say.

"He's still adjusting," I finally replied.

Dad nodded, expecting that answer. "How's his appetite?"

Aiden's desire for food other than blood was improving, but it wasn't where it should be. If he was truly going to master his vampyre side, he had to eat our food every now and then. We all knew that.

"It's getting better." It was a white lie, but I didn't want to say anything that would bring about my brothers' previous fretting.

"I hope so," Mason said. "I know he doesn't like eating deer and shit, but it's better than us. I've just stopped sleeping with one eye open."

"He's not going to eat you," I said. "He says you smell funny."

Mason started before sniffing his underarms. "What the hell does that mean?"

Dad poked him in the chest. "It means you need to bathe more. I'm always telling you that."

"He has to eat," Pierce said. His serious tone brought the light-heartedness to a halt. "We might need him in the weeks to come."

There were still so many unanswered questions. What did Ben want with the Hearthstone? What was his endgame? And even though I tried not to dwell on it, how much of what Ben had told me about the Conclave was true?

Those were answers we needed to find, and getting them was most likely going to lead us down darker paths than we had traveled so far. Having Aiden on our side, a powerful combination of fairy and vampyre, might turn the tide in our favor.

"Don't worry," I finally said. "You know me, always searching for solutions."

Dad finished Pierce's protein shake and tossed the empty plastic cup into the trash. "You'll find them, son. I have no doubt about that."

The pride that filled his eyes when he looked at me caused a lump to rise in my throat. When was the last time that had happened? "Thanks, Dad."

When he left the room, Mason returned to strutting around the kitchen like a peacock. As usual, Pierce took the bait. They wrestled and used their powers on each other while Drake read his book. He acted as if my brothers and their chaos didn't exist.

The old me would have glared at them disdainfully, telling them their antics were juvenile. But I wasn't that Thad anymore. My icy interior had thawed, and in its place now lived a warlock who wanted to hurl snowballs at his brothers and then run and hide.

Thad, come to the library.

I stiffened when the familiar voice spoke in my head.

After our last meeting with the Conclave, I'd been waiting for this. Gerald Wa was here, and he wanted to talk in private.

WHEN I entered the library, Gerald was waiting for me by the desk. On top of it sat the book he'd given me that documented the Conclave's findings on Ben throughout the years.

"I trust this has proved useful," he said.

He wasn't here to discuss Aiden. There were other subjects he wanted to tackle. "Yes, thank you," I said. "It's made the transition somewhat bearable."

"I'm pleased," he said with a smile that told me he wasn't quite ready to discuss what had actually brought him here. "I took quite a beating agreeing to let Aiden stay with you. The others wanted to take him back and study him. They are still debating this as we speak."

I got the message. He was asking me to make sure he didn't regret his decision. "Everything will be fine. Aiden's control is getting stronger. He spends more time in his fae form than as a vampyre. He only shifts to hunt."

Gerald exhaled. The news offered some relief.

"Tell the Conclave that being kept a prisoner for centuries drove Ben mad. I believe that is partially to blame for the problems we face today."

He averted his eyes and nodded. He felt the same way, and the burden of his guilt weighed heavily upon his shoulders. "That's why I'm here. To discuss Ebenezer Kane."

I had figured that out already. There had been more the wizard wanted to say when he was here the last time. The urgent look in his eyes told me that much, but he couldn't say whatever was on his mind in front of the others.

For whatever reason, this information was for my ears only.

"What is it?" I finally asked.

"Before I tell you, I need to ask you something." He crossed the room and stood before me. Worry hooded his usually kind gray eyes.

"There's something you haven't told us about your time in Otherworld, isn't there?"

There was. I had yet to reveal Ben's green pendant, the one he'd so lovingly caressed. It was a talisman of some power, and with my current distrust of the Conclave, I hadn't felt safe sharing what I knew with them. My gut told me to hold onto that information and keep it even from my family. I didn't know why, but one thing I'd learned since meeting Aiden was to trust my emotions and not hide from them.

When I nodded, Gerald returned the gesture. "As I thought. What is it?"

I still questioned whether I should speak of it or not. I'd been secretly searching magical texts for references to an emerald stone with a lily on its face, but my efforts had turned up nothing.

That wasn't a big surprise. Our texts certainly had proven incapable of holding all the answers we needed. The history of the fae had not been fully reprinted, nor what was truly known about the vampyren. Some unseen hand had effectively rewritten our history for a purpose I had yet to learn.

"You don't trust me," he said. He cast his eyes downward, hurt.

I didn't trust anyone besides Aiden and my family. I hadn't shared what I knew with them because I wasn't sure if knowing would put them in more danger. Ben had hidden the pendant for a reason, and if he knew others suspected it was important, I might place them even further in harm's way. "Let's just say I'm guarded," I said.

Gerald nodded. "I understand. Far more than you realize. I know you feel as if the Conclave has lied to you, and for all intents and purposes, we have. We have kept secrets and told half-truths in our attempts to protect our species and the Gate."

"And where has that gotten you?"

"Precisely where we are," he said, motioning between us. "It has wrought distrust, and in order for us to come out of this on the other side, we must rebuild that bridge. This is something I hope you and I can do together."

I would have liked nothing better, but I had my doubts of that ever happening. "How do we do that?"

"I possess information, and so do you. If we share what we know between just the two of us, we can begin to set things right."

It made sense, but I wasn't going first. "You start."

"Before I do, I must ask that you keep this between us. It is far too sensitive to be shared with anyone. Not your family or even Aiden. There is more danger afoot than you realize, and only by placing our trust in each other will we perhaps find the solutions we need."

It made sense, but it still begged an important question. "Why me? My father's the High Priest."

"He is," he said. "But before I joined the Conclave, you and I had a personal relationship outside what we have now. We have a history we drew on that forms a more solid foundation for trust, and trust is what I most desperately need right now."

He desperately needed trust? Whatever he knew had to be extremely dangerous if he felt he had no one else to turn to. "I promise," I said. "What we discuss right now goes no further than this room."

Gerald smiled in thanks before inhaling sharply. "When I told you we had discovered Ebenezer's cell was empty, I didn't tell you the whole truth."

I shook my head. Would the lies never stop? "So what is the whole truth?"

"What I didn't admit was that there had been no signs Ebenezer had used his powers to force his way out."

The ramifications of Gerald's words crashed upon my shoulders. No wonder he felt as if he couldn't trust anyone. "Someone let him out?"

He begrudgingly nodded.

If he was being held prisoner by the Conclave, then logic dictated one probable answer. "It was one of the Conclave?"

"That is what I suspect to be true."

I suddenly felt dizzy. My entire world turned upside down, and I no longer knew where to turn for stability. One of the most powerful in our ranks had betrayed us, but why?

"I'm uncertain of the motives behind this action," he continued, as if sensing my question. "Only that it reveals something far more sinister is in the works than even we can fathom."

No shit! "What are you doing with this information?" I asked.

"We are… investigating."

I arched my eyebrows in disbelief.

"The Conclave is a sluggish machine at times. Too cautious for its own good."

"There's a traitor in your midst," I said. "You should be doing more than investigating. You should be using your immense powers to ferret out the culprit."

"We've already tried that," he hesitantly admitted. "And turned up nothing."

That didn't make any sense. "How is that possible? You're the Conclave. The most powerful of us all."

"So what does that tell you?" he asked.

"That there's someone out there even more powerful than all of you?"

The fear that had hidden in the corners of his eyes leapt into full view. That was the reason behind the Conclave's inability to deal with our recent troubles. They had no clue how to handle a situation over which they didn't ultimately hold the upper hand. They were flying blindly in the dark as much as we were.

"That's why we must keep this to ourselves," he insisted. "We have no idea who this true enemy is or even where he or she might be."

He was right. If I spoke what I knew at the wrong moment, I, and everyone I loved, was in danger. "I won't say a word," I replied. "But we have to find answers."

"And that's what I'm hoping you might have for me," he said. Hope glinted in his eyes as he eagerly grabbed onto me.

I should have told him about the pendant. Perhaps he knew what it was and what it meant, but Gerald was right. There was no one for him to turn to, and if there was a being out there more powerful than the Conclave, I couldn't risk what I knew falling into the wrong hands.

"Ben told me some things about the Conclave," I finally said. "He told me not to trust you. That you only craved power and you had ulterior motives for forcing the fae to live in Otherworld."

Gerald scrunched up his lips. He'd been expecting more, and I felt bad about not upholding my end of the bargain. But I had loved ones of my own to protect. Aiden and my family were my primary concerns.

"And that's it?" he asked, waving away my words as if they were old and tired.

"It isn't much," I said, pretending to be hurt. "But it made me question my trust and faith in the Conclave, and after what you have told me, I'd say I've got reasons to be damn concerned, don't you?"

He folded his hands into his sleeves and nodded. "You do." His lips drew into a straight line, and his gray eyes turned hard.

"Is there something you expected me to learn there?" I asked. "Maybe I did see something, and I didn't realize it was important. If you tell me what you're looking for, I'll tell you if I saw or heard it."

Gerald shook his head before turning around. "There's no need. You don't have what I need."

Was he disappointed I didn't know more or that I did and refused to tell him?

"If you do remember something, please inform me at once. Information is the only weapon we have right now."

"If I come across anything new, I'll make sure you're contacted."

"Thank you," he said with a halfhearted wave. "It's dangerous out there, Thaddeus. The world we knew is changing. Stay safe."

A second later Gerald was gone.

He was right. Darker forces than I even realized existed were gathering, and no one had any idea why.

But I would stay safe. I was finally living my life again, and nothing and no one was going to take that away from me.

A FEW minutes later, I entered the bedroom Aiden and I shared.

The silk sheets lay draped across his naked form as he tossed and turned. As usual, he fought against sleep. His vampyre side didn't need to rest. We'd learned that from the Conclave's book, but we'd also discovered regular resting periods aided in controlling the vampyren instincts.

It gave his fae side time to recharge from the constant battle that waged internally.

I stood there for a few moments, relishing the comfort seeing him in my bed gave me. After what I'd just learned, I needed it.

But more important, I craved the comfort only Aiden's touch could bring, and I had something to offer Aiden that would hopefully ease his constant struggle.

I undressed and then crept over to the bed as he mumbled and thrashed. Aiden's sleep had been plagued by nightmares, which were apparently new to him. The fae only ever had pleasant dreams, the lucky bastards, so when he woke up screaming after his first bad one, I had to explain to him that sometimes they happened.

I crawled onto the bed, positioning myself next to Aiden. The warmth emanating from him washed over me in comforting waves.

He responded to my presence by scooting closer and draping his arm across my chest. I pulled him to me and inhaled the spicy cinnamon bouquet that lingered around him and ran my fingers up and down his back.

He settled down and let out a big sigh.

My touch still worked its magic on him, just the way his worked on me. It made me smile every time my kiss or embrace calmed his nerves. It only supported the argument my heart had already concluded.

Aiden and I were tied to each other in a way neither of us expected, and if I had my way, that bond between us would only grow stronger.

"When did you come in?" Aiden peered up at me from where he rested on my shoulder.

"Just a bit ago," I replied, kissing the top of his head. "I'm sorry if I woke you."

"Don't be," he said, draping his leg over me. He felt the need to get as close to me as possible, which was good. That was exactly what I wanted.

We hadn't had sex since the Arbor. Aiden still didn't trust himself completely. He feared his vampyre side might rear its head in the throes of passion. Since he was still struggling with control, I couldn't argue against that logic, but it was time for us to use the strongest power we had—our intimacy.

"Something's on your mind," he said. When he looked up at me, it took every ounce of restraint I possessed not to pounce. "What is it?"

"I have an idea I'd like to discuss with you."

Aiden sat up against the headboard. The sheets slid down his body, exposing the patch of dark hair that crowned the base of his cock. Fuck. How was I supposed to have a conversation with that wonderful distraction peeking up at me?

He hooked my chin with his fingers and brought my gaze to his. "My eyes are up here," he said.

"I know where your eyes are," I said, straining against his grip to get another look at his goods.

Aiden chuckled before pulling the covers up to his waist. "There. Can you focus now?"

I frowned. "Maybe after I have one more look." I was just about to pull the sheets off when he grabbed both my hands in his.

"Thad, we've talked about this."

"And we need to talk about it some more."

He released me and scooted to the other side of the bed. "It's not safe," he said. "And I won't put you in danger."

"Unless your feelings for me have changed, you won't."

"What?" he asked, his eyes wide in surprise. "Why would you say that? Of course they haven't changed."

I smiled and slid over to his side of the bed. "I know they haven't."

He gazed at me out of the corners of his eyes, holding tightly to the sheets around his naked lower half. "Then why would you ask me such a silly question?"

"Because I want you to realize that nothing has changed between us. What I feel for you courses through every vein in my body. It's a force that dwells within me and makes me stronger. And makes you stronger. Why do you think you've been able to exert as much control over your vampyren nature? It's your love for me that gives you that strength, that willpower to do what needs to be done."

"I know," he said. He released his grip on the sheets and laced his fingers with mine. "It's hard on me too, you know. Not touching you or kissing you in the way I want to."

"And that's why you have to do it," I said. I took his hand and guided his fingers across my chest, letting him feel the flesh he'd been denying himself. His fingers trembled in want, and his hardening cock created a tent in the sheets.

"I can't." He was breathless, and his cheeks were flushed.

"That's not true," I said. I threw the covers off me, and Aiden looked up and down my nakedness, devouring the light dusting of copper hair on my chest and the treasure trail that led from my belly button to my hard seven-inch cock. He licked his lips, hungry for my flesh, but if I had to guess, he was just as ravenous for my blood.

"Thad, stop." His protest was weak. He couldn't tear his gaze from what I offered.

"I won't." I sat across his lap. His bare flesh was still covered by the bedding, but his hard dick made its presence known. It pulsed while Aiden unconsciously thrust upward against me.

He gripped my waist, forcing my ass on his prick, and moaned. "I'm losing control." He gritted his teeth as he dug into my flesh.

"No, you're not," I said. I leaned forward and brushed my lips against his. "You're still you, Aiden. You haven't sprouted fangs and talons. Nothing has changed."

"Because I'm fighting it," he said.

"Don't fight it," I responded. I pushed my tongue into his mouth, drinking in the sweetness of his kiss. I moved my hands to his face, caressing his cheeks as Aiden relented to the kiss. "Take me."

Aiden growled and flipped me onto my back on the bed. He hovered over me, his muscles straining. He wanted to dive onto me, kiss me, make love to me, bite me, but he fought it with impressive fortitude.

But what he had yet to realize was that with me, he didn't have to.

"I know you think you have to hold yourself back because you might hurt me." I stroked his cheeks as I smiled at him. His chest heaved, and he bit his lip to keep himself focused on what he felt he had to do. "But Aiden, you're not going to hurt me. I can feel that as easily as I can feel my heart beat."

He groaned and turned away. Clearly talking about my heart made him focus too much on my blood, which was good. It was my blood he needed.

"There's a hunger within you that needs to be sated, and I can do that for you. My touch calms you down, my kiss makes you focus, my blood will appease your hunger."

"Oh no," Aiden said, scrambling off the bed. "I know where you're going with this, and I'm not going to feed from you. I could kill you."

"You can feed from me without doing that," I said. "I've been reading the book the Conclave kept, remember? A vampyre doesn't kill his victims because he has to. He has to want to. Ben wanted to kill all the people he did. He was so angry at the Conclave and his father that he went on a murderous rampage, killing innocent people and turning them into monsters like him. He then commanded them to do the same. That suggests unless they are being controlled by a stronger vampyre, not all vampyren want to kill."

"But I do." His muscular shoulders slumped in reply. "The impulse is so strong."

"Because it's new to you," I said. I got off the bed and decreased the distance between us. "But you and I can fight anything. That's why I think you need to drink my blood. It will show you that not only can you control yourself, but you can feed without killing. Then you won't be so terrified of yourself anymore."

He turned and faced the wall. The sight of my naked body once again threatened his restraint. "And if your theory is wrong?" he asked. "Have you thought about that?"

"I have," I said. I wrapped my arms around him, molding my front to his back. Aiden relaxed against me, and I skimmed my hands across his chest, down his stomach, to his throbbing hardness. "And if you lose control, which I know you won't, then you'll just have to turn me into a vampyre too."

Aiden spun around in my arms, his mouth a giant *O*. "Are you kidding me?"

I laughed it off. "I'll already be dead, so you might as well bring me back to life."

"I would never do that to you," he said, pressing me into his arms. The thought terrified him.

I kissed his lips. "Then you'll just have to control yourself as you've been doing. Take only what you need."

He rested his hands on my ass, pulling me close. "It's too dangerous."

"But it's nothing I wouldn't chance to be with you," I said. "If my blood can give you peace, then we have to at least try. I really think it will bring us even closer. You've got to trust in what you feel for me as much as I trust in you."

"I do," he said. He scratched his fingers up my back and pressed his erection against mine. "I want you, Thad. So bad."

"Then take me."

Aiden's lips found mine. I moaned into the kiss as he lifted me off the ground. I wrapped my legs around his waist; his cock throbbed against my crack as he walked us over to the bed.

He lowered me to the mattress. He slid his hands across my skin, clutching my shoulders, my side, my legs, as he rested on top of me.

The full weight of his warm skin on mine doubled my desire. It had been too long since our naked flesh pressed together. "Yes," I whispered. I bucked my hips against his, grinding our cocks together.

"I've missed this," Aiden said as he nibbled a trail from my lips to my chest. He drew moist circles around my nipples with his tongue, and I shivered from the pleasure.

"Me too," I panted. I stroked his shoulders, following the dip and curve of muscle. When he gently nibbled on my right nipple, I inhaled sharply. The pain was delicious. It brought my passion to a boil. What ecstasy would Aiden drinking my blood bring the both of us?

Aiden stopped torturing the pebbled flesh and licked a trail downward. When he reached my crotch, he inhaled my musky scent while he palmed my erection. He lapped up and down the shaft, teasing precum from the slit. He darted his tongue across the opening, and his eyes rolled back in his head. "Damn, you taste good."

"I'm sure you'll say the same about my blood," I replied.

He took the head of my cock in his mouth. The sudden warm moisture around my dick stole all breath from my lungs. I couldn't speak or even think. My entire world had been reduced to my hardness lodged inside Aiden's throat, and what a wonderful world it was.

He bobbed up and down on my prick, his saliva coating my shaft. It gave Aiden the lubrication he needed to suck and jack me at the same time. The pressure in my balls grew more intense, and he obviously sensed it. He grinned up at me as he increased both the strength of his suction and the grip on my cock.

I was getting dangerously close.

Just as I was about to come, Aiden released me, a satisfied smirk cutting diagonally across his lips.

"Shit!" I panted. "I was almost there."

"I know," he said. He blew warm air across my pulsing cock. "That's why I stopped."

I wound my fingers through his thick locks and gave them a small tug. "Tease."

He wiggled his eyebrows. "You haven't seen anything yet."

"What do you—?"

Aiden lifted my legs and dove face-first into my ass. I whimpered as his tongue fluttered across my opening before running around the outer rim.

"Fuuuuuck!" I gasped, thrusting against his tongue. When it slipped inside me, I threw my head back. When it began to worm and wiggle its way farther into me, I almost slipped into unconsciousness. "Please, Aiden," I begged. "Fuck me."

"I will," he said before inserting one finger inside me.

I gasped at the sudden intrusion. I tensed and my ass clenched the invading digit.

"Relax," he said, delivering feathery kisses across my thigh and up the length of my shaft.

After a few moments, my muscles loosened enough for Aiden to slip a second finger inside. He swirled them in circles, forcing them all the way in. He found my prostate and rubbed it. My hips thrust automatically to the rhythm his fingers played inside me, until a thread of precum dangled from my cock. Aiden slurped his prize from the tip as he continued the massage, coaxing more and more of the silky strings from my body.

The sensation grew even more intense. My entire body spasmed as waves of pleasure rippled within me in never-ending waves. It was as if I was having an internal orgasm, the way I tensed and relaxed at the same time.

When Aiden withdrew his fingers from my butt, I gazed down at where he kneeled between my legs. "Now?" The hope in my question couldn't have been any more apparent.

He grinned in reply and stood up. "Now."

I scooted farther up on the bed while Aiden crawled between my legs. He spat into his palm and coated my twitching hole. "Are you ready?" he asked.

I was ready for him to take my body and my blood. "Yes."

I could tell he wanted to say more, to offer one more warning, but I'd heard all the arguments and so had he. We had to trust in each other and the love that bound us together.

Aiden leaned forward, positioning his cock at my entrance with one hand while he slid the other to my shoulder. With one push, Aiden slipped inside me.

When my ass rested against his crotch, I let out a rush of air. Aiden's hardness filled up every available space in my body, but I wanted more. I gripped his back, using the leverage to grind my ass in circles on his dick. I wouldn't be satisfied until I had every inch of him inside me.

Aiden placed a hand on my hips to slow my pace and guide me to the steady rhythm with which he worked his prick in and out of me. He pulled his cock almost all the way out before slowly sliding it all the way back in until his dick slipped past my second ring of muscle.

I moaned and thrashed underneath his long, measured strokes. His eyes locked onto mine, and he gingerly kissed my lips as he picked up speed and force. His pace quickened a few beats, and then a few more, until he slammed into me faster and harder. With each moist collision of our bodies, his pupils grew wider.

He was getting close. He was losing himself to the pleasure that would not only end in release but in Aiden biting into my skin and drinking my blood.

I forced my hand between our sweat-slick bodies and palmed my cock, jerking myself to Aiden's frenzied pace. "Do it," I said. I turned my head to the side, exposing my neck. "Take me."

A sharp sting quickly followed my words as Aiden bit into my flesh. He let out a grunt as my blood flooded his mouth and his seed filled my ass. It was the most sensual experience of my life to have my body fluids enter the man I loved while his entered me. It sent waves of pleasure crashing into me. When I came, I almost blacked out.

Five volleys of spunk exploded out of my cock. I moaned and thrashed through each spasm, coating our dripping bodies with my cum.

When my orgasm subsided, Aiden pulled off my neck. He rubbed where he had bitten me and then studied me intently. "Are you okay?"

Of course I was, especially since his eyes were no longer mad with hunger. A serene calm now drifted across the field of green. "I'm perfect. How are you?"

"Pretty damn good," he said in surprise. When his retreating hardness left me, he rolled over and pulled me into his arms.

"I told you you could control yourself."

"And it was easier than I thought it would be," he admitted. "For a while there, I wasn't sure. As I got closer to coming, I felt the vampyre rising up, but all I had to do was look at you, and I was able to force it back down."

"As I suspected you would."

He kissed the top of my head and squeezed me tight. "Thank you. I can't believe you were willing to do that for me."

"I didn't," I said, rising on one elbow. "I did it for us," I added, repeating the same words he had told me after we'd made love in the Arbor. "Now you know what you can do, and the fear you've been living under shouldn't be as strong."

He smiled, craning his head to give me a kiss. "It isn't. But I'm not going to let down my guard completely. That would be too dangerous. I still don't know what I'm capable of." He pushed me onto my back and climbed on top of me. "There is one thing I do know without a doubt, though." He pressed his lips against mine and ran his fingers through my hair.

"And what's that?"

"You are damn tasty," he said, making an exaggerated show of smacking his lips.

I laughed. "Did you doubt it?"

"Nope." He nipped playfully at my nose, his cock coming back to life. "But I'm gonna need more of everything. Real soon."

"And you'll have it," I answered. I shoved him on his back and got between his legs. I brushed his sweat-matted dark locks from his forehead and ground my wakening cock against his butt. "But next time, I cum inside you."

He eagerly nodded his head. "Oh yeah. That's hot."

As I stared at Aiden's beaming smile, it was easy to dismiss all the potential problems we still faced. My conversation with Gerald cast even more shadows onto an already darkened road that stretched before us. Where it ended was anybody's guess.

As long as we had each other, though, the final destination didn't matter.

We were now tied by love and by blood, and what could be more powerful than the bond between this warlock and his vampyre fae?

The answer was easy. Absolutely nothing.

Stay tuned for an exclusive excerpt from

Soul Struck

The Warlock Brothers of Havenbridge: Book Three

Like the electricity he commands, Pierce Blackmoor streaks through life on raw power and pure sexual energy. His conquests on the battlefield and in the bedroom form his foundation, but that bedrock crumbles when his younger brothers' abilities surpass his own. Pierce finds himself at an all-time low, and clawing his way back to the top becomes his only concern.

Pierce's plan to reassert his dominance, however, takes a backseat when he wounds Kale Aquilo, an emissary of the Beast King, lord of all shifters.

Kale's beguiling nature shoots like a lightning bolt straight to Pierce's soul, and when the soft-spoken Kale relays that a virus is killing his people, Pierce abandons his quest for power to do something he has never done before—protect someone other than himself.

As Kale, Pierce, and his brothers struggle to find the root of the magical virus spreading plague across Aeaea, the shifter island, they face a gauntlet of old and new foes. Soul struck, Pierce and Kale must uncover the truth behind the conspiracy gathering in the shadows.

Coming soon to
www.dreamspinnerpress.com

CHAPTER 1

"I'M GONNA fry you like a chicken."

Blue arcs of electricity leaped from my clenched fists as I studied my opponents. They stood on either side of me, sizing me up. The cold bastard on my right had his hands folded behind his back, while the dipshit to my left stuck his thumbs in the front pockets of his jeans and sighed.

They no longer saw me as a threat.

A few months ago—hell, even a few of weeks ago—I was the powerhouse. One stray static discharge from my pinky finger snagged their attention. That was when the world was right. I was the oldest, the most powerful.

At least I used to be.

"Come on, Pierce," my youngest brother, Mason, said. He dug his gloved hands further into his jean pockets to scratch his balls. "Is this necessary?"

"Yes," I growled.

"He's got something to prove," Thad shouted to Mason from where he stood on the rear lawn of Blackmoor Manor. He combed his fingers through his strawberry blond hair before readjusting the green scarf around his neck. "We might as well drop our pants and get out the measuring tape."

Mason barked in laughter and, after removing his hand from his pocket, slapped it against his thigh. I didn't find it funny. My brothers needed to be reminded that after Dad, I was the baddest warlock in the family.

"Big talk needs to be backed up," I said. I funneled more of my magic to my hands, sending snaking lines of blue energy sizzling toward the cold ground.

"This isn't wise," Thad said. "Using our powers out in the open like this is a big risk."

Thad had to be shitting me. Blackmoor Manor was on the biggest, most isolated plot of land in all of Havenbridge. "Stop making excuses and power up."

"Or what?" Thad asked. His arched eyebrow issued just as much of a challenge as his tone. "You'll attack us anyway? What the hell will that prove?"

"Just. Power. Up."

"Come on, guys. All y'all are actin' foolish." That was Drake Carpenter, Mason's boyfriend. I usually found his Southern drawl soothing. Today it only pissed me off. Mostly because I could hear the pity in his tone. He felt sorry for me, and that only ticked me off even more.

I glared over my shoulder at where he stood shivering on the red-bricked porch. He had his hands shoved into his blue Northface jacket, and his sandy blond hair dangled across his forehead. "Stay out of this, Drake. This is a family matter."

His shoulders slumped, and he took a step back as if I'd punched him.

"What the fuck, man?" Mason asked. He stomped across the dead grass toward me. The shadows cast by the weakened December sun crawled across the lawn toward my brother, most likely in response to his summons. "That's *not* cool."

No, it wasn't. We were the only family Drake had now. Well, at least the only family that hadn't come back from the dead as a vampyre. I'd make it up to Drake later. Buy him a root beer or some other crap food that he and Mason loved to ruin their bodies with. All I cared about right now was that Mason was angry enough to fight.

One down. One to go.

"I'll tell you what's not cool," I said. "Having a fucking vampyre for a boyfriend."

Thad inhaled sharply, and his face flushed.

My brothers were too predictable. It had always been easy to get a rise out of them, but now that they were no longer single ladies, it was even easier to yank their chains. Thad hated that the family still didn't fully trust his newly vamped boyfriend. What the hell was a vampyre fairy anyway?

"Don't make me hurt you," Thad said in a quiet, measured tone.

I snorted. "You've got that backward, Brainiac." He had hated that nickname ever since he was a kid, and that was the straw that broke Thad's back.

Thad, who was usually the most reserved of us all, charged. The already-chilled Massachusetts temperature dropped a few more degrees as Thad clicked on his ice powers. An icicle formed in his right hand, and he hurled it at me.

I had to admit, I was pretty fucking disappointed. An icicle? From a man who'd recently summoned a fucking blizzard?

I didn't even have to move to shrug that attack off. I nudged one of the arcs of lightning from my fist in the direction of the icicle, shattering it before it could come within twenty feet of me. "You'll have to do better than that."

"I'm planning on it," Mason said before jumping on my back. His fists struck the back of my neck.

Since I had at least forty more pounds and a lot more muscle than my little brother, the blows were more irritating than anything else. I reached back, grabbed Mason by his coat, and hurled him off me. He landed with a yelp that reminded me of a scared puppy.

Now that was what I needed.

Ice formed around my hands, cutting off my power source. I turned just in time to see Thad's fist coming right at me. I stepped out of the way and stuck out my leg, letting his momentum trip him up and send him face-first into the dead grass.

Their powers might have grown, but they still didn't know how to fight worth a damn.

I pushed more power through to my arms. Lightning streaked from my fists, splintering the ice Thad had formed in his lame attempt at muzzling my magic. I glanced at my brothers, who were once again upright, their chests heaving.

"You're about to get your ass handed to you on a platter," Mason said. Black energy hummed around his fists. He was preparing to fire off a shadow blast.

Thad didn't say a word. His upper lip curled into a snarl as he took a deep breath.

He'd done that once before, back in fairyland. He exhaled a snowstorm that almost took out that dumb fuck Ben, who'd been a major pain in our asses for the past couple of months. Lucky for me, I wasn't as big of an idiot as everyone else thought I was.

"*Propellit*," I whispered with a flick of my wrist, and Thad and Mason flew backward ten feet before slamming back onto the hard ground and skidding another few inches.

Now that was fucking funny. I laughed so hard I almost pissed myself.

Thad and Mason eyed each other before nodding. They rose in unison and stood their ground.

"Finally ready to get serious?" I asked.

Thad nodded once, his jaw tense. Mason shot me a thin smile before saying, "This is gonna hurt."

Shadowy tentacles gripped me from behind. They coiled around my hands and legs, anchoring me to the ground. Another set wrapped around my chest, making it difficult to breathe. This was uncomfortable, but it didn't hurt one bit.

Pain exploded in my groin as an inky limb grabbed my junk, tugging and twisting in directions my cock and balls were never meant to travel.

I let out a cry of pain before ice formed across my lips, sealing them shut and sending sharp, stinging pinpricks coursing through my mouth. The agony was worse than fifth grade, when I kissed the flagpole in the middle of winter on a dare. It had taken me a week before I could whistle again.

I yanked against my shadowy restraints. My muscles strained, and perspiration slid down my cheek from the effort. They wouldn't budge, and the fucking tentacle between my legs wouldn't let my shit go. How the hell was I going to get out of this one?

"Just surrender already," Thad said.

"Screw that," Mason replied. "He has to do more than cry uncle. He's got to admit his days as king of the magical hill are over."

Thad nodded, a triumphant smile practically cracking his face in two. "I agree. Just admit we're more powerful than you are and we'll stop."

Like that was ever going to fucking happen. I'd rather nose-dive naked into a pile of dirty syringes. I narrowed my eyes at them in reply.

"Suit yourself," Thad said before turning to Mason. "Do you want to go first?"

He nodded and cracked his knuckles.

"Mason, stop!" Drake ran out to them. He glanced at me before turning his disappointed gaze upon them. "That's enough. I think you boys have made your point."

Oh fuck this! There was no way I was going to let a human come to my rescue. I liked Drake and all, but no one was going to pull my ass from this fire except me.

"He fucking deserves it," Mason complained to his boyfriend. "When he's not mouthing off about how powerful he is, he's shoving my face into his sweaty pit or something equally disgusting. I've had enough!"

"I hate to agree with Mason," Thad said, "but he's right. Pierce needs to be taught a lesson. He's not in high school anymore. It's time he grew up and acted like an adult."

"This isn't right," Drake added. "He's obviously tryin' to overcompensate because your powers have grown."

Who the hell was I? Shelby from *Steel Magnolias*? There was no way these bitches were gonna talk about me like I wasn't here.

I shut my eyes and blocked out the pain. It was a distraction. I had to focus only on the raw magic that had coursed through my veins since I turned twelve. I was the first Blackmoor to tap into my active power at such a young age, and I'd used that gift to get me out of tighter spots than being hog-tied and sexually assaulted by Mason's shadow puppets.

I willed the lightning within me to my fingertips. The energy crackled and burned my fingers, but I had to push past that too. I had to overload Mason's restraints, pour more and more power into my fingers until either it short-circuited my bonds or blew off my hands.

Either way, I'd be free.

"Pierce, what are you doing?"

I paid no attention to Thad. He was trying to distract me from getting free. I sent even more energy surging through my limbs. Not only were my fingers on fire, so were my arms and now my chest. I clenched my jaw so tightly my teeth started to hurt. It was like I was biting down on aluminum foil.

"You need to stop," Mason said. His voice cracked. He was clearly worried I was going to get free and kick his ass so hard he wouldn't be able to sit for a week.

More energy flooded my hands. The burning spread down my chest to my legs and up to my head. The usual low buzz of my power turned into audible crackles and pops that reminded me of a transformer ready to blow. I was almost there.

"Shut it down!" Thad screamed. "Now!"

"Listen to them," Drake yelled. "You're gonna hurt yourself."

"Fuck that!" Mason added. "He's gonna hurt us."

Damn straight I was.

Sweat ran down my face, and my body shook with electrical current. It was like I'd become a live wire. It was time.

When I opened my eyes, I didn't understand what I saw. Someone had replaced the world around me with waves of blue, orange, and yellow that formed people and trees.

What the fuck did my brothers do to me?

"Pierce, are you okay?"

I turned to my right. Someone mostly made of orange stood next to me. Lines of blue and green coursed through his body. It sounded like Thad, but it sure didn't look like him.

"Whatever you're doing, stop!"

A person made of yellow stood twenty feet ahead of me. Inside him flowed threads of silver and gold. Was that Mason? And who was that behind him? That person wasn't made of any *one* color. He reflected all colors at once, making him a being of almost pure white light.

"Do somethin'," the radiant figure said. That sure sounded like Drake, but why did he look so different from everyone else?

I switched my focus from the people to the world around me. The forest along the back of our property had been turned to a solid black with spots of green twinkling within. The sky above glowed yellow before turning to orange and then red. At the highest point in the sky, a dark blue slowly gave way to a deep violet.

In the distance, I spotted birds. A strange crystalline light surrounded them and alternating colors of yellow, blue, and green radiated off the bodies of all of them except the one flying in front. It was composed of a pink aura with threading lines of dark red and royal blue.

What made that bird so different from the others, and why did I want to go chasing after it?

"Will you listen to me, dammit?"

The orange Thad shook me by the shoulders before a brilliant blue surrounded him and sent him flying across the backyard.

What the fuck happened? I surveyed the backyard, looking for whoever attacked my brother.

"What did you do?" the yellow Mason asked as he ran to where Thad landed.

"Me?" I asked, but my voice didn't sound like my voice. Instead of words, I crackled and popped.

If only I wasn't still restrained by Mason's shadows, I'd go over and check on Thad. That was when I realized I could move my arms and my balls were no longer being squeezed to death. How long had I been free?

"Pierce, you've got to calm the fuck down."

Mason crouched by Thad, who moaned in pain.

"Is he okay?" I asked, but my voice still wasn't working right. It sounded like static.

I had to find a way to make myself understood. I pointed at Thad, planning on following the gesture with a thumbs-up to get my point across. Instead a brilliant blue line of energy exited my pointing figure and crashed right into my brothers in an explosive thunderclap. Their bodies flew across the lawn.

Holy shit! What did I just do?

"Pierce, listen to me." Drake, or the white energy that seemed to be him, slowly backed away from me. "You're out of control, man. Your power's goin' everywhere. You've got to discharge it now. Before it's too late."

What the fuck was he talking about?

I held my hand in front of my face, except it wasn't my hand. At least not really. The flesh, blood, and bone had been replaced with lines of surging energy that arced off my body and singed everything around me.

What the hell was going on?

"Do it!" Drake yelled. "Now!"

I aimed my hands at the sky and expelled whatever had gotten into me. Never-ending streaks of deep blue shot out of my body and crackled overhead, turning the once multicolored sky into an electric blue. The snaking trails of energy crisscrossed through the firmament like a lightning storm until they made their way to the innocent birds that had progressed just over the forest behind the estate.

I watched in horror as my power fried the birds that emanated varying colors. Their fluctuating spectrum stopped the moment the blue lines of energy collided with their bodies. The bird with the pink aura tried to avoid the crackling discharge. It dipped and angled, doing its best to escape, but there was too much energy released all at once.

A stray line of power shot through its body, and it fell from the sky until eventually the blackness that was now the forest swallowed it up.

"Pierce, are you okay?" Drake asked.

With each blink of my eyes, he flashed between the flesh-and-blood Drake and the glowing white aura he'd become. It made me dizzy.

I tried to shake it off, but reality continued to warp around me.

When I took a step forward, my world went black.

For bonus content from

THE WARLOCK BROTHERS OF HAVENBRIDGE

check out

www.havenbridge.me

Don't miss how the story started!

Spell Bound

The Warlock Brothers of Havenbridge: Book One

By Jacob Z. Flores

Mason Blackmoor just can't compete with his brothers, much less his father. They represent the epitome of black magic, strong, dark, and wicked, and though Mason tries to live up to his respected lineage, most of the spells he casts go awry. To make matters worse, his active power has yet to kick in. While his brothers wield lightning and harness the cold, Mason sits on the sidelines, waiting for the moment when he can finally enter the magical game.

When a dead body is discovered on the football field of his high school, Mason meets Drake Carpenter, the new kid in town. Drake's confident demeanor and quick wit rub Mason the wrong way. Drake is far too self-assured for someone without an ounce of magical blood in his body, and Mason aims to teach him a lesson—like turn him into a roach. And if he's lucky, maybe this time Mason won't be the one turned into an insect.

Not surprisingly, the dislike is mutual, and Drake does nothing to dispel Mason's suspicion that the sexy boy with a southern drawl is somehow connected to the murder.

If only Mason didn't find himself inexplicably spell bound whenever they are together, they might actually find out what danger hides in the shadows.

JACOB Z. FLORES lives a double life. During the day, he is a respected college English professor and midlevel administrator. At night and during his summer vacation, he loosens the tie and tosses aside the trendy sports coat to write man on man fiction, where the hardass assessor of freshmen-level composition turns his attention to the firm posteriors and other rigid appendages of the characters in his fictional world.

Summers in Provincetown, Massachusetts, provide Jacob with inspiration for his fiction. The abundance of barely clothed man flesh and daily debauchery stimulates his personal muse. When he isn't stroking the keyboard, Jacob spends time with his daughter. They both represent a bright blue blip in an otherwise predominantly red swath in south Texas.

Blog: jacobzflores.com

Facebook: www.facebook.com/jacob.flores2

Twitter: @JacobZFlores

Pinterest: www.pinterest.com/jacobflores2

Goodreads: www.goodreads.com/author/show/5142501.Jacob_Z_Flores

Google Plus: plus.google.com/u/0/+JacobFlores9595/posts

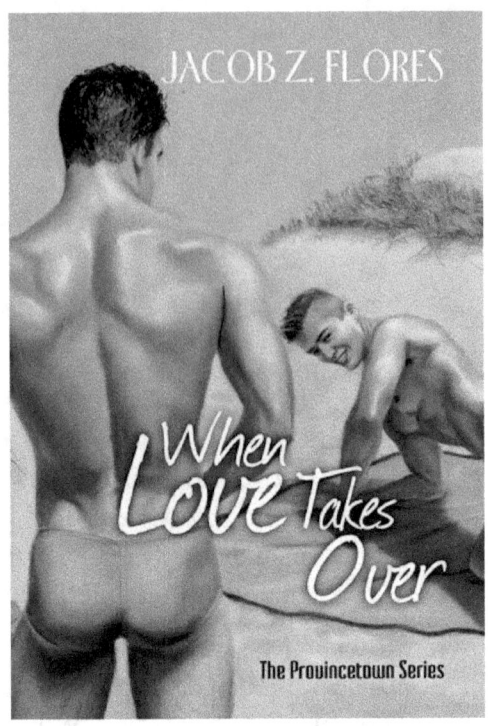

Provincetown: Book One

Zach Kelly's life is a shambles. His boyfriend of three years dumped him, and his writing career is going nowhere. On a whim, he heads to Provincetown, Massachusetts, to nurse his broken heart and figure out his next step. He's expecting to find rest and relaxation on the sandy beaches of Cape Cod. Instead, Zach meets a hunky porn star during a chance encounter at a leather shop he mistakes as a place to buy a belt that is definitely not for whipping.

Van Pierce is smitten when shy and inexperienced Zach crashes through a shelf of fetish gear. Though Van's got an insatiable appetite for men on and off the set, his porn persona, Hart Throb, hides a broken heart. He's struggling to find the reality the porno set doesn't offer, and Zach is fighting to find the fantasy that will set his writing on fire. The odd goofball and the suave beefcake may either find love amid Provincetown's colorful pageantry where summer never seems to end—or more heartbreak than either can imagine.

www.dreamspinnerpress.com

Provincetown: Books Two, Three, and Four

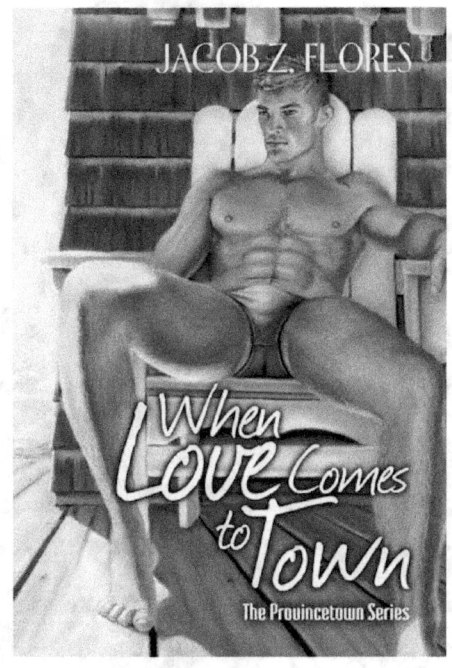